PW

Wedding
Bell
Blues ✀

By Linda Windsor

WEDDING BELL BLUES

Coming Soon

FOR PETE'S SAKE

Wedding
Bell
Blues

Linda Windsor

INSPIRE

An Imprint of HarperCollins*Publishers*

Excerpt from *For Pete's Sake* copyright © 2008 by Linda Windsor.

WEDDING BELL BLUES. Copyright © 2007 by Linda Windsor. All rights reserved. Printed in the United States of America. No part of this book may be used or reproduced in any manner whatsoever without written permission except in the case of brief quotations embodied in critical articles and reviews. For information address HarperCollins Publishers, 10 East 53rd Street, New York, NY 10022.

HarperCollins books may be purchased for educational, business, or sales promotional use. For information please write: Special Markets Department, HarperCollins Publishers, 10 East 53rd Street, New York, NY 10022.

FIRST EDITION

Interior text designed by Elizabeth M. Glover

Library of Congress Cataloging-in-Publication Data

Windsor, Linda.
   Wedding bell blues / by Linda Windsor.—1st ed.
      p. cm.
   ISBN: 978-0-06-117137-6
   ISBN-10: 0-06-117137-9
   1. Weddings—Planning—Fiction.
   I. Title.

PS3573.I519W43 2007
813'.54—dc22   2006028199

07 08 09 10 11 JTC/RRD 10 9 8 7 6 5 4 3 2 1

To my Jim: I can imagine you smiling at my use of some of the Shore's traditional sayings that illustrate extremes: the stubborn, no-win clash of "black gum against thunder" or "till a fly wouldn't pitch on it" (when we all know that flies will pitch on the most distasteful of things). This first book written without you has been difficult. Yet, thanks to the patience, diligence, and encouragement of my editor, Cynthia DiTiberio, and my dear friend and critique guru, Connie, here it is. And, in retrospect, I found that you were still with me through it all, within the pages and my heart. God is so good.

PROLOGUE

We dubbed ourselves The Bosom Buddies after performing in *Mame* for our senior class play back in 1989. I, Alexandra Butler, played lead and codirected the production about the free-spirited New York aristocrat who was struck down, but not out, by the stock market crash of 1929. With me as Mame, it was only natural that my best friend, Sue Ann Quillen, play Vera, Mame's flamboyant and sometimes promiscuous sidekick.

It was perfect casting. I fancied that I had Mame's rebellious and resilient spirit, while Suzie Q was truly a 1990s version of Vera Charles. Neither of us gave a hoot what anyone thought of us back then. Suzie Q doesn't to this day. And neither of us expected to meet two more soul mates between scenes.

Brainy, but clueless to fashion or anything apart from plants, dirt, and engines, tomboy Ellen Brittingham was perfect for the role of the frumpy, whining stenographer, Agnes Gooch. The snort when Agnes laughed came naturally to the local landscaper's daughter. But unlike the Agnes in the musical, Ellen turned out to be fun and witty, with a Brooklyn accent and Yiddish expressions from her Jewish mother's side of the family that never failed to crack us up.

The Cinderella–like role of Pegeen, the secretary who married the rich guy to live happily ever after went to Janet Kudrow, a die-hard believer in fairy tales. With her petite build and short blond hair, she'd even been called Tinkerbell by her classmates. Maybe if I'd been born into her dysfunctional family, I'd prefer to live in an alternate reality, too. Jan, like Ellen, didn't exactly fit into Suzie Q's and my circle of friends; but, like a shy, gullible kitten, she worked her way into our hearts and aroused our protective natures.

If we'd have admitted it back then, we weren't so different from Jan. We all longed for the man of our dreams and successful careers far away from sleepy, boring Piper Cove. But, to paraphrase the Scottish poet Robert Burns, "the best laid plans of mice" *and* bosom buddies went astray.

Yet, neither time, nor broken hearts, nor the call of dreams can destroy a friendship where it's a sworn duty for a bosom buddy to sit down and tell another the truth. Especially where a man is involved.

CHAPTER ONE

A *sundae* meeting was called for. Even though it was Wednesday, Alexandra Butler had put out the call to her friends. With a nostalgic smile at the celebration tradition that, like their friendship, had survived since high school, she pulled her Mercedes coupe into the parking space in front of the Piper Cove Country Club.

As of this morning, she had only one final payment to make on the loan that had subsidized her decorating business, one payment between her and financial freedom from her banker father's tight rein. To celebrate, hot chocolate and whipped cream were waiting inside, along with her bosom buddies.

Thank you, Lord, she prayed, grateful for the freedom, and her friends.

She needed her friends for more than a celebration. Her sister Lynn, whom their father called his *little surprise* when she was born twelve years after Alex, had called from a weekend trip to New York to announce her engagement to John Astor Whitlowe, Jr., a financial wunderkind just out of grad school. The couple was so excited, they'd even picked out Lynn's dress at a Fifth Avenue boutique. Alex's father, while overjoyed about the match, was determined to impress Lynn's future in-laws. They were not only from old money, but John's father was president of Mercantile One out of Bethesda, a large banking corporation that was taking Piper Cove Mercantile into its network. In other words, John's father was soon to be B. J. Butler's boss.

"I want us to nip in the bud that old notion that Eastern Shore men across the Chesapeake Bay are web-footed hicks," Benjamin James Butler—known as B. J. by the locals—had told Alex earlier that morning. "Which is why we are gonna plan the finest shindig my money can buy. You've got a knack for making a pig's ear look like a silk purse, and Lynn's so aflutter with love and finals that she won't be much help to your mama, so I'm depending on you, Alex."

I'm depending on you, Alex. It was probably the first time Alex had ever heard those words from her father, and satisfaction hardly described the emotion overwhelming her. Usually B. J. Butler assigned duties like a commander, expecting them to be carried out because he said so, not because he needed anyone.

As Alex swung open her car door, a male voice interrupted her thoughts. "Alexandra, allow me."

Alex lowered her sunglasses, peering over them. "Thank you, Will. Taking the day off, or are you headed to a business luncheon?"

Will Warren had graduated two years ahead of Alex's high school class and now worked for her dad's bank as head of the mortgage department. He made no secret of his ambition to replace B. J., and

Alex knew full well that Will's flirtation was nothing more than a potential rung on his ladder to success. It was futile, of course. Her father would give up his position only when they patted him in the face with a spade.

"Business . . . unfortunately," he added, his voice lowering in suggestion. "Believe me, I'd much rather spend an hour with you."

If her father heard that comment, or rather, its innuendo, B. J. would have shot Will on the spot. Alex kind of warmed to the idea, but she was forced by the restraint of the law to use verbal ammo on the would-be Romeo—

"Will Warren, if an hour's all you have to offer," a familiar voice interjected in a honeyed drawl, "a woman would as soon skip as bother."

As for stinging shots, that one would do. Alex grinned. "Hi, Suzie Q."

"Mrs. Wiltbank, good to see you," Will answered stiffly, as Sue Ann Quillen Wiltbank, of the Ocean City engineering Wiltbanks by marriage and the Piper Cove Quillen Realtors by birth, sashayed toward them in a smart black pantsuit, cut to accent her voluptuous curves. Although Alex's friend had gained a good twenty pounds since high school, it had all gone to the right places. "Tell Daddy I said hi, Will," Alex said, leaving the banker flushed from his white starched collar to his thinning brown hairline.

Suzie smothered her in a perfumed hug. "Alex!"

"You're bad," Alex chastised under her breath.

"That pig has had his nose stuck up my—"

"I know," Alex interrupted her, steering her toward the lighthouse-styled apex of the L-shaped building.

As one of Piper Cove's richest citizens, Sue Ann could say anything she wanted and not worry about reproach. Not that that had stopped her when she was merely an affluent realtor's daughter. Hers was the mouth always in gear, whether her brain was or not.

"Tush. I was going to say *tush*." Sue Ann's mischievous blue eyes twinkled like the genuine gemstones clustered on one of her many rings.

"Of course you were." Alex linked arms with her friend and ushered her through one of the double glass doors with a "Thanks" to the exiting customer who held it open for them.

"Why, Bobby McMann, aren't you the sweetest thing?" Sue Ann called over her shoulder to the man.

Alex could have reminded Sue Ann that Bobby was married and a practicing Catholic who'd perfected procreation by having six kids. But Sue Ann knew that. She simply couldn't help herself. Men brought out the flirt in her, no matter their age or shape. If Bobby had been sixty and balding, instead of a rugged, thirtysomething contractor, Sue Ann would have treated him just the same.

To the left of the entrance was the dining room, reflecting the formal elegance of Chesapeake Bay living. Alex steered her companion to the Coffee Café on the right. Its wildfowl theme and hunter green and beige color palette was in keeping with the natural habitat the area was known for. This room said smell the coffee, while the other suggested high tea served on the club's custom-designed china.

"There they are." Sue Ann pointed to a corner booth, where a brunette in a tank top and jeans jumped up and whistled.

"My gawd, Ellen," Sue Ann exclaimed. "Summon the Piper Cove Fire Department, why don't you?"

"Good to see you, too, Sue Ann," Ellen quipped, undaunted. She patted the bench next to her. "Take a load off those stilts you're wearing before your arches fall."

"Jan," Alex said to Ellen's quiet companion. "How's the new job going?"

Jan Kudrow had been the only one of the bosom buddies who even came close to keeping their high school pledge to leave their sleepy bayside community and never return. Alex and Ellen had come back straight from college. Sue Ann, who went into her parents' real estate business until she married into a family with even more money, never left at all.

Determined to be a star, the pixielike Jan had worked her way through a New York performing arts school and actually played a supporting role in an off-Broadway production. But in truth, her talent wasn't star quality and, after a steady stream of rejections and some horrible relationship failures, Jan came home.

The upside of Jan's New York experience was that she had learned to do something she really was good at while working her way through school—preparing sweet concoctions that were as artistic as they were delicious.

Jan's pale green eyes lit up. "Great! The supermarket loves my work. My boss actually said that he was considering making me head of the pastry department."

"He's not putting the moves on you, is he, Tink?" Sue Ann inquired, referring to the petite Jan's high school nickname Tinkerbell.

"Subtle, Suze, real subtle." Ellen rolled her eyes as she tucked a long, limp strand of dark hair that had escaped a haphazard twist and clip behind her ear.

"He's married and could practically be my father," Jan told her with that clueless, wide-eyed look framed by the blond fringe of her short haircut that made her a target of every lecherous jerk around. Sue Ann arched a perfectly plucked brow. "Your point being . . . ?"

A teenage waitress clad in white shorts and a green tee shirt with PIPER COVE GOLF AND COUNTRY CLUB emblazoned on it put four menus on the table. "While you ladies decide what you want, what can I get you to drink?"

Alex knew the drill. "Iced tea, lemon, no sugar, for me. Pepsi— *leaded*—for her," she added with a glance at Ellen, who ordered sodas like fuel for her Harley. "Water with lemon for my sidekick," she said, pointing to Jan, who smiled sweetly.

"And a lemonade for me." Sue Ann fanned herself with a napkin. "I—"

"Hate this heat," Alex, Jan, and Ellen finished together.

Sue Ann did not like to sweat. Never had. It ruined her makeup, and humidity was the worst enemy of her hair, which always looked like she'd just stepped out of a salon. She hadn't, of course. She had a hairdresser on her house staff. Living so close to the ocean, Sue Ann considered that a necessity, especially in the summer.

"That's going to go real well with a chocolate nut sundae," Alex said, when the waitress left.

A blank look grazed Sue Ann's cover girl face. "What? Is this a *sundae*"—she practically tasted the word—"lunch?"

Sue Ann didn't listen well either. All one had to do is mention one of the words *shopping, lunch,* or *dinner*—Suzie Q did not do breakfast—and she started coordinating what she was going to wear while letting the details go in one diamond-studded ear and out the other.

"Can you think of a better way to celebrate?" Alex challenged good-naturedly.

"Well what are we celebrating?" she asked, a little vexed.

"Who cares?" Ellen licked her lips, a wicked gleam in her hazel eyes. "I'm going bananas, as in banana split, three toppings, the *woiks*."

"You're killing me," Sue Ann wailed. "I was going to be a good girl and order a salad."

At Ellen's loud snort, the others dissolved into laughter, all but Alex, whose glare quieted them . . . eventually. "Well, just in case any of you are interested in anything besides how many calories are in ice cream, I just landed a contract to decorate a new condo on the bayside, big enough to pay off my business loan a year ahead of time. It may not sound like much, but I feel as if a giant weight is already lifting from my chest."

Jan squeezed Alex's arm. "That *is* good news. I'm so proud of you."

"Yeah, now you can tell your old man to butt out the next time he tries to butt in," Ellen agreed.

"Come on, guys, don't you think he does it because he loves her?" Jan asked, a trace of longing in her voice for something she'd never had. The word *dysfunctional* could have been coined for her family.

"B. J. Butler likes to run everything in this town, and his daughter's life is no different. I offered to pay that thing off a dozen times," Sue Ann told them, giving Alex one of her exasperated looks. "But no, Alex had to do it herself."

"It wasn't the same, Suzie Q, and you know it," Alex said in her defense. "I had to do it myself . . . on a loan and a prayer."

"But there's something else . . ." Alex paused until she was certain she had their complete attention. "I also need to call in the ranks. Daddy asked me to help Mama coordinate Lynn's wedding. I'm heading to the house tonight to discuss it. We have to pull this thing together before September."

"Lynn's getting married?" Jan squeaked—a shriek for her—fists clenched against her collarbone. "I've got to do the cake. Puh-leeze, let me do the cake."

"What's the rush? Is Lynn preggie?" Sue Ann asked.

"Oh get real, Suzie. This is my perfect little sister we're talking about," Alex chided. "Actually, the groom has a great job offer starting September, so he wants to get the wedding and honeymoon over while he has time off."

"I am so jealous." Jan sighed.

"Well, I'm not . . ." Alex said, denying the little green pang in her chest. "Moonstruck and gushy isn't my style." She'd outgrown that years ago—after her failed marriage.

"We don't usually do flowers these days, but Ma and I would be thrilled to do them for Lynn," Ellen offered, bringing the conversation back on track. "Ma always said Lynny would marry a rich doctor before she graduated from nursing school." Ellen snorted in amusement. "I think she was dropping hints for me."

Ellen was her father's daughter, a mechanic and lover of the soil. If she wasn't up to her knees in dirt and covered in sweat, she was covered in grease, working on the landscaping equipment, her houseboat, or the engine of her Harley.

"You know, I could make that happen for you," Sue Ann said, studying Ellen's face with its high cheekbones and valentine shape. "You've got one of those slight builds that photographers and, some men, love."

"That's Suzie's way of saying I got no boobs."

"That's because Suzie got your share and mine, too," Jan teased, looking down at her shortcomings.

Ignoring the banter, Sue Ann continued with her assessment. "I mean, it might not be a doctor, but with all the people buying those six-figure condos at full asking price before they're even finished, there's bound to be a man with money for you among them."

Ellen leaned back as the waitress approached with their drinks. "Hey, just because you got one doesn't mean you have to punish the rest of us. Besides, I like working."

"Hear, hear," Alex agreed. "Not all of us have the fortitude to spend our days pampering our bodies to maintain our youth for a man."

"The devil with all of you, then. See if I care if you wind up dried-up old spinsters." Sue Ann shoved a straw in her drink and made a show of sipping it through fire-engine red lips.

"What can I get you ladies to eat?" the waitress asked, giving the giggling Alex, Ellen, and Jan one of those aloof *will-you-people-act-your-age* looks that teenagers seemed to specialize in. But smugness turned to outright shock when they placed orders for three hot fudge sundaes with wet nuts, and a banana split.

"Who is that little hip-swinging thing?" she asked, after the girl walked away talking to herself. "That is, *if* she had hips."

One would think that Sue Ann had never eaten in the coffee shop. Although, usually, when they met for lunch or dinner, it was at one of the swankier places on the ocean side of the bay.

But in the middle of a workday Jan and Ellen weren't dressed for it. Jan, who'd just gotten off from working since before sunup in the supermarket bakery, couldn't afford those. And Ellen had a truckload of plants coming in that afternoon and could only spare an hour or so from the landscaping architecture business she owned with her parents.

"She's Hattie Mae's granddaughter . . . Candy, I think," Ellen answered. "You remember Hattie Mae's Diner."

"Oh, I loved that place," Jan said of the antique diner that had once stood on the main street of Piper Cove. "To tell the truth," she continued, "I hardly knew Piper Cove when I came home. Who'd have ever thought this sleepy little boondock would become a flashy resort?" What buildings hadn't been torn down, like the diner, were filled with specialty shops for the tourists, who flooded the condos built on canals and along the coast of Assawoman Bay. "Who would have thought sixteen years later we'd still be stuck here?" Alex mused aloud. "And you, the most timid of the bunch, were the only one who really followed her dream."

"Hey, I never wanted to leave," Ellen protested. "Small is good . . . comfy."

"And I didn't have to leave home to get my dream," Sue Ann pointed out. "I married a local rich boy."

"There's a lotta people who'd like to be stuck with a successful business like yours, Alex," Ellen added.

Alex nodded. She'd started the business as soon as she returned from earning her degree in interior design at the Philadelphia Art Institute. By that time, Sue Ann had become a real estate agent, so, between hers and Alex's dad's contacts, finding clients had not been a problem. Fortunately, Alex had the talent to deliver.

She lifted her tea glass for a toast. "To my last payment and getting out from under my father's thumb."

Her friends clicked their glasses to hers with a round of "Hear, hear."

"Not that your dad will stop his *buttinski* act," Ellen commented. She sat back at the approach of a tray of sinful-looking ice-cream delights carried by none other than Hattie Mae Taylor.

"I knew it! When Candy gave me your orders and described you four to me, I knew it was my girls." Aside from considerably more wrinkles, Hattie Mae looked the same as she had when she'd run the diner, still wearing a pink uniform slacks set and white apron. Most likely, Lady Clairol maintained the golden brown of her hair.

"I'd have thought you'd retired by now, Hattie Mae," Sue Ann said.

The sparkle in the woman's gaze dimmed for a moment. "Can't retire till I finish raisin' my granddaughter."

Sue Ann put her hand to her mouth in dismay. "Oh, Hattie Mae, I'm so sorry. I'd forgotten about Ruth Ann's cancer."

Hattie drew in a bracing breath, and her brightness returned. "She's with the Lord now, bless her, and raisin' Candy has been a joy. I'd best let you girls eat your ice cream before it melts. I hope you all will come in again real soon."

"Count on it," Ellen called after her.

Alex dug into the three-dip-high pile of ice cream, hot fudge, and whipped cream and glanced at the others. "And now another toast," she announced, holding up a heaping spoonful. "To the bosom buddies . . ."

"To old times," Sue Ann chimed in, doing likewise.

"And new times," Jan said.

Ellen scooped up a spoonful dripping with strawberry topping and whipped cream as her dark-lashed gaze shifted abruptly past Alex and Jan toward the entrance. "Uh-oh."

Sue Ann's eyes widened as if she'd seen a ghost. "Talk about a blast from the past."

Alex exchanged a bewildered glance with Jan. "Think we dare look," she teased.

"You'll have to sometime, honey," Sue Ann told her, as Alex popped a spoonful of frozen heaven into her mouth.

Jan turned and gasped so sharply that she nearly choked on the ice cream she'd licked off her spoon.

Unable to resist any longer, Alex looked over her shoulder and found herself nose to belt buckle with jeans-clad masculine hips. She followed the row of buttons up a chambray shirt and past a tanned throat to where a golden shadow of stubble covered a dimple she'd never forget as long as she drew breath. Above it danced a pair of pale blue eyes that she'd prayed alternately never to see again and to bask in their light just one more time.

But this was *not* the time.

CHAPTER TWO

"Well, hello Josh Turner," Sue Ann cooed from across the table. "What brings a big star like you back to Piper Cove?"

Honey dripped from her voice, but the blue ice in Suzie Q's gaze was cutting-sharp. She'd been the first to come to Alex's side when she heard how Josh Turner had abandoned his eighteen-year-old bride of less than a year in favor of life on the wild side.

Josh smiled, and Alex's heart turned over like a pup, throat up to a bigger dog. "A little business, a little pleasure. But, when I walked in and saw four of Piper Cove's prettiest gals, I had to come over and say hi."

Alex steeled her jaw and swallowed hard . . . before her ice cream had sufficiently melted. Josh had no right to look this good after the life he'd led. As the lead guitarist for the Southern rock band White Lightning, he'd made more money than he and Alex had ever dreamed of when they were together; but it had also led to drugs and alcohol. The least he could do was to have aged more, dried and shriveled like one of those has-been rock stars instead of looking like a poster boy for a soap commercial.

"So what kind of business and how long are we going to be graced with your presence?" No playing around for Ellen. Straight to the punch.

"I heard your grandma's farm has been sold to a big development company from Baltimore," Janet spoke up. "Must be hard, that being your old homeplace, and having so many memories." Her irrepressible sympathy earned a glower from Sue Ann. Alex watched an emphatic "Duh" register on Janet's face as she recalled that Josh's old homeplace had also been his and Alex's home during their brief marriage.

"Whatever Josh is doing here, it's none of our concern." Was that her voice, Alex wondered, as Jan shrank against the corner of the booth. It sounded so calm and collected.

No, don't look at me. Too late. Josh's mercurial gaze shifted to her. Like the weather, it could change from stormy gray to midnight, but today it was the blue of a summer sky—the kind that enticed the hardest of hearts to frolic.

Alex could have stabbed herself with her spoon to stop hers from rolling side to side. Frolic was the last thing she wanted from her ex-husband. Blood, sweat, and tears were far more preferable.

"Don't let us keep you from whatever it is you're here for, Josh." She attacked her sundae as though she expected him to grab it and run.

But Sue Ann wasn't ready to extract her claws just yet. "Well, I heard you got religion after your accident." She leaned forward on one elbow with a feline slant of curiosity. "Is that true?"

"What?" Ellen looked as though Sue Ann had just declared belief in the tooth fairy.

Alex continued to spoon ice cream into her mouth, needing to focus on anything but her ex-husband and his faith. When she'd first heard of his epiphany, she'd reeled with the same incredulity that Ellen showed now. Religion and the Josh Alex knew were not compatible. He'd only attended church out of respect for his grandmother, not God. Besides, stories of celebrities and criminals finding God multiplied like rabbits in the media. She could be happy for them and pray it was true; but believing it was true came harder when most used sudden faith as an op-ed rather than sincere testimony.

"I saw him in some church-sponsored TV commercial about saying no to drugs a little while ago," Sue Ann told her. "It's been on forever. You'd have seen it if you weren't out digging in dirt or fishing." No one could express distaste like Susie Q.

"Speaking of which"—Josh nailed Ellen with his attention—"are they catching any flounder in the bay? I've just bought a forty-two-foot Hatteras Sportfisherman."

Despite her loyalty to Alex, Ellen crumbled at the mention of both a boat *and* fishing. "What kind of engine ... Ow!" She clutched her rib cage where Sue Ann had delivered an elbow jab.

"My question first." Sue Ann propped her chin on her hand, a picture of mischief.

But the mild amusement in Josh's eyes disappeared. "I found Christ, if that's what you're asking. After my accident, there was only one way to look ... and that was up."

Could it be real? Alex wondered. One of Josh's hands had been crushed in a car accident. It ended his career as lead guitarist. White Lightning went on without him, and he faded from the gossip columns until the story broke regarding his sudden spiritual epiphany. It wasn't up to her to determine how genuine his faith was, but Josh in church? That was a concept as hard to believe as the fact that he was standing here close enough that she could smell his soap—some clean, shower-fresh scent. Josh was that, and pure male pheromones.

"Well, I think that's nice," Janet said. "Real nice."

"When was the last time you were in church?" Ellen challenged her friend playfully. "Not since you got back from New York, I can tell you that."

"Just because I don't go to church doesn't mean I'm not spiritual," Jan said, shrinking behind her sundae dish.

That was always Jan's excuse when Alex or Ellen suggested she might enjoy attending services with them.

"I think the proof will be in the pudding, if you get my drift." Sue Ann eyed Josh with skepticism. She didn't have much use for religion either, but Ellen and Alex both recognized that their friends weren't as far along on faith's journey as they and were willing to love the two, gently witness as best they could, and wait for God's timing to kick in.

"Or aren't you going to be around long enough for us to see how much you've changed?" Subtlety was not one of Sue Ann's strengths either.

Alex held her breath at the challenge, *yes* and *no* clashing on her mind. Never mind that she'd not seriously dated since Josh left. *Lord, don't let him find that out.*

It wasn't as if she'd been pining away. Unlike Josh, who for too long appeared on the covers of rag sheets with buxom bimbos clinging to his tattooed arms, she simply hadn't found anyone who held her interest. She'd had a business to build, one she was very proud of. She wouldn't have had time for a man, even if she'd wanted one—which she hadn't.

"We'll see," he said, undaunted by Suzie Q's interrogation. "I have a few commitments to see to."

Although it had been lonely. God, had it been lonely. And painful. As if Josh had ripped her heart from her chest and taken it with him. Even worse, the term *divorcee* was synonymous with *easy* in some men's eyes, which made Alex an even harsher judge of men in the aftermath than her marriage to Josh had made her. She scared them off, so her friends said. But it had been easier to put on a prickly veneer and place her battered heart in a cage, where nothing could get to it.

"Finding Jesus *and* honoring commitments. My you *have* changed." Her heart might be caged, but her long-suppressed bitterness flew the coop before she could stop it.

She wanted to evaporate before the four startled gazes that shot her way.

Hurt wouldn't let her look away, no matter how humiliation urged her to dive, facedown, in what little was left of her sundae. To her surprise, she saw no trace of anger in his expression. Actually, there was nothing to suggest what Josh was thinking.

Beneath his appraisal, Alex resisted the urge to rub her temples where an ice-cream headache was gathering from the three chocolate-smothered dips she'd force-fed herself in a matter of minutes. And there was no help from the ranks. All three of her friends took a confection retreat. Finally, Janet's spoon clanged against her ice-cream dish, shattering the strained silence.

A twitch tugged at Josh's mouth although Alex was hard put to discern if it was rooted in irony or humor. "I'd like to think I've changed," he said quietly. "Like Suzie Q said, I guess the proof will be in the pudding."

Reaching across the table, Josh took a napkin from the dispenser and added fuel to the blazing fire of Alex's humiliation by dabbing chocolate from her chin. This time there was no mistaking it. His lip twitched with humor, through and through.

"Then there's some things that never change." He winked at her.

Alex could have sworn her heart stopped, dropped, and rolled like her cat Riley begging for attention.

"Good to see you all again," he said, putting the napkin down and turning to saunter out of the coffee shop.

"Well, what do you think of that?" Sue Ann exclaimed, when Josh was beyond earshot.

"I think Alex put him in his place," Ellen replied, holding up her hand for a high five. "Changed or not, he used to be a real jerk."

Alex ignored it. She didn't deserve a high five. She should have been grace itself, as if Josh had done her a favor, not shattered her heart. She hated losing control, but then Josh was a master control-buster, as were her reactions to him or any mere mention of him.

It had been sixteen years since he'd abandoned her, and she'd given her heartbreak to God a long time ago. After that much time and God's healing work, she shouldn't feel anything for Josh. At least not anything meaningful.

She shook her head, trying to free herself from both the ice-cream headache and disgust over her own weakness. She probably just needed to spend some time in prayer about this. God had a reason for allowing this to happen. He always did. She just wished he would share it with her.

"Has he left?" She refused to turn around and give him the satisfaction of catching her looking after him.

"No," Janet whispered. "He's talking to Candy at the register."

"Got her falling all over herself," Sue Ann observed with interest. "It's got to be those bedroom eyes of his."

"Don't remind me," Alex groaned.

Janet stole another quick glance over her shoulder. "She's getting his autograph."

"Wonder what kind of engines he's got in that thing?"

Alex, Sue Ann, and Janet swung their gazes to Ellen, who relished a mouthful of chocolate sundae, a dreamy expression on her face. It took a moment for her to realize she was the center of attention.

"What?" she asked.

"Are you serious?" Sue Ann demanded.

Ellen threw up her hands in exasperation. "His boat. It's a Hatteras Sportfisherman," she said with the same awe that Sue Ann held for Prada. "There's gotta be at least two five-hundred-horse kickers under his deck."

Sue Ann fell back against the booth, palm against her forehead. "I think I'm gonna swoon."

Ellen jabbed her with an elbow. "Leave it to Suzie Q to have her mind in the gutter."

"It's all she ever thinks about . . . and she's *married*," Janet said in hushed amazement.

"Even if all I did think about was sex, that only means I'm not blind or dead." Sue Ann dug into her sundae. "Though sometimes I think I might as well be," she mumbled, shoving a dripping spoonful into her mouth.

"Martin gone again?" Ellen asked, at once sympathetic.

Spawned from a line of architects that had built half of Ocean City and most of Piper Cove's new developments, Martin Wiltbank III traveled at least two weeks out of the month. Sue Ann complained that the other two he spent buried in his office.

"Has he gone yet?" Ordinarily Alex would enjoy her friends' lively banter, but her day had been ruined.

"He left last week—" Sue Ann broke off. "Oh, Josh? Yes, he's gone." She peered through the blinds at the parking lot. "I wonder what he's really up to?"

So do I, Alex thought. Although, if she knew Josh—and she did, all too well—it wouldn't be long before she found out.

⚜

"Isn't it beautiful?" Lynn Butler held her wedding gown against her slender frame and twirled around in her parents' dining room that evening, so that Alex and her mother could admire it. "I am so glad it didn't need alterations."

The way her sister carried on, one would think that the shipping from New York's Fifth Avenue boutique to Piper Cove had somehow changed it since she and John had picked it out a few days ago. But then, the girl was in such a dizzy race for the altar, one might also think she feared that her fiancé might take back his offer.

"Just pinch me so I know it's real."

Having suffered Lynn's incessant bubbling from soup to dessert, Alex obliged her little sister, exacting a wounded squeal.

"You asked," Alex said in her defense.

Lord, forgive me. I am happy for Lynn, I truly am.

But their father hadn't even mentioned Alex's visit to the bank, much less the news that she'd landed a huge job decorating a new bayside condo, one big enough to enable her to pay her loan off early. Twice she'd tried to bring it up, but everyone's head rang with wedding bells.

"I was speaking *metaphorically,*" Lynn complained.

"Girls, please! We need to stop twittering and focus on this weekend's engagement party at the club. I don't know ... I just don't know." Nervous, Lenora Butler tapped the rich mahogany surface of the dining room table, now cleared of the dinner dishes and covered with wedding paraphernalia, including silver boxes of invitations to be addressed. "Where's the seating chart for the engagement dinner?" she fretted, moving one of the boxes, but not really looking. "Your father doesn't want Aunt Rose at our table."

Rose Butler McMann was one of Alex's favorite people. Unpretentious to a fault, which was why B. J. wanted her distanced from the Whitlowes, Rose was usually the life of the party.

"I think Aunt Rose would fit fine at Sue Ann's table," Alex assured her mom, not without envy of her buddies.

"That's probably a good idea," Lynn remarked, her long sigh a sign that she was torn between her love for her only aunt and her desire to make a good impression on her future in-laws.

"If things get too boring, we can always ask her to tell about the time she caught the prize at the White Marlin Open," Alex put in, grinning.

Instead of laughing as she usually did when the story of Aunt Rose outfishing a boatload of sport fishermen was mentioned, her mother lifted a delicate brow at the bride-to-be. "Have you spoken to your sister yet?"

Alex sat up at attention, alert to a something behind her mother's words. "Spoken to me about what?"

"About the wedding, silly." Lynn turned abruptly to hang up her dress.

"I've already said the Bosom Buddies are ready and able to take care of the flowers and cake. Suzie will help us fine-tune the seating arrangements at the reception and anything else we need."

"She is the hostess with the mostest," Lynn said, zipping up her gown as though closing a friend up in the protective bag.

"Lynn, you promised me that you'd talk to Alex before this weekend. For heaven's sake, child, you've been home a week."

"Mama, Alex has been busy wooing a client all week." Lynn spun around, as though stuck in fairy-tale mode, and floated over to the table where she settled in a chair across from Alex. "We've hardly had time to chat, have we?"

Alex tried to ignore the anxiety that crept up the back of her neck. She hadn't seen or heard from her little sister since she'd been home, except through their parents. "The engagement party is this weekend, Lynn," Lenora snapped in uncharacteristic impatience.

Alex glanced at her mother in surprise. Daddy was right. Mama was on edge about the wedding. Time was, Lenora Butler was Piper Cove's queen bee of the social hive, but a few years ago, she'd been diagnosed with depression and practically gone into seclusion. The medication helped immensely, but the idea of putting together an engagement party and wedding was pushing the envelope.

A pout formed on Lynn's lips. "Mama, you know I've had a lot on my mind, what with lining up my bridesmaids. The maid of honor is a given." Lynn smiled at Alex. With fair hair and a soft blue-gray gaze, her baby sister was Lenora's image, while Alex had inherited B. J. Butler's wild auburn hair and dark eyes.

"It had better be," Alex replied with relief. "Although I might back out if you choose that sickly pink number," she said, pointing to the color swatches for the bridesmaid dresses, "for my dress."

"My bridesmaids will wear the pink blush. Your dress is sangria." Lynn rolled the *R* in a way that would have delighted their Spanish teacher. "Mama insisted I use a jewel tone for you."

"Tea," Lenora announced, as much to herself as her daughters. "I think I'll fix some tea. The two of you can *chat*"—she shot Lynn a stern look—"while I prepare it."

Alex waited until her mother left the dining room before zeroing in on her baby sister. "Why do I get the feeling that there are two conversations going on here, and I'm only privy to one of them?"

Lynn grabbed a book of sample paper products. "Mama is all worked up because of John's choice for best man. She's certain it's going to upset you, but I told her past was past."

One by one, Alex felt the hairs on her neck begin to stand on end.

"I mean, you are *so* over Josh Turner, I hardly—"

"Josh Turner is John's best man?" Alex interrupted. No way. How had a guitar-plucking renegade like Josh even met a cookie-cutter-type stockbroker from Baltimore, much less become best friends with one? It made no sense. They were night and day.

"Crazy, isn't it?" Lynn said with a giggle. She always giggled when she was nervous, or when she'd done something wrong. And this was wrong, very wrong.

Alex let questions fly with her anger. "Just when were you planning to tell me, Lynn? Friday night, just before the party? Or were you going to let me walk in and see Josh seated at our table? Does Daddy know about this? Because one of them's going to wind up dead. Daddy'll either shoot Josh or have a heart—"

"Daddy knows," her sister told her. "Doesn't like to discuss it."

That was an understatement, given their past history. "And I did try to tell you once. I left a message for you to call me for lunch."

And Josh hadn't said one word today at the country club. He'd let Alex verbally slice and dice him, knowing full well that he'd have the final laugh. Alex clenched her fist, unsure if she was going to lose her dinner or give her baby sister a mother of a black eye to sport this weekend. Since Alex wasn't the violent type, her meal was more at risk.

"Didn't you get my message?" Lynn's face crumbled in despair. "I . . . I'm so sorry, Ally. I was afraid to tell you. I knew you'd be upset and I . . . I just didn't know how to tell you so that you wouldn't get upset an . . . and . . ." She reached for one of the sample napkins on the table and blew her nose. "It's not like *I* picked Josh. John did. I was shocked when John introduced me to Josh. Al . . . although he *has* changed."

"How—" Alex grasped at one of the questions swirling in her brain to no avail. All she could see was that smug smirk on Josh's face this afternoon. What was it he'd said he was in Piper Cove for? A little business, a little pleasure?

"John got in trouble with drugs in college," Lynn whispered, as though the walls had ears. "He met Josh at a Christian rehab center. Josh helped him turn his life around. John said that if it hadn't been for Josh, he'd likely be dead."

"But *Josh* had a drug problem," Alex argued.

"That was years ago." Lynn put her hand on Alex's arm. "I tell you, he's changed. He's a totally different man."

Alex would believe that when she saw it. And even if he had changed, that didn't change what he'd done to her, how he'd treated her.

How she didn't seem to have any control over her reactions to him.

"All you have to do is be civil until the wedding is over."

Lynn gave her arm a squeeze and smiled. One would think she was five again and asking for one of Alex's dolls, and Alex could no more tell her little sister no now than she had way back when.

"Fine then. I can do civil," she said grudgingly. "But you'll owe me your firstborn and anything else I might want in the future."

Lynn smothered her in a big hug. "Deal . . . at least full babysitting rights for our firstborn," she amended with a giggle.

"Here we are," Lenora sang as she entered the doorway with her grandmother's Haviland tea set steaming on a tray. But the fretful look she cast at Alex belied her cheery demeanor.

"Don't worry, Mama," Alex assured her. "I promised Lynn to be civil."

A relieved smile washed over Lenora's face. "That's my girls." She put the tray down and opened her arms. Lynn rushed into her mother's embrace, with Alex dragging behind.

"This is going to be the best wedding Piper Cove has ever seen," Lenora said, hugging them.

"I know it is," Lynn agreed, breathless with a joy that Alex tried not to envy. "I have the best mom and greatest sister helping me plan it."

Feeling anything but the greatest sister, Alex brandished a civil smile as she backed away. She was going to need all the practice she could get.

CHAPTER THREE

Josh Turner gave the mirror in the cab of his black Dodge Ram a civil smile as he ran a comb through his hair. Heaven knew he'd need a store of them to get through all of the hullabaloo associated with John and Lynn's wedding. Knowing the Butlers, it wouldn't be a small, quiet affair. Alex was planning it, or so Lynn had said.

Alex. Josh glanced over at the vacant leather seat next to him and, for a moment, he was no longer in his new expensive pickup truck, but the old rusty red Ford he'd driven as a teen. He could almost envision Alex Butler sitting beside him, clad in jeans and a tight-fitting top that revealed a trim, delectable midriff. She'd been so ticklish that all he'd had to do was give it a menacing look, and she'd dissolve into giggles. Part girl, part woman, and all wildcat—not at all like the business-suit-clad female he'd seen at the coffee shop the other day. Old B. J. had finally got what he wanted, a female clone of himself.

If the wildcat had survived their first year of marriage, maybe things would have turned out differently, he mused. A backwash of bitterness in his throat caught him by surprise as he slid off the smooth leather seat and onto the paved parking lot. It hadn't been long before the honeymoon was over and the arguments started. What she'd loved about him—music gigs, late nights, and uninhibited passion, she'd started hating. The dream he'd shared with her of making it in the music business became his alone.

Annoyance shouldered its way into his thoughts, pushing aside the blame he cast on Alex alone. He knew better than that. Or at least he should know better. They'd both been young, with expectations and dreams that couldn't survive the real world. He *knew* that....

It didn't help. At the moment his prayer for rationality and detachment seemed to be unheard, though he knew better than that, too.

How many times since seeing her unexpectedly at the coffee shop had he needed to remind himself it was just as well they had parted ways? If they'd still been together, Alex could have been killed in the accident that maimed his hands. Josh flexed his fingers, staring at the scars from the surgery that had saved them.

At least his dream hadn't been totally in vain. He'd made a boatload of money doing what he'd loved, and with some wise investment it had multiplied considerably. God had graciously saved him before he'd killed himself with drugs and alcohol, then revealed a new purpose for Josh's life by helping others survive, if not avoid, chemical addiction. Yep, Piper Cove's rebel from the wrong side of town had reformed, and returned in style and then some.

When he'd walked into B. J. Butler's office this afternoon, he'd been determined not to rub it in the old man's face. Much, anyway. But the forgiveness in Josh's heart over the ultimatum B. J. had given him sixteen years ago took a beating when the bank president refused to sell him the Turner farmhouse where Josh had been raised, where he and Alex had lived with his grandmother for almost a year.

"Boy, you don't have enough money to buy that place from me, I don't care how much you made playin' that guitar. I bought it fair and square. The auction was announced in the paper and through proper channels. It's not my fault you missed it in that *rehab*—" B. J. practically spat the word out in distaste. "—you got yourself into."

Josh's fists tightened, driving his fingernails into the flesh of his palms. It was his fault that he'd been in rehab at the time. That his grandmother left the place to Uncle Joe and Aunt Marie was only right. They'd taken care of Gran and sold it when they retired and moved to Florida.

It wasn't their fault, but he felt robbed of his victorious return . . . although not completely. Smugness tugged at the corner of Josh's mouth. B. J. had only bought the farmhouse and a couple of acres. The rest of the land had gone to a now overextended development company that was all too eager to pass it on to the highest bidder—which happened to be Josh's new development company.

"Just because you've cozied up to folks higher than you, doesn't make you one of them, Turner," B. J. had told him. "I'll be civil, but you can bet I'll be watchin' you a like a hawk. My Alex is still too good for your likes."

That comment definitely stung—Josh couldn't deny that there was an element of truth in it. Alex had been too good for him. She wouldn't have given up on their marriage so easily and hadn't deserved Josh's abandonment without explanation. If he had it to do over, that was one among his many transgressions that he'd have changed, no matter what her father said.

"Well you just do that, B. J."

Josh was so angry, it was a wonder his collar hadn't caught fire. There'd been a time he might have flipped the old man the finger and cursed him till a fly wouldn't pitch on him. Instead, Josh retreated, steaming until he was inside his vehicle, where he again prayed for rationality and detachment. He knew in his mind that forgiveness was the right thing to do, but B. J. Butler made it harder than he'd anticipated. When Jesus had said love one's enemies, old B. J. hadn't been born.

Josh gave in to a sheepish grin, imagining heaven's stern look at his errant thought. *I know, Lord. I have to at least be civil to the man, not just today, but during all the wedding-related shenanigans to come. One day at a time.*

Josh grabbed his suit jacket from the back, as a young woman rolled her motorcycle into a parking spot nearby. Tall, slight of build, and clad in a gray slack suit, she put down the kickstand and removed a red helmet to reveal long dark brown hair pulled up in a no-frills ponytail. Upon seeing him next to the Escalade, she whistled.

"Now *that's* a pickup," Ellen Brittingham marveled. The heels of her pointed-toed dress boots clicked on the asphalt as she approached. "Let me guess, three-forty-five horses, three-eighty pounds per foot of torque." Ellen was one of a kind, able to talk shop with the boys till the cows came home. And she could hold her own with a tool set.

"You sound like a talking brochure," Josh chuckled.

She smacked the hood. "Mind if I take a peek?"

"How could I refuse a Harley-riding vamp like you?"

He reached inside and released the hood. Before he could help her, it was up and locked into place. "Oh," she groaned as she ogled the engine. "I'm in love."

"If you're good, I'll let you drive her later."

Ellen's ponytail bobbed with the swing of her face toward him. "Not in this lifetime," she snorted. "First, it would spoil me. Second, you stiffed my best friend, and even if your toys are mind-blowing, she comes first. Besides, she'd kill me if she saw me with you."

"Gotcha." Josh always did like Ellen. She intimidated the heck out of guys, but when she met the right one, that brass would be appealing. "I'll see if I can get dispensation from the queen," he said, referring to Alex. If he'd had a little sister, Ellen would be his choice. In fact, he liked all of Alex's friends. He even liked her mom and sister. It was just her father he couldn't stand to be around.

Ellen cocked a dark brow at him, her dark eyes shining with mischief. "Pull that off, and you're on. Although," she said, straightening from her close examination, "you do anything, and I mean *anything,* to hurt Alex again, and I'll pull your plugs so fast you won't know what hit you."

Laughing, Josh threw up his hands in surrender. "You have my word, I have no intention of having anything to do with Alex, save act the best man to her maid of honor in the wedding. Past is past." Even as Josh said it, a note of skepticism niggled at the back of his brain.

"Ellen Brittingham, is that you with your head stuck under Josh Taylor's hood?"

Jan Kudrow approached them from the paved drive leading toward Piper Cove proper. Still clad in a white chef's coat with a mandarin collar, a baker's cap, and white sneakers, she carried a small duffel bag slung over her shoulder. "Shame on you," she chided Ellen, grinning all the while.

"What, is that pillbox pinned to your brain?" Ellen reached over and tugged off her work hat, ruffling Jan's short blond hair.

Josh always did think Jan looked like a cross between the Disney fairy and a green-eyed Goldie Hawn—all eyes, smile, and heart, too much of the latter for her own good. Like him, Jan hadn't had the easiest row to hoe in Piper Cove. She was always getting dumped on, first by her family, whose earned reputation as trailer park trash had carried over to their innocent daughter. Later it was men who took advantage of her and her willingness to believe the best of everyone.

"My, but don't you look all handsome and distinguished." Jan said, reaching up to touch the silk-linen weave of the jacket he'd slung over his shoulder as though it were spun gold. "And rich."

"Yeah, well you'd better put your hardworking tush in high gear. This thing starts in twenty minutes," Ellen warned her.

Jan groaned. "Don't I know it? I worked from four in the morning till two this afternoon at the market, then went to do some part-time work at the Baysider . . . the new hotel restaurant. It's catering its first wedding this weekend. I didn't think I'd ever finish all those tiny pastries."

"I was wondering at that getup. You look like a malnourished version of the Pillsbury Doughboy," Josh teased.

"I borrowed the coat from the pastry chef," she explained. "He complimented my work and said that when business picks up, I might be able to work full-time for him." She shrugged, lifting the too-big coat up and down on her small frame. "At least I learned something in New York besides how hopeless I am at acting."

"She's a regular duchess of sweets." Ellen grabbed her by the arm and started to usher her away. "I hope your dress and shoes are in that bag."

"See you soon, Josh," Jan called over her shoulder, as her friend rushed her into the side door of the coffee shop.

"Will do, ladies."

"Are you flirting with him?" he heard Ellen chastise in a sawmill whisper as the two retreated.

"Don't be silly," Jan shot back. "I'm not looking to be dumped *again*."

Josh exhaled heavily. It hurt to be thought of so poorly by the Bosom Buddies. For a moment, he wanted badly to call them back and explain what he'd done all those years ago and why. To justify himself.

He shook his head as he tugged on his jacket and walked toward the front entrance. Sue Ann had said it: "The proof will be in the pudding." Hadn't he learned that actions rather than words spoke the truth?

He had a feeling that he would be painfully reminded of that quite a bit while he was here. *Lord deliver me from my own weaknesses.*

After picking up a lime and tonic at the bar, where some locals were gathered, eyes glued to ESPN on the big-screen television, he meandered into the private dining room and stopped dead in his tracks.

Alex Butler commanded the centerpiece-toting waitstaff like a five-star general, moving about the room and checking place cards against a list.

"No, Stephen," she called out, her tone a velvet-coated steel, "the large arrangement is for the head table."

"You got it, Miss Butler," the young man said with a look that was nothing less than pure lust as Alex bent over to change a place card.

She was clueless to the boy's admiration. That much hadn't changed. There was no seductress in Alex Butler, though she oozed sensuality.

"Has the wine been opened? It has to breathe," she said, straightening to catch Josh in midgrin. Her brown eyes widened with recognition. "You . . . you're early."

"Need any help?" he asked, surprised to find his mouth had gone dry. The dress was hardly sexy. Sleeveless, it covered her from the soft drape at her neck to a ragged kind of diagonal hem that swung and clung to her long legs. But it fit like icing on a cake, smooth and tempting.

"No, I have everything under control, thank you." Alex shoved in the chair that blocked the remainder of his view. The tip of the dress ended just above the ankle strap of a pair of three-inch heels the same cream color as her dress.

Groaning inwardly, Josh took a drink of the lime and tonic before his tongue stuck to the roof of his mouth. Aw man. He was a sucker for high heels. He didn't know how women walked, much less walked gracefully in them, but he was glad they did. The sight of Alex in heels mesmerized him. "I—" He coughed as a trickle of the drink went down the wrong way. His voice was strangled as he finished. "In that case, I'll—" He cleared his throat "—I'll wait in the bar till it's proper for me make an entrance."

Okay, he could pass on the business-suited Alex, even with a smidgen of hot fudge on her face. But the sight of Alex looking like a Greek goddess in high heels was enough to send the wooden totem pole at the Ocean City inlet jumping in the water before it self-ignited.

The who's who of Worcester County enjoyed a meal of steamship round, grilled bacon–wrapped scallops, and Maryland backfin crabcakes as only local cooks could prepare it. At the head table with her family, her sister's future in-laws, and Josh Turner, Alex sat next to her fidgeting mother and carried on a conversation with Mrs. John Whitlowe, Sr., about a shopping trip planned for the following day.

"Of course, Ocean City is a resort town, so most of the clothing will be casual," she said. "And we can have lunch at the Harbor House on the inlet. There's a Coast Guard museum next to it; the view is lovely and food scrumptious."

Marilyn Whitlowe, a beefy woman in a tailored linen suit, clasped her bejeweled hands together. "My dear, it doesn't matter what we buy. It's the quest and the company that will make the day."

"My feelings exactly," her husband agreed. His smoothed, salted hair and blue suit fit the big banker image more than B. J.'s silvered auburn shock and sport coat. He winked at Josh. "It won't matter what we catch, it's the quest and the company, right, young man?"

"But if we happen to snag a marlin, you wouldn't complain, would you?" Josh challenged good-naturedly.

Josh had offered to take the men, B. J. Butler included, deep-sea fishing on his new boat. B. J. had little option but to accept. After all, it would be unseemly for him to decline an afternoon of fishing, not just with his daughter's future in-law, but his future boss. On the one hand, it pleased Alex to see her father being manipulated for a change. On the other, knowing that Josh was subtly tugging the strings annoyed her.

"We'll do breakfast at McMann's," Alex rallied. "You remember my dad's sister Rose's place."

"That would be great. I hope she'll be there. I could tell your aunt was a character the moment you introduced her," Mrs. Whitlowe confided with a hint of mischief that belied her demure appearance.

Clad in a bold red, white, and blue pantsuit with sequined anchors, Aunt Rose had been grace itself when Lynn introduced her earlier, but her aunt was what she was—a diamond in the rough.

"Why, you might just land one like B. J. has mounted over his desk at the bank," Josh was saying to the men.

"Hah," the senior Whitlowe exclaimed. "Wouldn't mind that at all, young man, not at all. Maybe B. J. here can give me some pointers."

"I believe his sister Rose holds the local record," Josh told him, casting a "gotcha" glance at B. J.

"That's right," B. J. answered evenly. But Alex knew from the beet red flush around her father's collar that Josh was getting his goat. "We'll make a fisherman out of you for sure. This is fishing paradise."

"And beach paradise," Lynn put in, distracting Alex from the subtle gaffing contest between Josh and her father. "Don't forget the beach."

If her sister were any giddier, she'd float, Alex observed. And she wasn't so certain the prospective groom was on the ground either. Tall, dark, and handsome in his tailored silk suit, John Jr. looked a little drunk every time he looked at Lynn—drunk with adoration.

Alex had been there, done that, and, confound it, she couldn't help but envy them. She prayed, for Lynn's sake, that it was the real thing and not what Alex had shared with Josh.

"Which is why," her father continued, his wily tone drawing Alex to full alert, "I have decided to give the newlyweds a summer house on the river."

Lynn's hands flew to her naturally rosy cheeks. "What?"

John Jr. was no less astonished. "A . . . a summer home? Sir, that's beyond—"

"Young man, if your daddy can buy you a fancy condominium in the city, then Lenora and I can provide a retreat for our daughter near the ocean." Punch proud, B. J. put his arm around Lenora, who looked at him with speechless astonishment. He gave her a squeeze. "Now, darlin', I know how it grieves you that our baby will be living across the bay, so this is for you as well as the newlyweds," he told her. "Lynn can come down here in the warm weather and you, young man," he said to John Jr., "can commute with that little plane of yours from the local airport."

"Why, Daddy, I don't know what to say," Lynn gushed, cuddling into the cradle of her fiancé's arm. "Where is it?"

A smile spread on B. J.'s mouth, a Cheshire cat's with a belly full of goldfish smile. What *was* he up to, Alex wondered. She fished a preemptive antacid out of her purse and popped it in her mouth.

Please God, make him behave.

"Now, now, it's not ready yet," B. J. said, drawing out the suspense with a Suzie Q finesse. "It needs some work, but I'm going to hire the best interior designer I know to make it just right for you two."

The antacid lodged in Alex's throat as her father turned the smile on her. She swallowed hard, more certain than ever that this wasn't something that she wanted to hear . . . especially when B. J. switched his smug attention squarely on Josh Turner and pounced.

"Of course, Josh knows the place well, don't you, boy?"

"Daddy, what are you saying?" Alex's annoyed question was rhetorical. Deep down in the churning mass that was her stomach, she already knew what B. J. was talking about.

"Oh, Daddy, you don't mean the Turner place?" Lynn tossed a disconcerted glance at Alex.

John Jr. clapped Josh on the back. "Man, did you know about this? You know, of course, that your having lived there makes it even more special to us." Clearly he was oblivious to the hostility that flowed between Josh and his future father-in-law, or the shock on anyone's face who knew the home's history.

"Didn't have a clue," Josh replied through a fixed smile. "This is *all* B. J.'s doing."

All was right. If her mother had known about this, she'd never have allowed it. And poor Lynn was too stunned to do anything but follow the dictates of good manners.

Alex clung to the straw of a thought as though it alone would keep her from slipping into the dark undercurrent flowing back and forth between the two men. God in heaven, she was caught in the middle after all.

Alex clenched her fists around the napkin in her lap, reeling back and forth between past and present betrayal. How could B. J. expect her to restore the home where she and Josh had shared so many memories, enough good ones to make it sacred to a part of her. If it had been all bad, she could have walked away unscathed and chalked their year together up to inexperience and bad choices.

God, You know I can't do this.

Beneath the table, Lenora Butler found Alex's hand and gave it a sympathetic squeeze. Alex forced a valiant smile to stem the worried flow of compassion and sympathy in her mother's gaze. She wanted to soak it up like a vulnerable and frightened child, but Mama was the fragile one. She needed protection more than Alex.

"I'd been thinking how great it would be to have a vacation

place down here once we got on our feet financially, but this is mind-boggling, sir." John Jr. drew Lynn against him with an enthused hug.

Whatever second thought her sister had for Alex's feelings dissolved in love's euphoria. "And I just love that old Victorian with the wraparound porch. It overlooks the river and has a little dock," Lynn told her fiancé. "It was grand in its day," she finished weakly as she glanced at Alex.

Lynn didn't like old homes. She preferred sleek and modern. Alex tried to tamp down a rising mix of anger and anguish as her sister cast another furtive look of concern and apology her way. Under the circumstances, there wasn't much else her sister could do with her clueless fiancé practically drooling with delight over the gift.

"Well, its day had long passed when Josh lived there, and no one's lived there since he left for fame and fortune. It's hard to keep a place like that up," B. J. reminded her.

"I know that Alex will restore it to a modern fare-thee-well," her sister went on. "I'll bet *Victorian Homes* will do a feature on it."

Lynn rose and planted a big kiss on B. J.'s cheek before going around him to smother her mother with hugs and kisses as well. "You two are full of surprises. Why I'm speechless ... utterly speechless."

Those at the table who knew Lynn's chattiness laughed. Alex couldn't. So much for the glimmer of hope that Lynn might turn down the gift, though it was unreasonable. Alex tried to muster a smile, but the way her emotions twisted and clashed, she didn't know whether she succeeded or not.

Acutely aware of Josh's steady appraisal from across the table, searching, yet unfathomable, Alex cast a longing look at a nearby table where her best friends had been seated with two of the county's new and most eligible bachelors. Next to her husband Martin, who'd flown in from Belize that morning, Sue Ann had relinquished her accustomed role of queen of the table to Aunt Rose. The center of attention, Rose spoke in a sawmill whisper that almost reached Alex's ear, causing her companions to erupt with amusement.

Alex glanced down at her plate, trying to swallow the antacid-coated blade of emotion in her throat. Her friends were laughing. She, on the other hand, was slowly dying inside.

CHAPTER FOUR

After dessert, guests mingled, moving from table to table to the music of a three-piece ensemble. The cluster of well-wishers around the head table was as oppressive from without as Alex's emotional turmoil was from within. Unsure of whether she'd lose what little dinner she'd eaten or simply pass out from the suffocating waves of body heat and assorted colognes, she worked her way away from the knot of guests and toward the rear terrace overlooking the river.

The evening breeze felt good to her flesh, evaporating the dampness from the heat of the close quarters. Alex inhaled the familiar mingle of salty ocean and river air, forcing open her lungs against the fists of tension constricting them, and walked down the steps to a gazebo, pristine white against a backdrop of starlit sky and water. To her left, the sleepy downtown of Piper Cove stretched around the curve of the harbor. Its clusters of onion-globed streetlights peeped through the pine trees of the city park.

To her right, beyond the mouth of the cove, the eastern skyline glowed from the lights of Ocean City's hotels, condos, and amusement parks. Thankfully the noise of traffic, the roar of the rides, and screams of delight and terror the rides exacted remained on that side of the bay. Not that Alex minded them. She'd grown up thrilling to the thrum of the resort. But tonight, she craved quiet to sort the thoughts and emotions turning end over end in her mind.

"Fancy meeting you here."

Alex started at the familiar drawl coming from the shadows beyond the latticed arches of the shelter. Her chest seized again. The last she'd seen Josh Turner, he'd been surrounded by some starstruck locals at the bar. Not that she'd been watching him. But that didn't matter. What was she going to do now?

"It's not intentional, trust me." Not a bad comeback. Alex forced herself to unclench her fists. "I needed some air . . . and quiet."

She debated walking straight through the gazebo, the halfway stop between the clubhouse terrace and the riverside, and down to the dock. But what if Josh followed her? What would she do then, jump in the water? Besides, it wasn't as if she could avoid him forever.

Instead of moving toward her, Josh leaned casually against one of the square posts and crossed his arms, head cocked. "Old B. J. blindsided you, didn't he?"

Alex shrank inwardly. She couldn't deal with the bomb B. J. dropped in her lap *and* Josh at the same time. Relying on instinct, she sought the only other defense she could find, an offense. "What are *you* doing out here?"

"Praying."

Now that was the last answer Alex expected. Curiosity stalling her other emotions, she sat down on one of the benches built along the octagonal rails. She wasn't prepared to believe Josh Turner had gotten religion, but the concept was intriguing. He'd never taken faith seriously when she'd known him. Only given it lip service out of respect for his grandmother. But all things were possible, Alex supposed. And heaven knew Josh had had enough knocks in his life to warrant the change knowing God personally could enable.

"Praying that I won't be tempted tomorrow to knock your dad overboard when no one's looking," Josh continued with a familiar edge that always entered his voice when he spoke of her father. "The old goat wouldn't sell the place to me."

"You tried to buy the property?" she asked, startled by the possibility.

Of course it made perfect sense. Why else would her father decide to give Lynn and John that particular house? He knew Lynn wouldn't like the house, but the possibility of striking a blow at Josh would override any other consideration.

As if reliving the past, Alex was torn. She didn't like B. J. and his domineering ways, but she loved him; even though he persisted in placing her squarely in the middle between himself and Josh and using her as the rope. It was impossible to count the times her father complained to her about Josh's worthlessness, forcing her to defend Josh—her choice of Josh as a husband. Or the times that Josh had railed at her for something B. J. had done or said. Sometimes her father had meant well for them, like offering Josh a position at the bank, but Josh saw it as intrusive or manipulating. Her love for the two men tore at her from both sides.

It had been a no-win situation for them all. *God, I don't want to relive this!*

Alex tried to shut off the flood of old feelings pouring into her chest.

"I can't for the life of me imagine why my father bought that old place when there are beautiful lots all over Piper Cove where Lynn and John could build just what they want. Or a no-maintenance condo would suit Lynn's taste to a T," Alex declared, as disconcerted by Lynn's reaction as her own. It was part of Alex's job as a designer to pick up on people's likes and dislikes. The Turner place was *not* Lynn.

"Lynn's always been a contemporary girl," she went on, "new and cosmopolitan, not the nostalgic Victoriana type. Love must have addled her, the way she was gushing about wraparound porches like she was ready to don a Scarlett O'Hara dress and suck on a mint julep." *Stop babbling. Get to the point.* "Besides, that place doesn't have the best track record for happy relationships. I can't imagine why *you'd* even want it."

She winced, wishing curiosity didn't have such a hold on her common sense. Some things were best left alone.

While Alex couldn't see the smirk on Josh's lips, she heard it in his voice. "Oh, I don't know about that. Generations of Turners had a legacy of love, work, and dreams on that land . . . before you set foot on it."

So much for the remote chance of his remembering any good times. Alex bristled. But to insinuate she'd brought an end to his so-called legacy was war. "If your generation had done more than dream," she said, rising, "Turners might still own it."

"I did dream," Josh took a step toward her. "And I worked till it came true."

"Well maybe you lost your legacy because you forgot the love part."

Josh shook his head in reprisal. "Ally, Ally, Ally," he chided, closing the distance between them. "Now you know full well that's not true. That old house probably saw more lovin' between you and me than its rooms had ever seen before."

The man still didn't know the difference between love and lust, but her heart did. It beat a mile a minute as he stopped in front of her. Undoubtedly, he smiled that know-it-all smile of his, when he didn't know diddly.

"That was lust, Josh Turner. You wouldn't know love if it up and bit you on the backside."

"Is that so?" He propped his hands on his hips, mocking her.

Alex's breath hitched. He was close enough to project his body heat on hers, close enough that his scent filled her nostrils with the pure tinder of soap and virile male. She thought about bolting or slapping him, but to do either meant to touch him and sparking a sensory flash fire.

No, a dignified retreat was much better. Besides, she didn't stand a chance if she let this get up close and personal. He'd play her just as he'd done in the past, as he was trying to do now, daring her to dance close to the flame. But she needed space, or she'd be caught up in it anyway.

Alex placed her palm against his chest and backed him away. "It's a moot point, Josh. We've both moved on."

"Hey," he said, lifting his hands in surrender. "You're the one who brought it up."

Had she? Alex paused at the gazebo steps, backflashing. Okay, she *had* brought up their soured relationship, but if they'd not been discussing the Turner homestead . . .

"No, B. J. did," she decided aloud as she turned to make her escape. "We were simply drawn into Daddy's wake."

"Yeah, well don't let him drown you, Ally," Josh called after her.

Head high, Alex continued toward the terrace, where some of the guests had meandered out to enjoy the pleasant evening. "I learned to swim a long time ago, Josh. That old place is just another job," she called over her shoulder.

Maybe *she* should have been the one to go to New York to become an actress instead of Jan. The Turner place would never be *just* another job to Alex . . . but Josh didn't have to know that.

∽

The bells heralding the opening service of one of the two churches on Church Street echoed through Piper Cove above the chatter of the Sunday worshippers leaving the other two blocks away. Having promised her mother that she'd be at the Butler home no later than one to help with preparations for the dinner that her parents were hosting for Lynn's future husband and his parents, Alex walked briskly past the mostly Victorian homes lining the back street.

So far, everything had gone smoothly, Josh and the Turner place notwithstanding. Mrs. Whitlowe was charm personified, so that Lenora Butler eventually relaxed in her presence and enjoyed the resort shopping and lunch they'd shared at the Ocean City inlet. When the men returned from a successful day of fishing, the senior Whitlowes and Butlers went out for a parents-only dinner, while the younger generation did their own thing.

Caught between the age groups, Alex declined an invitation to go clubbing at the beach. Instead, she spent her Saturday evening working on sketches for longtime client Lillian Laws, who'd given her two weeks' notice to do over a June 1st rental.

Walking through the four-block historical district which she'd helped preserve, Alex couldn't help but smile at the irony that she'd been the kid who was going to leave the hick town with its old houses in her dust at eighteen. The exteriors looked like the old Piper Cove fishing village, while the interiors were modernized to house specialty shops with posh upstairs apartments overlooking the park and waterfront beyond.

Odd how the terrible storm of 1933 that all but leveled the village and cut the inlet connecting the ocean to the bay had closed one door to the bayside fishing community and opened another—charter fishing and tourism. Alex slowed at the corner, taking a moment to enjoy the view. Memories of the place were countless for Alex. Band concerts and picnics in the pavilion, meeting her friends at the playground, her first kiss . . .

Josh. She couldn't avoid him in thought or in the flesh. This afternoon she'd promised to help her parents entertain the Whitlowes. Naturally, as best man, Josh would be there, just as he'd been in church this morning, looking as saintly as a choirboy in a coat and tie. He'd set the tongues of the senior members wagging by sending more than one playful glance Alex's way. By this evening, those who were new to Piper Cove would know the whole sordid story of her and Josh's past. She doubted a soul had focused on the minister's topic.

Talk about storms. Josh had blown in like a number five tornado, turning her life upside down. And it would take an act of God to put it right. Grimacing, Alex made her way to the awning-protected storefront of Designs by Alex and let herself in a side door that led up to her apartment. She emerged from the stairwell into a world of light. The sun flooded the whites and beiges of the room through the tall palladian windows fronting the street.

Her heels sank into the thick oriental runner leading past her tiled kitchen/dining area to the living room, when a feline trill from the box seat in one of the windows drew Alex's attention to where a large yellow tabby, stretched lazily and yawned, his nap evidently interrupted by his person's entrance.

"Hello, Riley. Did you miss me?" she asked, as the two-year-old tabby jumped down from his perch and approached her for his due affection.

Riley was Alex's golden-eyed rescue from Clamdiggers, the seafood restaurant at the edge of the park. No one knew where the little garbage scavenger came from, but at the rate that it kept sneaking into the restaurant kitchen each time the door opened, it was on its way to the animal shelter . . . until it ran from the business owner up and under Alex's car.

Still dressed in a chic skirt suit from an earlier business meeting, Alex had to lie on her back, shimmy under the vehicle, and retrieve the frightened fur ball from between two black hoses that connected heaven only knew what. Both looking the worse for wear, she'd left her car at the restaurant and walked through the park to her apartment, with the decidedly stinking kitten wrapped in a tablecloth that the restaurant owner told her to toss out when she was done with it.

Scooping him up in her arms, Alex walked through the open living area to her bedroom door. "I have to get moving, Riley," she told the cat, putting him down on the rose-print spread. It set the theme of the room, so that the paintings and other accessories tied into it.

"Yeah, I know," she said, when Riley gave her a look of consternation. "I'm as excited as you are about my leaving again, but a woman's gotta do what a woman's gotta do."

She stopped, catching sight of the floral garland that she'd woven around a train of gauze that was draped from the canopy frame over the bed. One string of flowers appeared to have been suspiciously rearranged by untrained feline paws. Alex straight-ened it, recapturing its whimsical, romantic look.

The extent of romance in her life, for all that.

"You have no sense of décor," she told the guileless feline. "And who needs romance?"

But the realization that Riley was the only steady male presence in her life, aside from her father, made Alex groan.

Lord, please don't let me wind up in another thirty or so years like one of those crazy cat ladies I've seen on cop reality television shows. You know, the ones living in isolation and litter?

Although they seemed happy. A little nutty, but content.

Still frowning, Alex had taken a sundress from the closet and laid it on the bed when the phone rang. Riley bolted for it. But instead of knocking it off the hook—a nasty habit Alex had finally broken him of—he sat next to it on the bedside table, waiting for Alex to answer it as if it never crossed the furry rascal's mind to forget his training.

"Hello?" she said upon picking it up.

"Hi there, future sister-in-law. This is John. I've got a quick question for you."

Alex lifted her brow in surprise. She didn't know John even had her number. "Shoot, future brother-in-law." Lynn had probably given it to him.

"How would you like to have some steamed crabs with the din-ner this afternoon?"

Immediately Alex pictured the mess—newspapers, empty shells, and chum. It was fine in a restaurant with concrete floors or commercial carpet, but in her parent's dining room on a Persian Kashan? Besides, she already had planned the menu with Lenora and Fran, the Butlers' part-time housekeeper and cook. Grilled steaks topped with crab imperial, Greek salad, Fran's scalloped potatoes, and homemade yeast rolls ... Steamed hard crabs hardly fit.

"It's a little early for crabs, isn't it?" She hoped John would detect the hesitation in her voice and take the hint. "They're usually poor this time of year."

"We have our sources," he said, clueless. "And Mom and Dad love them."

Alex could have sworn she heard a snicker in the background. Josh, undoubtedly. "Well," she began slowly. "If you already have them—"

"We do. Josh and I will take care of everything," John assured her. "You're the greatest, sis. We'll see you later."

Sis? "What do you mean *everything*?" Alex asked, as visions of mama's china and silver in the dining room gave way to newspaper and crab mallets in the Florida room.

But it was too late. John had hung up. She returned the handset to the base as Riley rubbed up against her, complaining with a three-syllable *Mr-r-ow*.

"My thoughts exactly." Alex gave the cat a head scratch and kicked into high gear. She put the sundress back in the closet and donned a more casual outfit in its place. Whatever those guys were up to, she wanted to be there ahead of time to organize it. The last thing she needed was her carefully planned afternoon turned into the chaos Josh was fully capable of.

CHAPTER FIVE

The Capri set that Alex had chosen to wear was damp with perspiration from setting up for a crab feast in the sunroom overlooking the back patio. Now she stood, gaping at the sight and scratching sound of the bushel basket filled with live blue crabs that Josh Turner unloaded from the back of his pickup. It was bad enough that he'd ruined her dinner plans, but the crabs weren't even steamed! That meant getting out a steamer and filling the Butler home with the scent of locally blended Old Bay seasoning and cooking crab. It wasn't an unpleasant smell, by any means. Nothing could tantalize the taste buds like steaming crabs doused in Old Bay seasoning, but the process of cooking and eating them conflicted with the genteel elegance that she'd meticulously planned for the afternoon.

"Where do you want me to put these?" Josh asked, his grin as wide as the barrier island resort across the bay.

"I don't think I can answer that honestly," Alex muttered under her breath. This was so typical. Josh never gave any thought to his actions. He just acted and left her to pull the pieces together. And then he'd left altogether . . .

His smile faltered for a moment. "Don't you worry about it," he assured her. "John and I figured we could set up the picnic table in the garage and set up the gas burner just outside."

Picnic table . . . *garage* . . . gas burner . . . Alex stewed. He just didn't get it. But then, he never did. For the last hour, she, Lynn, their mother, and Fran had been trying to figure how to convert the formal Sunday dinner into an informal but gourmet crab feast. While Alex and Lynn put away the china and silver in the dining room, moved furniture out of the sunroom, and set up paper-covered tables, Lenora and Fran changed the menu to shish kebabs and crab balls.

"Crabs!" Lynn's squeal drew Alex's attention to where her sister bounded out of the house. "What a delightful surprise." She threw her arms around her fiancé's neck as though the young men had brought a basket of gold doubloons instead of crawling live critters with pincers that, once clamped on a toe or finger, would not let go. A crab bite gave a whole new meaning to *till death do us part.*

"Don't thank me," John replied. "It was Josh's idea."

It was hard to believe that just moments before, her schizophrenic sister was grumbling in sympathy with Alex as they covered the tables with brown paper, a far cry from the exquisite linen-and-lace tablecloth they'd put away. Leaving the love-besotted couple chatting by the tailgate as though they'd not seen each other in years instead of hours, Alex followed Josh to the one of the open garage doors, careful to keep her voice down.

"Have you lost your mind?" she demanded, maintaining a respectable distance from the bushel of crabs he deposited on the paved driveway.

Once bitten, twice shy was an understatement for her when it came to the live crustaceans. A bite when she was seven ended her summer fun crabbing with the other kids off the bulkhead. The only crab she trusted now was steamed red-orange and smothered in Old Bay seasoning. That kind could only give an open cut or hangnail a burn to remember.

"I promise, they're nice, not locals." Josh told her, as if she didn't know that the area's preseason catches were poor of meat and often filled with mud from being dredged from the bottom in the still-cold waters. "These babies came in from Carolina this morning. Your aunt Rose gave me a deal I couldn't refuse . . . wanted to put on the dog for the Whitlowes."

"Bless her heart." Guilt pinged Alex.

Okay, Lord, my tone didn't exactly imply blessing. She loved Aunt Rose, and getting prime crabs in May *was* a treat, but only under different circumstances. Her ire more fixed on Josh, Alex counted to ten. But ten wasn't enough to negate, not just today's ire but that hitting like hailstones from the past. The man was a loose cannon when it came to the orderly life that made her tick.

"*This* is your idea of putting on the dog?" she challenged. "Did you ever think to check with me before you did this? No," she answered for him. "Did it cross your mind that this wouldn't go with what Mother and I had planned for dinner? No, of course not. And now you've ruined—"

At that moment, the Whitlowes pulled up in a silver Mercedes sedan and guided it into a paved area set aside for guest parking. Alex bit her lip as John and Lynn walked over to greet them.

"Well, well," B. J. Butler's voice boomed behind her "Looks like we've got our work cut out for us." Her father and mother came out of the house through the garage, arm in arm to meet their guests. "You ever steam crabs, John?" he asked the senior Whitlowe.

"Oh, I've done a few in my time, although," John Sr. added with a chuckle, "it's been a while."

It was a disaster, Alex thought. The Whitlowes looked as though they were still in their church clothes, clearly not dressed for a crab feast. The first time her father had asked for her help, and it was turning into a disaster. "I could just die," she muttered under her breath to her mother. "Everything is falling apart."

"Nonsense, dear," Lenora answered. "Just follow my lead."

Her mother's composure in welcoming her guests left Alex dumbfounded. Granted, Alex had warned her parents ahead of time that the young men were bringing a bushel of crabs, although not even Alex had guessed they'd not been steamed. Now, the woman who'd barely kept frustrated tears in check as they'd gone over the invitation list was acting as if this was what she'd had in mind all along. If it was a new medication, Alex wanted some.

"B. J. dear," Lenora announced with the aplomb of a queen, "I'm leaving the outdoor cooking to you and the men. Why don't you set up the burner on the patio, where there's already furniture for everyone to sit in? Meanwhile, Marilyn, I, and the girls will be inside, if you need anything. We'd started out to have a Sunday dinner in the dining room," she confided to Marilyn Whitlowe, as they entered the house through the utility room, "but the boys came up with the crabs at the last moment, so . . ."

"So it's fall back and regroup," Marilyn finished for her. "Don't worry on my account. I can't recall the number of times I've had to do the same thing. I can't decide if learning to shift direction in

midstride has kept me young or added some of this gray to my hair."
She laughed. "But that's what keeps our marriage interesting."

"I know exactly what you mean," Lenora agreed, shooting a
strange look in Alex's direction. "But, are you sure your John won't
mind cooking outside with the men?"

Was Mama trying to tell her that this confusion made a marriage interesting? And why, for heaven's sake? It wasn't like Alex
was going to jump into that fire again. Besides, constantly shifting
feet got old when the shifting was one-sided.

"Mind?" Marilyn made a snort that didn't go with her flawless
sophistication. "Darling, he's in his element. There's something
about fire that brings out the primitive in men, even city-born and
-bred ones. All I have to do is mention the grill, and John, who
couldn't cook a decent meal in the kitchen if his life depended on
it, suddenly becomes the master chef."

"Pay attention, girls," Lenora said, leading the way into the Florida room. "The sooner you learn to go with the flow, the less you'll
need a counselor to deal with the other sex."

She was more prone to need an attorney; a criminal one, Alex
fumed in silence as she made her way to where Fran had set up a
refreshment bar to serve iced tea and lemonade.

⥈

"Well hello there, pup," Josh said to the dog who bounded around
the house, seemingly from out of nowhere, with a well-chewed
Frisbee in its mouth. He gave the chocolate Chesapeake a head rub.
"I didn't think you liked dogs, B. J.," he said to his host.

"He's not mine," B. J. answered as he put the first steamer full of
crabs on the gas unit that Josh had brought along. "Sparks belongs
to the neighbors, but the moment he senses there's food around,
he's Johnny-on-the-spot."

"Not a dog person, eh?" John Sr. asked from one of the patio chairs they'd circled around the burner. "I thought everyone in this area had hunting dogs."

"No, I'm just never home to give one the attention it needs," B. J. replied smoothly. "Like my work too much, I suppose. Then there's Lenora's allergies . . ."

Josh smiled to himself, tossing the Frisbee toward the waterfront where Lynn and John Jr. sat on the small dock that jutted into the water. Ignoring an unsolicited pang of envy, Josh zeroed in on B. J.'s act. He was quick as a fox, Josh gave him that. And he was bending over backward to impress his future boss. Time was, Josh might have reminded B. J. of his disparaging remarks regarding the mixed Lab and Shepherd puppy that Josh had given Alex for their first Valentine's Day together.

As Sparks brought the Frisbee back to Josh, the dog was distracted by the movement of the remaining crabs in the basket that B. J. had set on an upside-down bucket for ease of reach.

"Whoa, back off, boy. You don't want your nose nipped." Josh tugged the dog away, picked up the disc, and threw it again.

"A little bird told me you were thinking of sticking around in Piper Cove for a while, Josh," B. J. said, drawing Josh from his preoccupation with Sparks. "Why on earth would you want to leave the West Coast? I thought you'd burned your bridges back here a long time ago."

No, B. J. had burned all those bridges, or given it his best shot, Josh was tempted to say. But he didn't. He could have chosen not to go along with B. J.'s plan. At the time, with all the bickering between him and Alex, it had just seemed like the right thing to do. He and Alex had been too young and immature for marriage, at least in his twenty-twenty hindsight.

"Let's just say I'm thinking about building a new bridge," Josh sidestepped. "How does it go about taking the country boy out of the country, but you can't take the country out of the boy?"

John Whitlowe, Sr. snorted. "Now don't be modest, young man. No *thinking* about it. Our *country boy* pulled off the deal of a lifetime. If I'd gotten wind of it first, I'd have beaten him to it, but he had inside information."

B. J. eased into one of the plump-cushioned patio chairs, his neck growing red from the polo collar of his shirt and spreading upward. "Inside information for a deal around here?"

"Tell him, son." Whitlowe beamed with pride like the father that Josh had never known.

"I bought the Bainbridge Construction project."

B. J. started as if one of the crabs had latched on to his toe. "The one developing your farm? A Baltimore company bought them out before it went to auction."

"My company," Josh informed him.

It had cost an outrageous sum, but the look on B. J.'s face was worth every penny. And in time, Josh would easily double his money. There was only so much waterfront property left and even less that had been approved for development before the moratorium. Bainbridge had been undercapitalized and overextended.

"I knew I should have grabbed that property when your aunt and uncle put it up for sale, but at the time, I had my hands full with this development," B. J. grumbled. He gripped the arms of his chair as though it might be pulled out from under him like the rest of the Turner land had.

A dart of guilt pricked at Josh's conscience. *Lord, I know I shouldn't be enjoying this so much, but that old fox has had it coming for a long time.*

"We can't catch them all," Whitlowe commiserated, unaware of the hostile history between his companions. "And this is one fine-looking development. Marilyn and I took a ride around it before coming here."

"And you *did* get the homeplace," Josh reminded his ex-father-in-law. Beside him, Sparks gave Josh an eager nudge. *And you got your daughter,* he thought, distracted by the sight of Alex emerging from the Florida room with two pitchers.

"Refresh your tea or lemonade?" she asked.

"None for me," Josh answered, rising to check on the crabs. They didn't need checking, but it was hard to act like nothing had ever happened between them. He'd never told the Whitlowes about his marriage to Alex, partly from shame, partly because he wasn't one to share his private life. He figured that since the family never asked, John and Lynn hadn't volunteered the information either. Or maybe the senior Whitlowes were too tactful to bring up the past.

"This first batch should be ready in another twenty minutes," he said to no one in particular.

"This is the best lemonade I've had since my mother used to handpress the lemons," John Sr. told Alex as she freshened his glass. "Don't tell me your mother does the same thing?"

"Don't let on to Mama that I told you, but it's really a mix," Alex confessed. "Mama adds a little sugar and a fresh-squeezed lemon to dress it up. Then leaves the bruised rinds in the pitcher. That's the secret that makes it taste like homemade."

The playful note in her voice played like little fingers up and down Josh's spine, evoking memories and more. Alex as a teen had been a hottie, but as a woman, she was a knockout.

"Daddy?" she said, turning to B. J. When he didn't respond right away, she prompted him again. "Yoohoo, earth to Daddy." B. J. stirred from what Josh assumed to be a wallow of consternation over the news that his ex-son-in-law now had his property neatly hemmed in by the land surrounding it.

As much as Josh wanted to revel in the man's discomfort, when Alex bent over to refill B. J.'s glass, Josh looked toward the dock where Lynn and John Jr. started to stroll back to the house. A glimpse of that charming presentation was enough to rob him of the satisfaction of the moment and put ants in his pants for the rest of the day . . . maybe the night as well.

"I think I'll see what the lovebirds—"

"Sparks, no!" B. J. shouted, cutting him off.

Josh turned in time to see the friendly dog prop his front paws on the basket rim, his weight pulling it over. With a yelp, Sparks dashed away from the green-backed crabs scattering to freedom in every direction. The clatter of their hard shells on the flagstone was broken by the crash of the two acrylic pitchers Alex dropped.

Although it clearly wasn't her intent, the rolling pitchers diverted the side-scrambling crustaceans around her stone-still form. Chewing what Josh knew to be choice words for the dog and the situation, B. J. grabbed the basket and started picking up the escapees from the back, avoiding their ready claws, and tossing them back into the container.

With a few deft kicks to avoid the pincer-brandishing flow headed in his direction, Whitlowe pitched in as well. "Got one!"

Meanwhile, Sparks barked enough for three dogs, darting in at the crabs, then back in retreat.

"Lynn, get that blasted dog," B. J. ordered as her fiancé joined the quest.

Josh made his way toward Alex, remembering all too well her

unreasonable fear of live crabs. Her face ashen, she swayed like a sapling in the wind, the terror betrayed in her eyes strangled silent in her throat. Just as he reached her, it thawed. With an ear-piercing scream, she came to life and started scaling the front of him in blind panic.

"It's all right, I've got you," he assured her, as she wrapped her arms around his neck so tightly that breathing was an effort. In spite of her frenzied attempts to get traction on his legs and climb higher, he managed to drag her away from the chaos. "Stop it, Ally, or I'll be deaf and singing soprano next Sunday."

But there was no reasoning against her longtime phobia. Alex was bent on climbing him like a monkey up a palm, shrieking all the way. He had to get her somewhere where she couldn't see the blasted crabs. Protecting himself as much as he could with a hysterical female hanging from his neck, Josh hobbled toward the nearby garage. For all her soft, dangerous curves, he'd forgotten just how wiry she was when she wanted to be.

"Ally . . . Ally!" he protested, pulling her so tightly against him that his shins and feet took the worst of her panic as he ducked inside. "I've got you, girl. Look! No crabs in here."

As his statement sank in, her voice quieted, and her feet stopped flailing.

Her answering babble was hot against his collarbone and the crush of her softness against his chest was enough to make a man want to cry "uncle." But so did the bite of her fingers into the pressure points of his neck as the rest of her went all soft and needy in his embrace.

CHAPTER SIX

With a grimace, Josh relinquished his hold just long enough to pry her hands away. "You're killin' me, babe," he whispered, suddenly hoarse. Whether it was from the pain or the clutch of desire around his throat, he didn't know. What he did know was that Alex, realizing at last that she was out of harm's way, melted against him, weak with relief.

It seemed natural to touch his lips to her forehead, still as cold from shock as the hands that now folded loosely about his neck. She smelled like heaven . . . or at least what Josh recalled the heaven they'd shared in each other's arms smelled like. Sweet Pea. He still remembered the name of her fragrance. Other memories shot through him, awakening something he'd nearly drunk himself to death trying—*wanting*—to forget.

Josh stiffened, trying to override the compulsion to draw Alex closer by moving backward. But the desperate need of the fingers that fisted about his collar blew his intention to kingdom come.

Alex in need was a rare Alex he'd never been able to resist. He'd have hung the moon and stars for her if she'd *needed* him to do it. Alex inhaled shakily against his chest.

He should say something, but everything that *should* be working wasn't. He licked his dry lips, resting his chin on the top of her head. Alex shifted, looking up at him, causing his lips to come entirely too close to her ear for comfort.

"Uh . . ." His paltry attempt at coherent speech made her jerk away, but he never could think straight with Alex around.

"Did I hurt . . . oh!" Her gaze widened, meeting his, then retreated as though scorched. "Omigosh," she groaned, taking a step back and crossing her arms between them.

Color crawled up her face as she stared up at him, vulnerable enough to make him fight a dragon on her behalf. "I . . . I'm so sorry. I don't . . . I didn't . . . they must think—"

"It's okay," he assured her. Still, Josh tried to make out the mix of emotions swimming in her eyes. Had he been right? Had memories stirred her as well or was it all the aftermath of her childhood phobia? "I remember how you are about crabs."

Alex took another step back, blinked, and the confusion disappeared, veiled by a scowl. "Then blast you to bits," she swore with a stomp of her foot. "Why did you bring them? So that you could watch me make a fool of myself?"

Josh's empathy faltered. "Whoa, babe. Don't try spinning this thing so that it's suddenly my fault."

"It is your fault, Josh," she told him. "But you never wanted to accept responsibility for anything, did you? You haven't changed a bit."

"Well, you have. You're more like B. J. than you ever were." His gibe hit its mark. Her arms tightened about herself. He couldn't count the times he'd heard Alex swear that she'd never be like her father. "You're a control freak, Alex, just like him."

"And you're totally undisciplined, thoughtless, irresponsible—" She broke off, her narrow nostrils flaring in frustration as she groped for more barbs to throw at him.

"Excuse me. Am I interrupting anything?" Empty pitchers in hand, Lynn stood by the jamb of the open garage door, glancing uneasily from Josh to Alex.

"No!" Alex snapped.

"No!" Josh chimed in.

❧

Alex wanted to crawl under the car, anywhere to get away from Josh Turner. He'd brought the bloody crabs, and the next thing she knew she was clinging to a male body that jarred the memory of every female sense she had. That was more humiliating than turning into a screaming Mimi in front of their guests. She had a reason for the latter. There was none for the butterflies beating back and forth between her chest and stomach.

"Daddy wanted me to check on you, Ally," Lynn said from her side. "We know how you are around—"

"I'm fine, no thanks to Josh and his cockamamie ideas," Alex added, aiming a hostile glare at Josh. She wanted to go home, escape, but that was out of the question.

"He said to tell you the crabs have all been caught. They're steaming as we speak."

He said to tell you . . . What was this, some flashback from the days when her baby sister was B. J.'s puppet, not to mention spy? Alex wondered how long Lynn had been standing there before she let her presence be known.

"Go tell Daddy that I'm fine." B. J. had no worries on that part.

Alex took the pitchers from her sister's hands. "Then come back inside and get the pitchers. I'll fill them for you and stay in to help Fran in the kitchen."

"I'll tell him," Josh volunteered. "Wouldn't want to start tongues wagging about us, now would we, Ally?"

Lynn raised her brow at Josh's innuendo, searching Alex's face.

"Yes, it *would* be a shame to have the scandal of a murder in the midst of all the wedding plans. Or did you warn your future in-laws that Josh and I were no strangers?" Alex challenged her sister. *Lord, I know I'm being a witch, and I can't help myself. Where is all this anger coming from? It won't stop bubbling up and over.*

Lynn avoided her gaze. "John and I thought it best not to complicate matters," she answered softly. "For everyone's sake."

"I think I'll go check on those crabs," Josh announced. He turned to Alex. "And, for what it's worth, I'm sorry for my part in ruining your day."

He wasn't being smart now. Sincerity deepened the color of his gaze, creating a new and devastating shade of blue.

But Alex had seen it before, too many times to count. His brand of regret lasted only until the next time he royally turned her life upside down. Taking a deep breath, she pivoted toward the house entrance from the garage. "Apology accepted," she called over her shoulder. It was the thing to say. Meaning it would require divine intervention.

❧

Monday was never Alex's favorite day, but this week it was more than welcome after yesterday's anything-but-restful Sabbath. And the night hadn't been much better. She'd argued with Josh in her mind round the clock, catching a bit of sleep, then picking up where she left off. It wasn't over the crabs, but over the many hurts and injustices she'd suffered after his abandonment.

Spending the morning pulling up Lillian Laws's files on her computer and working out a new color and accessory theme for the rental had been a welcome distraction. But then, work was a refuge. Since all of the Laws's units were identical and always painted off-white, the diversity had to be in the furniture and accessories. With no particular client taste to design the rooms for, decorating rentals wasn't much of an artistic challenge to Alex.

Except that as she looked at relaxed, comfortable, but easy-to-maintain seaside themes and color palettes, visions of the Turner place invaded her concentration, robbing Alex of her last safe haven.

Lord, I don't want to go there. I know I have to, but not yet. Please.

Determined to steer away from the thoughts that poured acid into her stomach, Alex pulled up jpegs of the condo she'd decorated ten years earlier according to the date of the files. Usually her greatest challenge came in convincing Lillian when a piece of furniture had seen its best days and needed to be replaced, but Lillian surprised Alex this time by stating up front that the sofa bed in the living room needed to go.

After ten years of use, no wonder. Renters didn't always treat the resort furnishings like they would their own, resulting in more staining, wear, and tear than usual. Then there were the inherent dampness and UV factors, especially in ocean- and bayfront units. But the jpeg of the living area's green-and-beige palm-print décor faded out on the screen of her mind. In its place was the octagonal parlor that had been her and Josh's living room in his grandmother's farmhouse.

"No, no, no, no, no," Alex said, blinking until her focus was on the condominium picture.

The tinkle of the bell over the front door made Alex look up from her desk. Sue Ann sashayed in.

"What brings you out and about this early?" Alex teased.

Taken aback, Sue Ann paused and glanced at her Black Hills gold and diamond-accented watch. "It's eleven-thirty. I'm always on the go in time for lunch."

Alex's quick look at the corner of her monitor confirmed it. Where had the morning gone?

"Speaking of which, how's about pulling your head out of that computer monitor and grabbing some lunch at Phillips's? This is the third Monday of the month, you know."

To Sue Ann, that meant that her favorite dress shop in Fenwick had gotten in new stock.

"Ellen and Jan are working," she went on, idly fingering the top of some fabric swatches Alex had on display in the sitting room section at the front of the store.

"Some of us do work, ya know." Alex grinned as Sue Ann poked her tongue out in response. "Now that's lovely. Did they teach you that in finishing school?"

"So are you coming or not? Well, hello, Riley," Sue Ann said, her impatience turning to sweetness as the yellow tom leapt up on one of the chair cushions and rolled over, in a belly-up bearskin imitation. "You are just too cute for your own good," she cooed, rubbing the fur tufts of Riley's tummy. "It's a shame Alex had you fixed, honey. You'd be a regular ladykiller."

"Not everyone is as obsessed with the opposite gender as you, Suzie." Alex closed the Laws file, relieved at an excuse to get away.

Besides, bologna sandwich upstairs in her fridge or a fist-sized backfin crab cake at the Phillips Crab House? No-brainer.

"So you're coming?"

"But I'm good for lunch only," Alex warned. "I'll drive separately so that I can go on and take some pictures of one of Lillian Laws's rentals while I'm oceanside."

She also really needed to go by the Turner place and see what her father had done so far so that she could start pulling ideas together. Alex groaned. Was there no keeping it down? Just the idea of going back there made her want to draw into herself. But she couldn't. Running wasn't her style, particularly where business was concerned. And that's all it was, all she'd allow it to be, she decided. But her head and her heart were incommunicado.

Alex switched the answering machine on. "You'll have to put Martin in further debt without me. Not that the Wiltbank fortune can't handle it."

"I have my own money, I'll have you know." And Sue Ann did, an ample annuity for her share of her father's real estate agency. "Although I always charge whatever I buy to Martin's accounts. Saving for a rainy day, you know. A gal can't be too careful."

Alex tucked her purse under her arm and grabbed her camera bag, ready to go. "Amen to that, sister."

Sue Ann couldn't possibly know how true that was. Let a man into your heart, and he stays there forever.

⚭

A meal at the Phillips Crab House was more than satisfying the appetite with food, it was an experience. The multilevels of the restaurant were decorated with eclectic flair. Its restored carousel horses, paintings, fishnets, and tools of the hearty watermen who'd first settled in Ocean City made up a collage of the resort's past and present from work to play. Seated in a private nook next to a gorgeous white carousel charger bedecked in ribbons, Alex and Sue Ann each enjoyed one of Phillips's renowned crab cakes with side salads.

"I never thought about your having had crab imperial yesterday," Sue Ann observed as she separated the fried cake to expose the steaming white lumps of sweet backfin.

"I didn't," Alex told her, watching as a nearby patron hammered a crab claw to a mush of shell and meat—obviously not a Shore native. "Not imperial anyway. We had to nix the Filet Chesapeake menu when Josh showed up with a bushel of live crabs."

Sue Ann's gaze lit up with interest. "Tell me!"

So Alex did, the whole story, even her humiliation in Josh's arms. "I don't know what came over me, Suz. In Josh Turner's arms was the last place I wanted to be. I'd have been safer standing *in* the blooming bushel basket of crabs."

Sue Ann laid her fork and knife across her plate with a satisfied, "I thought so."

"Thought so *what*?"

"That, no matter how much you protest to the contrary, you are so *not* over Josh Turner."

Alex wanted to object, but Suzie had struck a chord of truth, a double-edged one that wedged in Alex's throat. There was still something there for Josh, even if Alex didn't want it to be. She took a drink of water, hoping to wash it down.

"But the bright side is, you're both still available. Can you imagine how hard this would be if Josh had married one of his groupies . . . or worse yet, one of those starlets he used to sport around on his arm?"

"I wish he had," Alex said. "Then a summer of seeing him all around Piper Cove wouldn't be nearly as . . ." What was the word? Tempting? She heaved a sigh. "At least then, I'd know it was really over . . . you know, with closure."

"Honey, wedding vows don't always mean closure . . . at least not to some people."

Alex latched on to the melancholy note in Sue Ann's voice and added it to her earlier comment about being careful with her money. She didn't like where her conclusions were taking her. "Is Martin traveling again?"

"Left this morning," Sue Ann answered, "but I'm not talking about him, silly." She folded arms on the table, leaning in. "I envied the daylights out of what you had with Josh," she went on. "That boy taught you how to live, girl. You're where you are today because he helped you throw off your daddy's reins."

"And he left me with no more good-bye than a note that said he'd send for me when he made it big."

If there had been any hope of finishing her meal, it was gone now.

"Okay, there *is* that," Sue Ann conceded with a frown. "But, would you have let him go if he'd discussed his plans with you? Face it, Alex, you two were like black gum against thunder when it came to having your ways."

Alex toyed with the other half of the crab cake on the plate. Josh *had* discussed his dream with her. And, in the beginning, supporting his music had been an adventure for Alex. The late nights, sleeping half the day and loving each other the other half had been heaven. But the money Josh earned in local gigs wasn't enough to pay the bills. Some nights it barely paid his bar bills. It was Alex's job at a Berlin furniture store that carried them—barely.

Six months into the marriage, B. J. grudgingly offered to take

Josh into the banking business and teach him the ropes. It seemed perfect to Alex, a nine-to-five income with weekends for Josh's beloved music. That was when the fighting began.

Josh accused her of trying to make him into a little B. J. and began to drink more heavily. Finances became even more strained. There was no way that Alex would consider Josh's idea of leaving home and depending on that income alone to support them. It was too unpredictable. She'd warned him that if he didn't start acting like a responsible adult, that he should leave. And that if he left, he'd leave alone. Fool that she'd been, she believed in their love enough to think that he'd come around to accepting his responsibilities to her as a partner.

Instead, he'd sworn that he'd never set foot in this hick town again, then taken her at her word. Her chest constricted, opening the old wound.

"But you're older now . . . wiser," Sue Ann pointed out, oblivious to Alex's pain. "Who knows? Maybe this is fate's way of giving you two a second chance."

CHAPTER SEVEN

Second chance? How could Alex even consider a second chance when Josh had not been man enough to tell her to her face that he was leaving? And after he'd made it big, did he send for her? No! She might have been able to forgive him if he had.

Alex raised an incredulous gaze at Sue Ann, bewildered and more than a little annoyed. How could her friend, who'd been there to help Alex pick up the pieces of her broken heart, even suggest such a thing? "You swore you'd scratch out his eyeballs the next time you laid eyes on Josh Turner. Why the change of heart?"

Oblivious to Alex's sarcasm, Sue Ann reached across the table and gathered Alex's hand between hers. "It's not *my* heart that matters, honey. It's yours. I saw the way you two kept stealing looks at each other Friday night. I put my money on love then and there. Of course"—her fine-lined brows knit, certainty wavering—"Ellen's thinking revenge. Jan stayed on the fence."

That sounded like her friends, Ellen the aggressor and Jan the peacemaker. "So what am I, the new lotto?" Alex forced a laugh as Sue Ann let go of her hand and reached for her designer bag.

"Besides . . ." Sue Ann took out a tube of lipstick. "I was looking for my wandering husband after dinner and happened to see the two of you *chatting*—" Her inflection suggested more. "—in the gazebo." Smacking her lips together, she checked the result of her efforts in the tiny attached mirror. "So I had inside info to start with. Your telling me about your nose-to-chest-hair experience in Josh's arms confirms it. Your feelings aren't dead, honey. They were just suffering from that thing that people get when they're in cold water for too long."

"Hypothermia?" Leave it to Sue Ann to make Alex smile, even if she didn't agree with her.

"That's it. And yours are starting to come back to life."

"Then hand me one of those crab mallets and let me put them out of their misery before it gets any worse."

Sue Ann lifted her baby-smooth brow. It was an attribute the admittedly envious *buddies,* with thirtysomething hints of wrinkles that became visible on close examination, attributed to living a pampered life without financial worry or marital conflict. Sure, Martin's job took him away a lot, but when he was home, he worshipped his wife.

For a second, Sue Ann's comment about marriage and closure played back through the volatile stir in Alex's head, but it disappeared in the turbulence.

"He didn't even come back for me, Suz. No letter, no *nothing.*" Raw anger and hurt cracked her voice and pummeled her.

No! She couldn't—*wouldn't*—go through this again. Alex seized at the anger, whatever it took to blunt the pain. "I will never forgive Josh Turner . . . *never!*"

Sue Ann wagged a reprimanding finger at her. "Never say never. And from what I hear," Sue Ann continued, squirming like Riley when he was about to pounce in triumph, "Josh is going to be around for more than the wedding."

Alex's indignation withered into wariness. She knew about his business venture, but that didn't require his sticking around. Stockholders weren't usually hands-on. "What are you talking about?"

"I hear from one of our agents that he's looking to buy a home."

"*What*?" The prospect of Josh living in Piper Cove rather than visiting would have taken out Alex's knees if she weren't already sitting. No, no, not this.

"I hear he tried to buy his grandmother's house, but B. J. wouldn't sell it."

"Probably out of spite, knowing Daddy." And from the look on Josh's face the night B. J. announced that he was giving it to the newlyweds, it had hit a bull's-eye. Unless Josh's quiet, but steamed reaction was strictly from B. J.'s getting the upper hand and had nothing to do any emotional ties to the homestead. *Did* he have emotional ties? The notion took another swipe at her knees.

"So it looks to me like maybe Josh might be working toward that second chance."

"Or working to become a major thorn in Daddy's side," Alex mused aloud, still reeling from her thoughts. No, she didn't believe in fairy tales like Jan did. Once burned, twice shy as the saying went. When it was all boiled down, the hometown boy made good returning to rub it in the faces of those who doubted him made far more sense . . . and she was one of them. A queasy feeling swept through her belly. It shouldn't matter—not a whit. Why should his motives, or his plans, matter to her at all?

They shouldn't. They wouldn't. She'd not allow it!

"Sue Ann, I don't want to go through this again. Even if I could forgive Josh for what he did, I don't want to get caught between Daddy and Josh's power games. It'll be history repeating itself."

"Would you ladies like some dessert?" a young, blond waitress asked.

Alex shook her head. Her mind was whirling in a sea of questions. *He's back for more than the wedding, but what? And why do I have to care?*

"Just the check, please." Sue Ann flashed a platinum credit card between her fingers. "I'll get it this time," she insisted, even though Alex was too involved with introspection to offer. The check was the last of her concerns.

"Well, I'm not going to run," Alex declared, as she and Sue Ann left the dark cedar-shingled restaurant to the parking lot across the street. If there was even *anything* to run from.

Sue Ann's flowery earrings swung, glistening in the sun as she swiveled toward Alex. "Say what?"

"I am not going to let Josh Turner make me a fugitive in my own hometown . . . hiding from him, staying in because I might run into him." No matter how tempting it was.

"Well I should hope not. You are a mature, *successful* woman now . . . impervious to the likes of Josh Turner. You picked yourself up, went to school, made something of yourself, built your own business—"

"Yes, I did. And as far as Josh knows, I'm better off for his leaving."

"Even if you are still single—"

Alex checked her step as her friend's words registered.

"—with no good prospects in view . . ." Sue Ann left the sentence dangling, something else that annoyed Alex, at least when it was dangled in *her* face.

"And that is relevant *how*?"

"If you were married," she said, stopping at the door of her sporty BMW, "and had the recommended two-point-five children, that would *really* show him how little you missed him."

"Don't be ridiculous." Alex rounded the hood of her car, heels clicking on the pavement. "If I was all that, I wouldn't likely be where I am today."

"Alone?"

"You're married, and you're alone half the time." The minute the words were out, Alex regretted them. Sue Ann was trying to support her in her own not-always-helpful way. "I'm sorry, Suz. That was a cheap shot."

"It was a desperate one," Sue Ann responded, seemingly unaffected. "Besides, my life isn't the point."

"*Besides,*" Alex mimicked, "Josh is still single, too. This isn't our parents' day, you know. There's no stigma to being single at thirtysomething."

Sue Ann opened her car door and slid into the seat. "And you know as well as I do, honey, that Josh could have any woman he wanted, *if* he wanted one."

Now *that* stung. Maybe she'd apologized too early. "*If* I wanted a man," Alex shot back, "I could find one." Although, she didn't exactly have members of the opposite sex fawning over her like Josh did with those bedroom eyes of his. Sue Ann always said she was too aloof and scared them off. "I'm just particular."

"Looks like Josh is, too."

Alex wanted to wipe that I know more than you do smile off Sue Ann's lips.

"Think about it, sugar." Sue Ann closed the car door before Alex could respond. Not that she had a ready retort.

As her friend started the BMW's engine, Alex slid into the leather interior of her own car in a snit. Whether she was married or involved in a relationship had nothing to do with anything. It simply wasn't relevant; though, blast it all, it *felt* relevant.

❧

Headlights on, as required on the single-lane expressway that by-passed the congestion of downtown Ocean City, Alex sped back to Piper Cove after finding that the keys to the Laws's condo were in Will Warren's hands for appraisal purposes. She bit her lip in frustration as she crossed the Route 90 bridge. Beyond her, the calm silver-blue bay gave way to wooded and rush-edged wetlands. There, thick drab marsh grasses, fern, and deciduous growth burst with new life amidst the gangly evergreen of pine.

With her window cracked so as not to blow, and hence frizz the natural wave of her hair, Alex breathed the salt air deeply. The ocean had been balm to her for as long as she could remember. It could take her worlds away from the concerns surrounding her at home. If only she had time to take a walk on the beach for a full anxiety treatment, instead of rushing back into the thick of her problems.

As she exited onto the state road that became Piper Cove's Main Street, Alex slowed to its 25 mph speed limit. The town looked as lazy as ever on this spring weekday. But when the tourist season kicked into full gear after school let out, the street would be filled with meandering visitors from the hotel and rental condos along the waterfront with vacation dollars to spend.

While the influx gave the cove an appealing Bohemian popula-tion, a part of Alex mourned the loss of the mom-and-pop businesses she'd frequented as a child with her parents. The drugstore, the combined tiny post office and coffee shop, the hardware and wallpaper/paint store, the grocery, the butcher shop, the childrens' clothing shop, and independent dress shops . . . all gone. There were no strangers back then; although newcomers who took up residence there didn't stay strangers long. Piper Cove was too friendly for that.

Shaking the pang of nostalgia, Alex drove past the drive-thru of Piper Cove Mercantile and parked near the back entrance. Sheila Barnes, the secretary Will Warren shared with her father, was not at her desk, and Alex could see that Will was not in his office either. The blinds in her father's were drawn. As she walked into the railed sanctuary outside the offices, she heard raised voices coming from her father's, B. J.'s booming one in particular. Although she couldn't make out exactly what he was saying, he was definitely on the warpath.

Luckily Alex was there to pick up the keys to Lillian Laws's condo from Will. Hoping to avoid her father in his rage, Alex started toward the front of the bank to find someone who might know where Will was, when B. J.'s office door opened. Will emerged. His stony expression broke into a smile upon seeing her.

"Alexandra, I was expecting you," he said smoothly. "Come into my office."

Beyond him, B. J. Butler sat, fists folded on his dark cherry desk, staring at them as if he was about to blow again. His face and neck blended into the red of the silk tie knotted at his thick neck. Alex knew better than to ask him if he was okay when he clearly was having trouble containing his anger. She mustered a tentative smile.

"Hi, Daddy, just dropped by to pick up some keys from Will."

She didn't know why her stomach did a somersault. After all, she'd done nothing. It was Will's head that was on a chopping block for whatever reason.

B. J. grunted in acknowledgment as Alex followed Will into his adjoining office.

"Trouble?" she asked in a low voice.

"Loan gone awry," Will answered, dropping into his seat and pulling out a desk drawer. He withdrew a ring of keys and put them on his desk pad. "Confidential, of course."

Alex picked them up. "Of course. I just hope Daddy's blood pressure medication is working." Thank heaven her mother hadn't seen him like this. Mama worried herself sick if her husband got a hangnail.

"This new merger with the Baltimore bank is going hard on him. Besides, it's going to take a new breed of banker to stay on top of things."

"Over his dead body, you mean."

Will shook his head, an odd smile haunting his lips, given he'd just survived a blast from Mount B. J. "I wouldn't be so sure of that, Alexandra. You just heard him along with half of Piper Cove. I'm not so sure he's up to the stress and changes about to take place."

"Daddy was born red-faced and screaming, Will," Alex said, tucking the keys in her purse. "His retirement is wishful thinking on your part."

Will pressed his hands together, fingers fanned, and propped his chin on them. "Maybe so, maybe so."

"Well, I have to get—"

"Speaking of wishful thinking, the Rotary Club is having a meeting at Clamdiggers this Friday evening. Would you like to go?"

The man never gave up. Alex had to give him credit for that, no matter how annoying it was. "I have plans, Will, but thank you anyway."

"Josh Turner is our guest speaker."

Her polite smile thinned. Even Will could detect the way Josh affected her?

"In that case, I'd make other plans ... even if I didn't already have some. You get my drift." But Alex had promised Ellen at church that she'd attend this month's meeting. As president of the Rotary Club, Ellen was going to announce something big about her pet project—a youth center.

"One of these days," he said, getting up from his desk, "you're going to change your mind, Alexandra."

Not if he kept staring at the front vee of her cotton sweater like that. Alex beat it to the office door rather than give Will an excuse to touch her as he escorted her out. He wasn't always overt in his unsolicited attention, but, for some reason, he made her skin crawl.

"Why don't you ask Barbara Carrington?" she called over her shoulder. "I hear you two have a thing going."

Sheila, back at her desk, gave a little gasp that revealed she'd been eavesdropping. For how long, Alex had no idea. B. J. had closed his office door.

Alex hesitated, surprised that her father hadn't beckoned her in. Usually if she were in the bank, her father made it a point to call her in and debrief her on her business. Was he avoiding her?

"Barbara is one of our biggest customers," Will said, catching up with her, "and I've escorted her on a few occasions, business-related only."

"Bye, Sheila," Alex called to the secretary watching them.

"Bye, Miss Butler." Having been caught, the secretary pretended to run a total on her calculator, blank paper curling in a cluster behind it.

Alex stifled a groan as Will ushered her toward the door, hand pressed to her back.

"Speaking of business, I'm going to need to see your sketches for Lillian Laws's place . . . to put with the appraisal." At the lift of Alex's brow, he hastened to add. "I'm sure they'll be perfect, but I need it to justify the higher value I have in mind. Your father taught me to dot my i's and cross my t's."

Eager to escape Will's invasion of her personal space, Alex pushed through the door before he had the chance to open it for her. "No problem," she said, "I'll send them as soon as they're finished."

"Let me know if you change your mind about Friday."

Alex retreated to her car. "Sure thing," she replied as she pulled open her vehicle door and got in. *Just not in this lifetime.*

CHAPTER EIGHT

Rather than drive back to the Laws's oceanside condo, Alex considered heading for the Turner property on the north side of Piper Cove. She had plenty of time this afternoon to take her initial measurements, although every square foot of the home where she'd spent a year as a teenaged bride was indelibly etched in her memory.

And with them a myriad of memories, some too heavenly to think about and others too painful.

You are being a sentimental fool, she told herself. *It's just a stick-and-frame dwelling.* It wasn't like her memories couldn't haunt her anywhere else. Josh's arrival had stirred them like a hornets' nest and kept them buzzing about in her mind no matter what she was doing. She might as well face the past straight on. Besides, she'd need pictures in case the renovations that her father had commissioned had changed anything. This was mind over matter. End of story.

Her mouth set, she turned onto North Point Road. Maybe she could even use some of the sketches she'd done many years ago when she was working at the furniture store. She used to daydream about how some of the new inventory would be perfect for this room or that. Never quite able to part with them, she still had the notes and drawings in the hope chest her grandmother had given her.

Her hope chest. Now that was an oxymoron. Alex's heart constricted, not nearly as detached as she willed it to be. This was not going to get to her anywhere. Maybe just facing up to it, doing the job instead of thinking about it was the key. That was what she'd done before. Picked up the pieces of her life, assembled them as best she could, and forged ahead. A year behind others her age at the art institute, she'd attended year-round to get her degree. Dating was a disaster, as she'd been too bitter over Josh to trust any man. So, placing her hope on herself, Alex had worked long, determined hours to build her business. Nothing was going to set her back again. Not Josh's abandonment, not B. J.'s disapproval, and, now, not Josh's return.

Three Creek Road ran parallel to the river and crossed three creeks, two of which were only navigable by the shallow draft boats used by outdoorsmen. What had been primarily a hunter's paradise of the marsh and woods of the Turner farm was now Piney Banks, a housing development built by Josh's company. Thinking of Josh as a successful businessman was as big a challenge as accepting his religious epiphany. Money used to slip through his pocket like a sieve, especially on band gigs. She'd hoped that working at the bank, being around responsible people, would remedy that, but . . .

Oh, what was the point? He hadn't changed for her.

As she drove past, Alex noted that most of the new houses were already sold and occupied. She supposed it was only right that Josh benefited from the growth on the bayside of Ocean City. It had spread to Piper Cove like wildfire making a gold mine out of what had been considered worthless not so long ago. One thing for sure: His grandmother would never have believed that people from all over the States would want to live in her little neck of the woods, much less year-round. But then, it had been beyond Amanda Turner why civilized folks considered it fun to lie half-naked on the clingy beach sand in the hot sun, too.

The memory of her late Sunday school teacher and ex-in-law warmed Alex as she slowed and turned into the cedar-lined driveway leading up to the farmhouse. While not as grand as the older homes in Piper Cove, its hexagonal front corner and the lazy, wraparound porch spoke of a more genteel time when people dressed for dinner and Sundays were set aside for worship and visiting. Nestled between four giant oaks that kept it cool in the summer, it looked like a haven from the nine-*till* mayhem of Alex's world.

And for a while, it had been a haven from her father's world, where everything Alex did and said reflected upon B. J. She had to do daily battle over dress, behavior, and her choice of boyfriends. Preppies like Will Warren, who had the personality of a fire hydrant, had been her father's choice.

The changes in her honeymoon home brought Alex back from the past. There was new vinyl siding and trim that had preserved the house's Neo-Victorian detail and charm. Done in bisque with winter-river gray and slate blue accents, it was the perfect exterior palette for the waterfront home. Following the driveway, which circled the house, around to the back overlooking the St. Martins,

Alex saw a truck belonging to one McMann Construction's teams of carpenters parked in the yard.

"Hey, Miss Butler," P. K. Brooks, called out from a ladder where he and another hand were hanging screens. "I heard you were coming around to fancy this place up."

It was hard to believe that the weather-ruddied, work-buffed man was one of the same snotty-nosed kids that Alex had baby-sat for during church fund-raisers. Like the pictures of her former charges in the local paper beneath engagement and wedding announcements, the sight of P. K. made her feel old.

"Looks like you boys have been doing some fancying of your own," she replied, getting out of the car. "It's beautiful." Although she was going to have to give Ellen a call with regard to the over-grown shrubs and flower beds that had been trampled during the renovation process.

"Me 'n' Pete here were just about to call it day, but we can leave it open for you if you want."

Duh. She hadn't thought to pick up keys to the farm. "That would be fine, P. K.," she answered. "I'm just going to take some pictures and measurements of the inside." Alex reached in the back and retrieved the bag containing her tools of the trade—camera, measuring rule, and notepads among them. "Do the lights work?"

"Sure thing. New wiring, new plumbing, new wallboard . . . shoot, B. J.'s got himself a brand-new hundred-year-old house."

Now how had her father done all this without her hearing about it? Alex wondered, shoving her purse under the seat. Despite its growth and the fact that Alex hadn't been out this way in a good while, Piper Cove still had a sound gossip circuit. Maybe she'd sim-ply not been listening, she mused wearily. Most of her focus as she'd built her business had been across the bay in Ocean City.

Her low-heeled pumps felt as though they'd turned to lead, yet the designer in Alex quivered in them with an increasing mix of curiosity and anticipation. She let herself into the porch and entered the kitchen through the entrance to the utility room, which had once served as a laundry room and bathroom. Built before indoor plumbing, the house had no other practical place for the powder room except where plumbing had already existed. Suffice it to say, no one spent more time than necessary in the necessary, for fear of back door visitors.

But now the room was plumbed for a washer and dryer and a laundry sink only. Wondering where the powder room had been moved, Alex went into the wide central hall, where her suspicions were confirmed. One end had been sealed off for the bathroom, just enough space for the sink and commode. And exactly where she'd envisioned the room should be.

Back in the kitchen, she put her bag on the counter. The walls were primed with white, as was the wood trim, providing a blank canvas for her to work with. The wide reproduction moldings of the period, including the vertical beaded board of the kitchen wainscot, put a nostalgic smile on her face. The original woodwork, with its multiple layers of paint, including one that Alex had put on herself, had probably been split and beyond use after it was taken off for wiring, plumbing, and insulation.

While the carpenters fired up the engine of their truck to leave, Alex envisioned the room with white glass-paned cabinets, granite counters mocking Victorian marble top, and red accents. Red stimulated the appetite; although Miss Amanda's fire-engine red cupboards and rooster wallpaper had been overkill. It was a wonder that Alex had survived a year eating in that kitchen and still kept her trim figure. Oh for that metabolism again.

Blinking away an unbidden mist from her eyes, Alex walked over to where a narrow staircase rose to the second-floor bedroom that had been Josh's grandmother's. Alex could still see Miss Amanda ducking as she came down the last three steps into the room, her blue eyes twinkling from beneath folds of age.

She'd been, what, eighty-something when Alex eloped with Josh and moved in with her. In fact, Miss Amanda was the main reason Alex and Josh had gone to Elkton on graduation night instead of following local custom and heading to Ocean City with Alex's fellow grads for a weeklong party. Josh's grandmother wouldn't have let them in the door without a marriage certificate although it pained her that they'd not had a church wedding. Nonetheless, Amanda Turner was the only one who approved of the union and welcomed Alex with open arms.

"Maybe between us," she confided with a wink one day to Alex, "we can straighten that boy out."

Not that Amanda thought ill of her only grandson. She'd loved the orphaned Josh more than life. But, like Alex, she thought Josh could be so much more than a guitarist in a local band.

Josh again.

Alex turned from that *come hither* look beckoning to her from the past, visualizing instead Miss Amanda on the sunporch, where she'd loved to sit and sew instead. Somehow, Alex couldn't imagine Lynn getting that sort of use from the small closed-in extension off the kitchen. Mama had done all the sewing in the Butler household.

But the room would be a lovely breakfast nook. Take out the wall under the back stairway, frame it with a wide-angled arch for support, and it would be adorable. Plus, it would allow for an island workstation/breakfast bar in the kitchen instead of the old red Formica table that had once taken up so much floor space. Two people had to slide sideways by each other in order to pass. Not that she and Josh had minded—

That hornet's nest in her mind started buzzing again, threatening her professional train of thought. Of course the change would cost more, she rationalized, determined to stamp her feelings out with business. But her father should have consulted her *before* the inside renovations were practically completed; and he *had* said spare no expense.

Alex wavered under a broadside of guilt. Resorting to revenge on her father's purse wasn't the most Christian of motives, but his total disregard for her feelings on this project made Alex feel anything but saintly.

Oh Lord . . . The prayer ended. Alex hardly felt worthy at the moment to ask for any divine help.

Measurements, she thought, digging into the bag slung over her shoulder. No matter what her motivation, her intention was to do the best job she could. Alex sketched a rough floor plan of the home from memory, a simple foursquare with a wide central hall and staircase. That done, she took out a tape measure and stretched it across the room.

"Hey, need any help?" A male voice from the utility entrance gave her such a start that she retracted the length of tape she'd just unwound.

Josh. Again. In the flesh, this time. That it was him, *here,* of all places, would not allow her startled heart to settle. "Maybe a nitro-glycerin pill if you have one on you," she quipped. It was a wonder that her voice didn't vibrate from the commotion in her chest. "I didn't hear you drive up."

"I didn't." Too sexy for Alex's good, he leaned against the doorjamb in a way that took her back to another time. "I walked over from the model home in the development next door when I saw your car pull up. I'm living there temporarily."

Josh living next door? This job was going downhill at lightning speed. "I thought you'd stay at the new hotel." Despite her inner chaos, she at least sounded indifferent. "Not that I really thought you'd stick around at all. You hated Piper Cove as I recall."

"Had enough of hotels to last a lifetime. And I didn't hate everything about this place." Before Alex's piqued thoughts translated to a question, he squashed them. "I love the waterfront, the hunting, and fishing."

And why did he have to wear those faded jeans slung low on his hip and a tee shirt that showed the benefits of regular workouts in a gym?

"Anyway, I thought it would be a chance to take a look at the place," he added, "if you don't mind."

It was like being caught in a flashback, but with a flesh-and-blood Josh, blue eyes twinkling with a mischief that Miss Amanda never dreamed of. He slowly took in Alex's appearance from head to toe and back again. Palms suddenly damp, Alex wiped them on her slacks—and dropped the measuring tape she'd held in one hand.

"I'll get it." Josh sprang to life as she mechanically stooped to retrieve it.

His head struck hers on the way down, the resulting pain shocking her from her stupor. "Hold on there, Ms. *Independence*," he said, grabbing Alex by the shoulders to steady her as she stumbled a step back.

"I ... um ... I was going to take some preliminary measurements." Like *that* wasn't obvious. Dropping to one of the narrow steps leading to the second floor, she rubbed her forehead. From the ache, it was sprouting a knot the size of her fist. "Your head is as hard as a beaten biscuit." And many was the time that Alex had been tempted to beat it like Gran did the tough dough for the old Eastern Shore specialty. With the air beaten out of the dough, the result was a dense, pool-ball-sized biscuit that Gran often dipped in coffee or broth to soften enough to eat.

"You sound like Gran."

As Alex wrestled with just how to take that comment, Josh scooped up the tape.

"How about if I take the measurements for you, and you write them down?" he offered.

Alex scowled. It wasn't wise to spend another minute with Josh in this place. It could only lead to no good. But how could she say no without admitting that he still made her heart squirm like a worm on a hot brick.

"It'd save that smart-looking outfit from getting all dusty . . . unless my being here makes you uncomfortable."

A deaf person might lip-read consideration into those words. But Alex heard the innuendo, as if he assumed that he could still turn her knees to Jell-O, making her body betray reason.

Okay, he could, but there was no way she was going to give him the satisfaction of showing it. *Lord, please help me through this.*

She met his searching gaze head-on. Funny, she expected to see smug there. "Why should it? The past is past." Alex gathered her sketchpad from where she'd put it down on the steps leading to Gran's second-floor bedroom. "The rule is yours. I appreciate the help. Besides," she said, using the third step as a bench, just as she'd done gazillion times when talking to Gran or watching her cook. "The sooner I get home, the better."

"Got a hot date tonight?"

Alex's stomach clutched. She could almost see the angry hornets taking off in her mind. "No, not tonight. I have a lot of work to catch up on."

"So there's no one special yet, huh?" Josh hooked the tape on the baseboard and stretched it across the room. "I noticed you came solo to the engagement party . . . *and* the crab feast."

"So did you," Alex reminded him, terse. But instead of leaving well enough alone, the hornets stung her into continuing. "However, *I* didn't delude myself into thinking that you had pined away without romantic interest since you left me and Piper Cove in your dust."

The edge of Alex's voice made Josh lift his head. "Who said anything about pining? I'd think that'd be the last thing a looker like you would do."

Although if Josh were honest with himself, even if he hadn't exactly pined away in loneliness, Alexandra Butler had never been far from his thoughts. Neither the girls who flocked to his dressing room nor the drugs and alcohol had been able to drive her out of his system, no matter how much he'd indulged in them all.

"This is sixteen feet," he said. "And I really hadn't thought about whether you were involved with anyone or not."

It was a white lie. He had thought about it more than he cared to admit, especially when John started dating her baby sister. Talk about bizarre. Who dreamed that fate would bring Alex back into his life again, much less that the sight of her would make him feel more alive than he'd felt since he'd left the stage? She was as indelibly etched under his skin as his tattoos.

"But since you brought it up," he said, "have you been seeing anyone I know?"

Hoping he sounded more polite than interested, he glanced over to see Alex hovering over her sketchpad like a grade-schooler, taking pains to write down the numbers just so. Or was she crafting her reply?

"Some yes. Some no."

"So are you busy Friday evening?"

Her pencil froze. "I can't believe you're asking me out." No question there, just a statement.

"I wasn't asking you on a date. I was *inviting*." Or fishing, he admitted to himself.

Alex looked up, those beautiful brown eyes wary. Josh didn't dare delve into them too long, or he'd sink.

But now that he'd cast his line, he might as well see what was on the other end. "I'm speaking at the Rotary Club meeting Friday night down at Clamdiggers and thought you and your date might like to come as my guests," Josh explained. He snatched up the rule and set it down to measure the width of the room. "It'd be kind of nice to get together with the old gang at the old place."

A recent lunch with Bobby McMann at their former hangout had shown that the place had changed but not lost its local appeal. The restaurant side looked like any other bayside tourist eatery, but the bar was still a big room with pool tables, shuffleboard, darts, and a jukebox on one end with tables on the other.

"Actually, I'm going to be there."

Josh wondered if the way she shifted on the worn step plank suggested physical discomfort or some other kind of unease.

"*With* someone," she added pointedly.

"Good deal." Josh beat back a twinge of disappointment. He didn't think someone like Alex would be left on the shelf too long. She was smart, successful, and attractive, even if she did power-dress her charms. Although with that prickly, got-to-have-her-way temperament . . .

"That was sixteen full," Josh said, oddly annoyed as he repositioned the tape to account for steps of the corner stairwell that jutted into the room. "And this should be—" he knelt, ignoring the stylish turn of her ankles, and read off the measurement. "Yep, thirteen-six by—" He paused, allowing Alex to swing her feet out of the way so that he could measure the steps' width.

"Umm . . ." They were just ankles, he told himself, having to glance at the measure again because his mind went blank. "Two-six," he said. "So who's the guy?"

Instead of answering right away, Alex got up and walked into the front living area. "I haven't really accepted his offer yet. I was going to call him this afternoon."

Josh chuckled. "You never were good at mysterious, Ally. What, is there some reason you want to keep his name a secret?"

"No, I simply can't see how it's any of your business. You have no right to question me about my personal life. You didn't care when we were married, so why now?"

Josh held up his hands in surrender. He didn't want to go back there. "Hey, I was just making conversation." He focused on stretching the tape from the front to the back. "Sorry I mentioned it."

Maybe he should rethink settling back in Piper Cove. There was too much temptation to show those who'd looked down their noses at him that he'd become more successful than the lot of them. The names he'd been called, the disdain for him and his dream. The memories screamed at him from every corner of his mind, trying to drown out the better part of him that would leave it in the past where it belonged.

Josh didn't want to backslide to his former self, bitter, vindictive, angry at Piper Cove and his past. Those things had driven him deeper and deeper into darkness. He sought light now . . . and maybe love.

Love? The tagalong thought shook him. *Lord, help me.*

"I don't need this kind of help . . . or conversation, Josh." Alex put her foot on the tape as he locked it. "Just finish your tour on your own. I've had enough problems today without playing head games."

"Head games?" Josh echoed, a mix of confusion and indignation penetrating his voice. "How can you turn my asking you who you were going to the Rotary dinner meeting with into playing head games?" He rose. "It was just a simple question, Ally, polite conversation. What is it with women? You can take a simple question and read something more into it faster than a guy can get the words out."

"I was *not* reading anything into anything, Josh Turner. You"— she poked an accusing finger at him—"butted your nose into my private life, and I nipped it in the bud."

"Alex . . ." Josh shoved his hands in his pockets lest they yield to the temptation to shake that high-and-mighty look off her face. But he didn't back down from her glower. He looked directly into it. "I didn't come over here to argue."

"You could have fooled me." She took up the tape and pivoted toward the kitchen. "Reading something into your question," she grumbled under her breath. "*Really!*"

"Ally—"

Alex shrugged off the restraining hand he'd placed on her

shoulder to stop her retreat, continuting to shove her things into her leather satchel with a vengeance. "Be sure to lock up and turn off any lights."

Exasperated, Josh gave it up. All he'd asked was the identity of the guy Alex was going to the meeting with. It wasn't like he'd wanted the guy's social security number.

"Go ahead then," he shouted after her. "Run off, don't discuss this like the mature adult I *thought* you'd have become by now." The moment the words were out, Josh wanted to reel them back in. *Lord, how'd I get back here?*

"If that is not the pot calling the kettle black, I don't know what is. *You* set the speed record for running off, Josh Turner. As for maturity"—bitterness saturated her short laugh—"let's not go there."

"Fine." He couldn't agree strongly enough with that. Better he run because he was sinking fast in his past. If Ally stayed and verbally duked out that past, he was a goner. And he might just tell her more than he was at liberty to say.

Josh tried to sound nonchalant. "What about your measurements?"

"I'll get them later," she snapped, hauling the long strap over her shoulder. "I can't deal with you *and* the house at the same time. I just can't."

Hoping to restore civility, Josh followed Alex out to the porch, but she was so intent on getting away from him that he remained there as she struggled to open her car door and get in, with the big satchel still strapped to her. This behavior just didn't fit the Ally he knew. Did she hate him that much?

A plea for Alex to stay bobbed in the stew of emotions simmering from the past, engulfing the present. No matter how Josh rationalized leaving, deep down inside he knew Alex had a right to her anger. He'd left her without saying good-bye. Instead of making a coward's retreat, he should have thought of something to tell her, even if he couldn't divulge all the reasons for ending their relationship. Ill-fated love would have worked as an excuse. Heaven knew that was the truth. Maybe it still was. But ill-fated love wasn't *all* of it.

CHAPTER NINE

"I cannot believe you came here with Will Warren," Sue Ann exclaimed as she checked her lipstick in the mirror of Clamdiggers' ladies' room after an Eastern Shore surf and turf dinner—lump backfin crab cake and fried chicken. "I mean, I know you called and warned me, but I just couldn't believe you'd go anywhere with Wet Willie till I saw it." Will had earned the nickname in high school for his reputation among the girls for slobbery kisses.

Alex scowled at her friend's observation in rebellion. "It's all *your* fault, you know. If you hadn't made such a big deal at lunch about my being so pitifully alone, I wouldn't have given Will's invitation a second thought." And if Josh hadn't stirred the pudding Sue Ann had made of Alex's self-esteem with the bleak assessment of her nonexistent romantic life.

And now she was blaming others for her mistakes. Alex didn't think she could sink any lower, but here she was.

"Well"—Ellen came out of one of the stalls behind them—"you've certainly given the town something to chew on for a while." She snorted. "Talk about *desperate*."

"Yes, I was desperate, Ellen," Alex snapped, pricked by the truth. "I shouldn't have been, but I was. Josh backed me into a corner, and I had to do something so I wouldn't look so . . ."

"Lame?" Ellen filled in, followed by Sue Ann's, "Pitiful?"

"With you two as friends, who needs enemies?" Alex said wryly. But they were right. Alex hated the idea of Josh seeing her as alone or desperate. Worse, that his return made her feel that way. "Anyway, Will had just asked me to this thing, and it was the first out that popped into my mind." What was left of it.

"Just be careful," Jan warned from Sue Ann's other side. "The guy's a jerk. Everyone knows he's been chasing Barbara Carrington, and just the other day, she was hinting to me about needing a wedding cake in the near future."

Sue Ann snapped the cover over her lipstick. "Do tell."

Jan met her expectant look in the mirror. "The woman's completely silly over him. He's got her over some kind of barrel, if you ask me."

"You dated him, if I recall correctly," Ellen reminded her.

"Once," Jan pointed out sharply. "Just because my daddy worked for his, Will *thought* he owned property rights." With a dismissive sniff, Jan switched from uncharacteristic hostile back to her top-of-the-world and take everyone else with her demeanor. "I've developed better taste since."

After meeting Jan at the engagement party, Scott Phillips, coowner of the new hotel/restaurant at South Point on the cove, had been dating her. Alex hoped the bronzed blond tennis jock was for real. His reputation with the ladies gave her cause for concern, but who was she to judge when her own choice for a date was less than stellar? What was she thinking?

"I thought Josh would dislocate his neck when you walked in with Will," Jan said, "so your crazy scheme is working. He turned green around the gills."

Except it hadn't been a scheme. Had it? Alex was a head-on kind of gal, straightforward, no games . . . until now. But all she'd wanted to do was show Josh that she'd not been sitting on a shelf, not make him jealous.

"Like you could take your eyes off your date long enough to notice," Ellen teased Jan. "Just don't invest your heart in that eye candy if you know what I mean."

"You know," Sue Ann said, glancing at Ellen through the mirror. "For a gal who spends so much time around men, you really have a thing about trusting them, don't you?"

"Hey, they make great buds," Ellen replied, "but I'm saving my heart for someone special."

"You've been saying that since high school," Jan teased. She heaved a wistful sigh. "All I want is someone to really care and take care of me for a change."

"I'll know my guy when I see him," Ellen said in her defense, "and I haven't seen him yet."

And if Alex had followed Ellen's pragmatic course instead of listening to Sue Ann's innuendo that she was alone and pitiful, she'd not be sinking faster than a stone in water now.

"There is nothing wrong with coming here with Will, Alex," Sue Ann said, picking up on the downhill plunge of Alex's thoughts. "It will do Josh good to see you with someone else."

If that had come from anyone but Sue Ann, mistress of feminine manipulation, Alex might have taken some heart from it.

"I thought your dad would not only dislocate his neck but pop his eyeballs when you walked in with Will," Sue Ann continued. She gave her appearance a nod of approval before turning to Alex with a puzzled twist of her lips. "I thought your dad was always pushing Will at you."

Alex shrugged. Dinner had been an Oz-like experience. Without her mother to temper his humor, B. J. shifted his glower between Josh and Will. "I can't figure Daddy out. He's been on pins and needles with the wedding and the bank merger . . . but I think he and Will had some words the other day," Alex recalled aloud. "And you know Daddy. He holds a grudge like a bulldog with a hambone."

Ellen tapped her watch. "Hey, the business meeting is about to start." As president of the Rotary, she was to run the meeting. That meant it would be short and sweet, provided Josh didn't get too long-winded—not usually a problem for him. Today, Alex was thankful for that. The sooner this was over, the better.

She lagged behind the others, but when Alex entered the room, Josh caught her curious glance at his table as if waiting for it and waved. *Darn his picture,* she swore in silence. It was the harshest vow she'd ever heard his grandmother Amanda make, *picture* being her genteel substitute for *hide.*

Upon reaching her table, Will rose and pulled out her chair with a flourish. "Milady." He took her hand and, once she was seated, raised it to his lips. Sue Ann, seated across from them, nearly choked on her cheesecake.

Oh *wonderful.* Alex resisted the urge to pull away from his damp grip. She'd set the parameters of the evening by insisting she was going straight home after the meeting, but who dreamed Will would play Sir Lancelot. *God, how could You let me lower myself to this?*

You didn't consult me.

The unexpected answer popping into her mind took Alex back. It was true. Bad enough that her reason had been addled, but her spirit, too? Not that she was a saint, but—

"Good evening, ladies and gentlemen," Ellen announced from a small podium at the front of the room, drawing Alex from her distraction.

A waitress refreshed Alex's coffee, affording the opportunity to retrieve her hand without making her distaste for Will's contact obvious. *Lord, I can't help it. He's shallow as a tin can.* She moved the cup and saucer closer and added the remainder of cream from an already open plastic container.

Ellen concluded the reading of the minutes and treasurer's report, then moved on to the current fund-raiser as she cast a warm, hazel-eyed glance around the room. It was a shame that her black-rimmed reading glasses all but hid naturally thick dark lashes that most women used tons of mascara to mimic.

"From the bottom of my heart, I'd personally like to thank everyone who pledged his or her financial support for the community center project," she said. "The local kids really need a place to hang out apart from Ocean City."

A junior leader in 4-H in her teens and lifetime 4-H All Star, Ellen was committed to the leadership and welfare of kids of all ages. For a year, she'd pushed for the local clubs and city council jointly to finance the purchase of the old car sales building at the edge of town for a community center. So many local youngsters were lured across the bay to the shadier side of the family ocean resort, where, despite the city's concerted efforts, illicit sex and drugs could be found.

"*Busy, Not Bored*, right?" she challenged with the motto of her project. It was the one bumper sticker Alex allowed on her car. To the nods and applause of the audience, Ellen stepped aside for Treasurer Joe Phillips, brother to Jan's date Scott, to report on the progress of the project.

Even though the Phillips brothers were from out of town, they'd assimilated into the community and its concerns. The opposite of his fraternal twin in personality and coloring, the shy, dark-haired Joe announced that the town was three-quarters of the way to reaching the goal to purchase the car dealership building for the center.

"So we've got to keep on this, people," Ellen followed up, as Joe returned to his seat. "For the kids . . . your kids." She let another round of applause die down. "And now, I'd like to introduce our speaker, Josh Turner, even though he's no stranger to some of us," she added with an impish smirk. "On behalf of the Rotary Club and Piper Cove, welcome back, Josh."

Alex couldn't help but glance at her father, a few tables away. B. J. sat, hands folded on the table, more engrossed in them than in Josh's warm reception or what he had to say. It reminded Alex of his behavior the night before last, when she'd gone over her preliminary decorating ideas with her sister and mother. He didn't even grouse about having some of the new work torn out and re-done for the breakfast room, a suggestion that Lynn and Mama loved. At the time, Alex assumed it was because the decorating angle wasn't his thing.

But he thrived on business-related affairs like this. By now, he'd have worked all the tables, greeting and advancing whatever was on his current agenda. She frowned, puzzled.

"Piper Cove has changed a lot since I left it," Josh said from the podium. "But its heart hasn't. I believe it's possible to keep that community heart and accommodate a growing city population."

He leaned in on the podium with an earnestness that demanded full attention. "And because I believe in Piper Cove, because my heart is a part of its heart, and because I've been where many of your kids are headed, I'm prepared to help ensure that they don't make the same mistakes that I did."

The inflection of emotion in his voice locked Alex's gaze with Josh's. Heart? Mistakes? Of course he was talking about his drug and alcohol addiction. But her own fanciful heart, for just a half a beat thought that maybe—

No. She wasn't going there. Didn't want to. Didn't need to.

"I am going to pledge the balance needed to provide our youth with a place for recreation," he announced, following up with an abrupt, "Thank you."

The room went wild with approval.

Alex rose to her feet with the rest, clapping as Ellen raced up to the podium and bear-hugged Josh before he could retreat to his seat. Alex couldn't hear what her friend said over the cheering and scraping of chairs being abandoned, but knowing Ellen's passion for the project, she was babbling.

"Excuse me, Alex. I need to catch your father before he leaves," Will told her above the commotion.

B. J. had abandoned his seat and now walked against the flow toward the exit like a whipped puppy, Alex observed with a pang of concern. Josh had trumped him again.

"I'll be right back," Will promised.

"I'll make sure she doesn't run off," Sue Ann shouted across the table.

Was her father pale, or was it the artificial lighting that made him seem so? Alex wondered. Although, her mother would have let her know if B. J. were ill. By sheer instinct, Mama could detect if something as little as a pimple was in the works with any of her loved ones.

Sue Ann sidled next to Alex. "You look like you could use a drink from the bar."

"You are so bad," Alex accused, fetching her handbag from under the table. She was met by a mischievous gleam in Sue Ann's eyes when she straightened. "It's enough that I agreed to come with Will. Did you have to encourage him as well?"

"I couldn't help myself. It's not often I can catch Ms. Cool, Calm, and Collected in a fix like this." Her friend draped her arm over Alex's shoulder. "Come on, now. You know I love you."

As annoying as Sue Ann was at times, when the chips were down, she was always there, tearing through them like a Tasmanian devil.

"Can you stick around for a little while?" Jan asked, closing in on Alex's other side. "A bunch of us are going to hang out on the other side, just like old times."

"That sounds like fun," Will said behind them.

Alex turned, surprised. That was a short exchange. "I thought we'd agreed to an early night."

"C'mon, Alex," Scott Phillips cajoled, producing a toothpaste commercial smile. "All work and no play makes Alex a dull girl."

Alex felt the hair bristle on her neck. What would a *move-in-er* like Scott Phillips know about her?

That she was a dull girl. Or at least he thought she was after she'd decorated his hotel and ignored him when he'd hit on her for dates. Undoubtedly, he'd have been fun, but Alex had no interest in casual dating, and that's what it would have been. Despite spending lots of time together on the project, the *click* hadn't been there, physically or intellectually.

"Besides, Jennifer Campbell was asking for any of us from De-catur High to stick around and discuss ideas for the class reunion," Jan told her. "Isn't it weird to see so many of the kids we went to school with running the town businesses now?"

"True," Will replied. "I'd say two-thirds of the Rotary Club members now are of our generation."

And Alex was one of the business owners and on the reunion committee, but she really didn't want to stay. Jennifer Campbell was a chatterbox who would drag the meeting out forever, when all Alex wanted was to get away from here.

Sue Ann linked her arm in Alex's. "C'mon, Alex. Relax a little. It'll be fun . . . and it certainly beats going home and cuddling up with Riley and a good book."

Alex could have debated her friend on that, but not now.

It was almost like the old days, Josh thought, glancing at the checkered-cloth-covered tables where the Piper Cove High re-union committee met. Except that everyone had matured, and the lines that once separated jock from geek and beauty queen from plain jane were less visible. And Alex wasn't at his side.

Josh had been glad he was sitting when she entered the restau-rant with Will Warren. Not that Will was a bad guy, but what on earth could the Alex that Josh knew possibly have in common with a *yes* man like him?

Or was B. J.'s hand in this? The old coot had always wanted Alex and Will to date. He'd compared Josh to his brown-nosing assis-tant constantly.

"Got ya!"

Ellen Brittingham, who'd opted to play shuffleboard while lis-tening to the conversations going on around them, nailed his piece, knocking it out of bounds. It would never occur to Ellen to play the docile companion like her friend Janet, who stuck as close to Scott Phillips as a rescued pup, utter adoration in her eyes.

"I win." Ellen exclaimed, raising her arms in a little two-fisted victory dance. "You gotta buy the paint for the center."

"You drive a hard bargain, Brit." If Josh had won, she only owed him an alchohol-free beer from the bar.

"Tell you what," she said, linking her arm in his. "I'll even buy you that drink."

Josh pulled her back. "No way. When I'm beat, I'm beat. I'm buying. Then I'm going to whup your butt at billiards."

Ellen snorted. "You wish," she said in a not-so-low voice as they passed the cluster of tables pulled together for the impromptu meeting where Jennifer James gave her a scolding look.

Jennifer *Campbell*, Josh corrected himself. She'd married Jay Campbell, the former football captain who now owned a local drugstore franchise.

"As you all know," the former high school cheerleader said, increasing the volume in her voice, "we decided at our last meeting that this was going to be a joint class reunion so that classes that are too small to have their own can participate. So tonight, I'd like to settle on a theme. My committee"—she declared, lest anyone question her authority—"has narrowed it down to three. Country Hoedown, Beach Party, or *Puttin' on the Ritz*." Jennifer gave the last option her best touchdown enthusiasm.

"I vote for Country Hoedown," Ellen spoke up from the bar, where she had settled on a stool. "Line dancing was the rage when we graduated, and I don't have to have a date to dance."

"You mean you won't have to dress up," Jan teased.

Ellen broke into a mile-wide smile. "That, too."

"My thought is that *Puttin' on the Ritz* will enable attendees of all ages to dress up and not feel *dated*," Jennifer countered, as though Ellen had the IQ of a slug. "Does anyone else have an opinion?"

"Who won the game?" Bobby McMann asked Josh, turning from where he watched the television over the bar with local attorney Tony Richardson and bar owner Jerry Fitzgerald, aka Fitz.

"She did," Josh told him above the discussion that ensued over the reunion theme. "She puts a mean spin on that thing."

"Hey, Fitz," Ellen said, as the bartender set her up with a soda. "Don't you think it's time you replaced these games and tables with new stuff?"

Fitz, whose shaved head resembled a cue ball, wagged his finger at her. "Aw no, I see what's coming. Donate the old ones to the youth center and get new ones for here, right?"

"Okay," Ellen conceded, "maybe not *all* the old ones. We'd be thrilled with anything . . . and it would be a good tax write-off."

"I take it this is the *outlaw* section of Decatur High." Joe Phillips took the stool on Ellen's other side.

"Let's just say, we didn't quite measure up to standards back then," Bobby McMann explained.

"One Pepsi and a cranberry martini for the lady over there," Joe told Fritz, pointing to Sue Ann. "That lady is a trip."

"Don't worry," Ellen assured him. "Sue Ann's harmless. Happily married."

"It's like this," Bobby went on. "Me, Josh, and Tony used to hang out here at Clamdiggers when it wasn't the nice place it is now."

"Either here or at my dad's filling station at the end of Main Street. It's a strip mall now," Tony added, with a touch of irony.

"Does a man's heart good to see all these preps in here, don't it,

Josh? Used to be, nothing short of Ocean City was good enough for them," Bobby said.

Josh nodded, remembering how Alex had broken away from her clique and become a regular when Clamdiggers was just a local joint where ne'er-do-wells hung out.

Joe put a straw in the Pepsi Fritz served him. "For coming from the wrong side of town, neither of you appear to have done too bad," he observed. "What, we have a lawyer, the biggest contractor in the area, and one of the best guitarists I've ever heard. I have all your albums, man," he told Josh in admiration.

Josh tore his gaze from Alex.

"Thanks," he replied. And Josh meant it. There was a time that he'd grown cocky with talent and success and accepted praise as his due, but his accident and subsequent surrender to God's will had remedied that. It had all been a gift—given, squandered, and taken away. "I still pick a little. Not like I used to," he said, flashing the scars on the backs his hands, not with resentment, but wonder and gratitude. "As you can see, I'm lucky to have any use of them at all."

"Okay, okay, listen up." Alex pounded on the table to get everyone's attention. "Why don't we just take a vote and get this settled? The beach party is out because it's been done over and over, so it's between Hoedown and Ritz."

"I'm betting the game will go to the cowboys," Joe said under his breath as he gathered up the drinks to leave. "There are more men in attendance here than women."

It was a good bet, Josh observed, continuing to watch Alex from the corner of his eye. The way she flipped the handle of her purse back and forth, she was ready to bolt or move Jennifer aside. It was good thing that she and Jennifer had been separated by a year

in school, or the clash would have gone down in the high school annals.

"Is there any more discussion, or is everyone ready to vote?" Jennifer asked, rising at the head of the table as if to retrieve the authority the impatient Alex had seized.

Or maybe the annoyed set of Alex's mouth was because Will kept whispering in her ear or touching her on the shoulder. Not that Josh cared one way or the other. Those two just did not fit together in the same puzzle.

Having bided his time as long as possible, Josh turned to Ellen. "So what's the deal with Alex and Will Warren, Britt?"

A deer in the headlights look claimed Ellen's face, but only for a flash. "What do I look like, Dear Abby? How should I know?"

"First time I've ever seen them together," Bobby observed.

Ellen narrowed her gaze at Josh. "Besides, it's not like you care, right?"

Josh did a mental backpedal. It was always hard separating Ellen from the guys. She used to hang at Tony's father's garage with them, talk shop and engines. No one knew a big bike like Brit. But she was also one of the inseparable Bosom Buddies.

"Home run!" Tony shouted, slamming both fists on the bar.

Bobby swiveled toward the TV to watch the player run the bases. "It's about time."

The distraction gave Josh a moment to collect himself. "I was just curious."

"All in favor of Country Hoedown raise your hands," Jennifer said with an annoyed look in the bar's direction. It didn't lessen when the majority of hands went up in the air.

Aware of Ellen's forthright appraisal, Josh feigned interest in the hand count. He hadn't lied to her. But he'd not exactly told the truth either. He *was* curious. As to whether he cared, it was a moot point. It didn't matter one way or the other. At least that's what Josh told himself.

"That's it then." Jennifer's overbright voice was one of someone who was used to getting their way and hadn't. "The theme is Country Hoedown." She looked at Alex as if it were her fault. "So I suppose we'll have to get out the jeans and polish those old boots."

As if on cue, one of the guys fired up the jukebox and a boot-scootin' song rang out.

But if it didn't matter, Josh reasoned beyond the music and resulting yee-haws rising from the group, why did it feel like his heart was trapped in some unpredictable balance between reality and show?

❧

Alex's head hurt. She was so ready to leave. The other side of the bar area, a small enclosure that had once been an open porch, was not smoke-free, and no ventilation system could keep the smoke from drifting over to the *smoke-free* section where the games were.

"I think we should make Josh Turner an honorary alumni," Jennifer Campbell said, casting a dreamy look toward where Josh, Ellen, Bobby McMann, and Tony Richardson had started a game of partner pool. Josh, as if sensing that he was topic of conversation, lifted his drink in acknowledgment and flashed a smile that would have made Alex's tummy go all warm and fuzzy . . . had it been for her.

"Given his contribution to the community, it seems like a good gesture," Will agreed.

Always the *yes* man.

"I'll go ask him." Jennifer took off toward Josh as if she'd been waiting for an excuse.

And to think, there was a time Jennifer wouldn't give Piper Cove's bad boy a second look . . . at least one that she'd admit to. Although, Alex observed, after Josh offered to fund the balance of the money needed for the community center, he'd have everyone in his pocket. Except B. J. And Alex, of course.

"So are we ready to go now?" Alex asked Will, leaning back against her chair. She stiffened as Will curled his arm around her shoulders and leaned in.

"Take it easy, sweetie pie. Isn't this what you brought me along for?" Will whispered in her ear.

Was it *that* obvious? Alex groaned inwardly. How did the proverb go about tangled webs woven with deceit? The last thing she wanted was to be caught in a web with a brown-noser like Will. Yet, here she was, reduced to his level . . . no, lower.

"Don't worry, it's working." Looking past her in Josh's direction, Will produced a gloating smile and tightened his arm around Alex's shoulders. "Your ex nearly missed the pool table with his drink."

Enough was enough. Alex had made a mistake in accepting Will's invitation for all the wrong reasons. No way would she compound the error with dishonesty. "Look, I have an early appointment tomorrow morning, and the smoke from the other side of the bar is giving me a mother of a headache." She raised her voice for the others, adding, "I'm interviewing to replace my deliveryman, so if you know of a reliable person with a strong back, send him my way."

Her former deliveryman was now on workman's comp from straining his back moving the new sofa bed into Lillian Laws's condo.

Alex's move prompted the others to leave as well. Scott Phillips tried to cajole Jan into going to the racetrack at Ocean Downs, but she had to be at work the next morning at four. It was all Alex could do to keep from giving him an attitude adjustment, when he referred to Jan's job as a loser and suggested she quit and work full-time for him, but Sue Ann beat Alex to the punch.

"Now that is downright ridiculous," Sue Ann declared. The daggers in her gaze glistened over a saccharine smile. "Our Jan's too smart for that."

Leave it to Susie. Alex gave her saucy friend an atta-gal wink. So far Alex's instincts regarding Scott Phillips were dead-on. He was a candy-coated jerk. "Will and I can drop her off," she offered.

Alex had been wondering how to avoid the prospect of leaving alone with Will. There was just something about him that always made her feel sleazy.

Tonight she felt doubly so for using him. Tonight *she* was sleazy.

Lord, I am so sorry. I've not been this mixed up and miserable since . . . well, You know. Just get me through all this. Please . . . just get me through the next two months.

CHAPTER TEN

One month down and one to go, Alex thought. She pulled into the bank parking lot in the stepvan she'd driven to Baltimore that Wednesday on her monthly buying trip. Although it hardly seemed like a month had passed since she'd made a fool of herself at Clamdiggers with Will Warren. Nor did it seem possible that out of all the interviews she'd conducted, not one had produced a deliveryman.

Each time she'd glanced in the rearview mirror, Alex was reminded of that fact by the furniture neatly packed and tied down in the back. The problem was that, while the area was filled with young people looking for summer jobs, most needed full-time work to meet the resort's cost of living. Or they were there for the fun and not reliable. Alex needed a *reliable*, part-time deliveryman year-round.

Fortunately, her work on the Turner home had been more in the planning stages until now, keeping her busy with orders for window treatments, furniture, carpeting—all enthusiastically approved by her mother and sister. Too enthusiastically, Alex mused, as she climbed down from the van. They were trying to compensate for the emotional drain the work had been for her.

Yes, it had been a drain. And there had been tears at times. But the designer in Alex had risen to the challenges of the project with more than usual zeal because of her ties to the place. Of course, she'd become a workaholic Jekyll, alternating with a weepy Hyde. Thankfully, the advance from the new hotel project was paying off her business loan today. It helped level out the emotional swings and boosted her battered self-esteem, especially now that her second advance was in the bank.

"Is Daddy with someone?" she asked her father's secretary upon entering the reception area.

B. J.'s office door was closed and the blinds semiclosed so that it was hard to tell for sure. With her last payment on the loan for the building on Main Street in her purse, her downtown business office and home were now totally hers.

"No," Sheila told her, brightening. B. J.'s secretary for twenty years, she knew as much about Alex as B. J., maybe more. "Is this the big day?"

Alex nodded with a mile-wide grin.

"Congratulations! Just knock and go on in, sweetie."

Alex did knock and open the door, but instead of going in, she peeked around it to make certain B. J. wasn't on the phone. He wasn't. At his inviting wave, she stepped inside.

"Morning, Daddy. Isn't it a beautiful day? Looks like the Fourth of July shindig is going to have great weather."

B. J. looked at his digital desk calendar. "Is it the first week of July already?" A smile broadened his lips.

Beaming, Alex produced a check from her purse and laid it on his desk. "Paid in full!" Her dream was realized. Her spirit ballooned straight for the ceiling.

"*Prepaid* ahead of time," her father observed, grinning. "That's my girl. It's a shame you didn't take up banking. You have a good business head on your shoulders."

A compliment? No more snide comments about buying an old building and refurbishing it, instead of building new? If Alex had been elated before, she was about to pop on the dentil molding overhead.

"Thank you, Daddy. That means a lot coming from you." More than B. J. Butler could ever know. Emotion thickened in her throat, but she swallowed it. She'd waited so long for his approval. Fought hard for it.

"How about celebrating over dinner tonight at that new hotel restaurant . . . just you, Mama, and me?" He hesitated. "Or do you have other plans? After all, it's Friday night."

If she had, Alex would have canceled them in a heartbeat. "No, nothing Riley wouldn't mind postponing." She'd even call off this afternoon's sundae luncheon at the club with the Bosom Buddies for this.

"Sit down," he said, motioning to a plush leather side chair that matched his own executive model.

Alex's surge of joy hitched in her chest. This was, after all, her father. And from his sobering grimace, he had something else on his mind, something that didn't bode well.

"What's wrong, Daddy?"

B. J. averted his gaze. "You girls are both well established now . . . even though you aren't married."

Alex grimaced. Not the *women have to be married to be well established* again.

"But I can see that you can take care of yourself," B. J. went on before she could object. "It's time I spent more time with your mother. I think she has that woman's thing going on."

"Menopause?" Alex ventured. Where was this going? B. J. loved his job. He thrived on it. He'd go crazy without something to do, someone to manipulate. And heaven knew, he'd drive Mama nuts, too.

"No, that bird thing that happens when her babies are gone."

"Empty nest syndrome."

"Yes, that." B. J. lost himself in thought for a moment. "You know, Ally, I love you and your sister, but I've got to let you go sometime—same with work. Like the Reverend Beauchamp said about seasons last Sunday . . . one for everything."

Her father paying attention to a Sunday sermon? Usually church was more of a social hour for B. J. Butler. Lenora constantly had to punch him to keep him from talking while the reverend spoke. As for retirement, he always sworn he'd retire when they patted him in the face with a spade.

Alex thoughts jumped back to last week's conversation with her mother. "Daddy, are you feeling okay?"

She and Mama had met to pick out the wedding menu at the caterer's. Her mother had expressed some concern about his health then. According to her, B. J. had been distant and lethargic, staring at the television without watching, going to bed early. But Alex attributed it to marrying off his baby girl. Lynn had always been the apple of his eye.

"I'm finer than frog hair," B. J. answered without hesitation. "A little tired of working, but, shoot, I've worked since I was old enough to tie my own shoes."

She'd heard that before. While the other young men his age

were surfing, B. J. was in business school year-round *and* working at the bank. The bank was practically his lifeblood. Heaven knew he'd spent more time there than he had with his family.

"Have you discussed this with Mama?" she asked.

"I thought you might help me tell her tonight. You always seem to know the right thing to say . . . how to explain things."

Alex's balloon of elation flattened with its last gasp. So tonight wasn't about celebrating Alex's accomplishment after all. It was to engage her help in telling Mama that he was going to retire. And it hurt more than he'd ever guess.

"It sounds to me like you can speak for yourself"—she said through the constriction of her throat—"but, of course, I'll be there."

Wasn't she always?

Swept in a tide of shock and disappointment, Alex made her way out onto the black, heat-radiating asphalt of the bank parking lot. The stepvan she used for hauling furniture was a veritable oven, but she was too distraught to fuss at the overwhelmed air conditioner.

She didn't know which bothered her the most—her father's plan to retire or her delusion in thinking he really wanted to take her out to celebrate. She should have known his suggestion for dinner had nothing to do with her elation, but how could she have guessed he wanted her to help tell her mother about his retirement?

It shouldn't hurt anymore, but it did. It hurt terribly.

Of course Lenora would interrogate him beyond what Alex had as to his reasons, and B. J. never had liked explaining himself. Alex could take some of the heat off, distract her mother with the wedding plans.

She glanced over her shoulder. In the back were her latest purchases from yesterday's day trip to an auction house in Baltimore. One dresser and matching bed frame needed refinishing and would be set aside, along with some unique accent pieces, for future decorating projects.

But the dainty Queen Anne armoire, with its antique painted finish, was ready to go. With a mirror panel on one door, framed in delicate, hand-painted flowers, it was the perfect centerpiece for the smallest bedroom at the Turner house. Since that room had no closet space, having yielded what it had to the larger adjacent bedroom during the renovation, the armoire would provide clothing storage for guests. The moment Alex saw it, she'd fallen in love with it. If only—

Don't go there. You're in enough of a funk as it is.

As she had so many times over the last weeks, when working on her sister's summer-home-to-be, Alex shoved her feelings aside before they overwhelmed her. If she was going to lament over something, it might as well be the fact that her interviews had yet to produce someone to help her unload this stuff.

Alex started the truck and shifted it into reverse. Her rusty familiarity with the manual transmission jerked the entire vehicle as she pulled out of the parking space to the warning beep of the backup lights. Not for the first time that week, she wondered why she hadn't spent a little more for an automatic.

Compared to her small sports car, driving the delivery van was like maneuvering a tank through Main Street traffic, which was now thick with tourists gathering for the Fourth of July weekend. Twice the engine cut out on her, resulting in a few impatient horn beeps. And who could blame them, as hot as it was? Despite the valiant efforts of the van's air-conditioning, Alex sweated, vexed enough to blow the horn at herself.

But relief was on the way. Envisioning a tantalizing image of a tall parfait glass filled to the brim with chocolate nut sundae and whipped cream, she turned onto North Cove Road toward the country club. More important than the ice cream was the fact that her friends would be there. She could cry and vent all she wanted without judgment hovering over her. And they would give her advice, whether good, bad, or absurd. And the absurd would make her laugh.

The hint of a smile tugging at the corner of her mouth froze as she cleared the corner and the van's engine began to cough as though it had something terminal. Alex steered toward the side of the road, but in her haste to downshift, she didn't give it enough gas.

The motor died before she came to a stop.

"No, no, no!"

Chewing on a prayer, she hit the ignition, but the engine didn't turn over and catch as it had before. It made a pitiful show of protest, then nothing. Cars whizzed around Alex with beach buckets and boogie boards stuffed in the windows, the drivers shooting her annoyed looks. She tried the engine again, but for all its bluster, it would not start. Maybe Ellen wasn't at the club yet and would see her and stop.

With a groan, she opened the truck window to a humid blast of heat—the downside of an Eastern Shore summer. It enveloped her, smothering, like life of late. She had a truckload of furniture and no one to help her unload it. And her father was quitting a job he loved and wanted her to explain why to her mother, when Alex really didn't understand it herself. B. J. wasn't the kind of man who was attuned to the needs of others, much less to empty nest syndrome, or that *bird thing*, as he called it.

Despite the sob sawing at her throat, Alex chose to think it was sweat blinding her eyes instead of tears. She was made of stronger stuff than this, she thought, digging in her purse for her cell phone. But the sight of no bars on the battery indicator—she'd forgotten to recharge last night—heaped the last straw on what was becoming a mountain of burden. Her shoulders collapsed under its weight. Her world spinning out of control, she folded her arms on the wheel and leaned on them.

After she pulled herself together, she'd walk to the club, she decided, ignoring the beeping horn of a black pickup blurring its way past. Until it pulled over in front of her and backed up.

CHAPTER ELEVEN

Josh parked his Dodge Ram in front of the white stepvan marked DESIGNS BY ALEX sitting on the side of North Cove Road. To his surprise the boss lady herself was at the wheel. A bolt of alarm prodded him out onto the shoulder and into a run until he saw Alex raise her head and wipe her eyes.

He paused, taking a deep breath at seeing that she was all right, trying to dull the blades of panic and fear that had torn through him at the thought of her being hurt and helpless—

God, it's supposed to be gone by now. I shouldn't be feeling this way. I can't feel this way about Alex. Not this gut-wrenching fear that something might be wrong with her. That she might not be somewhere on the same planet and in the same life as I am.

Panic receding, he jogged up to the open door of the van. "Hey, good-lookin', what's cookin'? Aside from you," he added, noting the wilted cling of her blouse and prudently not mentioning the tear streaks on her face.

Those, too, bothered him, tempted him to brush them away. *Echoes,* he told himself. *Just a few stray bits of "if only" hanging around to cause havoc.*

Alex cleared her throat of the emotions that had reddened her eyes and splotched her face. "I can't get it started," she told him flatly.

Again resisting the instinct to brush a sweat-soaked strand of hair off her forehead, Josh inhaled the heavy scent of gasoline cloaking the vehicle. "Now what did I teach you about flooding the engine?"

When Alex was upset, and he could clearly see that she was, the best way to pull her out of it was criticism.

"I must have put that away with all the things I've tried to forget," she rallied. "I've tried everything except pushing the bloomin' thing."

"You always were hard on manual transmissions," Josh teased.

"Oh yeah?"

Josh's grin faded as Alex slid out of the seat and onto the ground in fight position, fists clenched at her side.

"Well, you're just as clueless as ever about me, aren't you, Josh Turner?" She cocked her head up at him. "Do you think that I'd be hard on the transmission on purpose or out of carelessness? Maybe I flooded it because my head is full of a gazillion other things," she declared with a ferocity that drove Josh back a step. "I have a demanding father, who knows just which of my strings to pull to get me to do what he wants—" She gathered a shaky breath. "And he wants more than I think I have the heart to give. I paid off my business loan today . . . *ahead* of time."

Not certain where this was going, Josh nodded. "That's good. I'll bet B. J. was proud as pun—"

"He invited me to dinner," Alex shouted, her face growing B. J. Butler red as she followed Josh's sidestep around the fender to the hood. "But not to pat me on the back," she went on. "He wants me to explain to my mother that he's retiring to stay home with her because she has empty nest syndrome! Have you ever heard of anything so ridiculous in your life?"

Josh felt for the hood release, the vehicle's white metal super warm to the touch. "Doesn't sound like B. J.," he said, hoping his comment was acceptable, because Alex was about to fly apart like an overwound clock.

Her eyes widened a fraction more. "Of course it does! It's all about him . . . always about him. I h—" Her voice, already raw, cracked. "Hate h . . . him."

Aw, man, there goes the chin thing. She wasn't going to blow. She was going to crumble. Abandoning the hood mechanism, Josh encircled Alex in his arms. "Now, babe, I know that's not so."

While Alex was independent enough not to let B. J. determine who she was, Josh knew that she loved her dad and secretly yearned for his approval. With Alex crying in his arms, wounded by her father, the angry wolf of revenge began to gnaw hungrily at Josh's resolve to forgive and forget.

Lord, don't let me feed it.

There was a time when Alex's hurts about her father had fed the darker side of Josh's heart, before the light of Christ had entered it. But Josh wasn't fool enough to think that the wolves weren't still there, hiding in a recess where righteous thoughts didn't go, waiting to devour it. It would be easy to make his return about revenge and showing off just how well he'd done in spite of all those who'd dubbed him worthless trash. With God's help, he'd learned to deal with his own hurt, but Alex's was another story.

And she'd come into his arms as if she'd never stopped trusting him. It was incredible the way Alex could make Josh feel ten feet tall and make him feel as if he were melting inside at the same time. And the sun overhead had nothing to do with the implosion in his belly. It was from the warm, sweet-smelling woman pressed against him, needing him . . . at least for the moment.

He saw it in her tear-reddened eyes, recognized the raw yearning to be taken away from it all. Her trembling lips parted as he lowered his mouth and assuaged them with a tenderness that made her breath catch. This was exactly where Alexandra Butler belonged—in his arms.

The way she swayed against him in surrender was all the evidence Josh needed that she knew it was true. The ignition of passion beneath the flutter of her lashes fired its counterpart in Josh, so that the muscles in his arms seized, trapping her against him as if to draw her into his skin.

Not that she'd ever been anywhere else but under his skin from the first day he'd seen her, a dark-eyed sophomore giggling over a school lunch tray. Although, head to head while trading secrets with her friend Sue Ann, the curious glances Alex slid in his direction made Josh vow to be the man to answer every one of those feminine questions. But the school cafeteria hadn't been the place, and neither was the side of the road in broad daylight for all the world to see.

"Damn you, Ally, I still love you," Josh moaned against her lips, his words drowning in the roar of blood in his ears.

Alex's eyes opened, stared at him with an expression he couldn't read—

A loud, prolonged beep, quickly told Josh that he was mistaken about the source of the roar. Startled, Alex shoved away from him and plastered herself against the front of the stepvan as Ellen Brittingham shut down the engine and swung off her idling Harley. Clad in cut-off jeans and a tee shirt, she pulled off her helmet and set it on the bike, grinning at them.

"Ya know, for two people who"—she made quotation marks with her fingers—"*hate* each other, you have a funny way of showing it."

"The van won't start, Ellen," Alex said, tucking her blouse into the waistband of her slacks. "A . . . and here I am, stuck in this heat in this worthless four-wheeled piece of junk loaded with furniture and I . . . I can't find anyone who wants to work part-time for deliveries," she said in a rush, babbling to cover up her embarrassment and confusion.

"Yeah, well maybe I should take a look and do what I do best, while Josh here does what he obviously does best." Covering her mouth and nose too late with her hand, Ellen snorted at her humor.

Josh fumbled for the hood release. "Ally's having a bad day," he explained, eager to change the direction of the conversation. This was between him and Alex.

With a knowing smirk, Ellen found the release and popped it without the least trouble. "Doesn't look like it to me," she replied in a singsong voice.

"*Uncle*, Ellen, *uncle*. Enough already," Josh said quietly as he watched Alex cross her arms over her chest and walk around to the driver's door, avoiding his gaze.

Why didn't he just lay his heart down in the road and let Alex run over it with the truck? Josh wondered wryly, as Ellen zeroed in on the problem.

"Ah, there's it is." Ellen pointed to a wire that had come loose from the ignition coil. "I tell you, the way Alex drives this tank, it's no wonder it shook loose. Stop, go, jerk!" Peeking around the raised hood, she pointed a playful finger at Alex, who by now was behind the wheel. "And that doesn't count the number of curbs you take out."

Alex's wan smile froze as a horn blew from behind them. Coming to a stop in Sue Ann's bright red convertible were the other two Bosom Buddies.

"What's going on?" Sue Ann called from behind her designer sunglasses.

"Is that Alex in there?" Jan asked.

Josh slammed down the hood as Ellen practically skipped toward her friends. "Engine and man trouble," he heard her say, not without a tinge of delight.

He met Alex's gaze over the hood. "Try her now. You should be good to go."

Sure enough, the engine caught on the first turn. Alex visibly relaxed, but her brown eyes were troubled, as though she were as unsettled by what had just happened between them as he.

"Hey, we're on our way for a sundae celebration," Ellen said to Josh as she headed toward her bike. "Want to join us? That is," she said, glancing hastily at Alex, "if it's okay with the queen of paid-off mortgages."

Josh shook his head. "I don't know, I was trying to run down Bobby McCann."

"That's where Bobby usually gets lunch," Alex spoke up. A becoming shade of pink crept over her cheeks. "I guess we'll see you there then." She shifted into first gear, accelerating and sending Josh and Ellen running to get out of her way before she let up on the clutch.

Uncertain about the invite, but determined to follow Alex, just in case she had more trouble, Josh climbed into his Dodge and pulled ahead enough to give her plenty of room to pass. The way he figured it, he thought as she clutched, accelerated, and jerked by, he might have done something right for a change. She hadn't tried to sideswipe him.

⸎

Josh still loved her? At least that's what it sounded like Josh had said to Alex above the roar of her pulse and Ellen's bike. *Still love you.* That was more information than she'd wanted. Way more. It opened up too many reactions, too much emotion . . . and need.

Dear God, I don't know what to do with it all. It's not supposed to be like this . . .

But here she sat, lips still tingling, in the coffee shop side of the country club, between Josh and Jan. Who was she kidding? Her whole body tingled. But then Alex couldn't count the number of times he'd made her forget her troubles, rallying her spirit with his stirring brand of CPR. With him on her side, she'd been able to knock all her concerns out of the ballpark.

Then he'd left, and she'd had to learn to fend for herself. Something she'd done very well, she reminded herself. She popped a spoonful of heavenly, fat- and sugar-laden ice cream into her mouth and, stealing a sidewise glance at Josh, really wishing he'd leave so she could straighten out her thoughts. Had he said what she *thought* he'd said?

Well, if so, he was years too late, and she wished she'd had the presence of mind to tell him so—flatly, without a shred of feeling to show she had none where he was concerned.

Oh yeah, that would have worked after the kiss she'd melted into. He'd felt so good. Strong. Protective. Steady—

He'd never been steady during their marriage. She really had to remember that. And she really ought to be joining in the conversation, to prove to everyone and herself that she wasn't all hot and bothered—on several levels.

At Ellen's prompt, he was giving everyone an update on the progress of the community center. "The kids have been great," he said. "We've managed to prepare the walls and get a new coat of paint on."

"And Burns Heating and Air donated a heat pump system, used but reconditioned," Ellen added. "If that and things like Josh's coming home and donating the balance to buy the building isn't God's handiwork, I don't know what is."

Josh coming home . . . God's handiwork? Alex shook herself. She was just grasping at straws to keep her heart afloat. So Josh had been at church every Sunday. But he'd always gone when they'd been married, too, although his grandmother was his motivation then.

"All I can say is this is the best sundae celebration yet," Jan observed. "Alex is debt-free and doing grand in the business she loves. Ellen's dream of a community center has come true . . . and I am so in love, I can't see straight."

That jarred Alex out of her self-absorption as she swung her gaze to Jan. "Hold up on that last one, Jan. Are you *sure*?"

Jan practically bubbled over. "Scott asked me to move in with him."

"After the way he dumped you on his brother a few weeks ago to go to the track?" Sue Ann exclaimed, incredulous as Alex. "Can't see straight is right, sugar."

"Hon, think hard about this," Ellen pleaded. "He doesn't think about anyone but himself. Tell me you didn't quit your job at the grocery."

Jan swelled maybe a half size larger than her petite size two self. "No, I'm not *that* stupid. I don't want my job dependent on him, too. At least not yet."

"Hey, Jan's a big girl. You all sound like a bunch of ruffled hens," Josh chided, as Alex and her friends swelled with more dissuasion.

"Mind your own business, Josh Turner," Sue Ann snapped. "When it comes to love, Jan hasn't always had the clearest thoughts."

"And, no offense, buddy, but you don't have the best track record either," Ellen reminded him.

Poor Josh. Alex was reminded of an antelope surrounded by pride of lions on nature TV as he rose, hands held up in surrender.

"I was going to add that Jan might want to reconsider moving in with Scott until he'd made a more tangible commitment than *come on in*," he said, wriggling his left ring finger.

Not only was he was quick on his feet, he was adorable when he wanted to be. Alex found herself grasping the edge of the table to keep from thinking past the point of no return.

"But I'm clearly out of my element and outnumbered. Besides"—Josh glanced toward the parking lot—"I see McMann's truck pulling up."

"And I never said that I'd decided to move in with Scott," Jan announced smugly. "All I said was that he asked me to."

"Case closed." Josh gave Jan a conspiratory wink. "I'll catch you all later."

"Thanks—" A sudden need to keep him here—close and within reach—hitched Alex's voice. "Thanks for everything," Alex said with an attempt at prim and proper gratitude. She pretended she had something caught in her throat . . . something besides her heart.

Josh winked, that slow, sexy grin riveting her till her brain rattled. "Actually, I have an idea that might help you out," he told her. "Me and some of the older boys could come over this evening and unload your truck for you. I'm thinking it would give them a little extra income and keep them busy . . . at least until you find someone."

"Brandon and Kyle would love it," Ellen agreed. "They're trying to raise money for a mission trip to Nicaragua in August."

Alex sorted the words she'd heard above the commotion of her senses. *Boys, help, mission trip, Nicaragua.* "G . . . great." *I think.*

"How does five o'clock sound? Meet you at your place?" he asked.

Boys, help, mission trip, Nicaragua. Yes. With the boys present, she'd not be alone with Josh. That was not such a great idea. She was too vulnerable.

"Perfect," Alex said, wondering if all the marbles rolling around in her brain were cracked. Some of them had anticipation written all over them. "No, wait." She'd forgotten about dinner with her folks tonight. "I have a previous engagement tonight . . . but tomorrow evening would be great. If it's okay with you and the boys."

Mimicking fake pistols with his hands, Josh pointed at Alex in affirmation. "You're on, partner. See you tomorrow night, five o'clock sharp."

He looked as good from the back as he did face-to-face, Alex mused, as Josh walked away.

"Boy, would I love to be a fly on the wall tomorrow night," Sue Ann said with a playful purse of the lips. "Remember what I said about second chances?"

Alex snapped to, squirming under Sue Ann's keen perusal.

"Wait a minute," Jan said, drawing it way from Alex. "How come it's okay if Alex has second chances, but I don't?"

"You're right, Tink," Alex conceded. She put her arm around Jan and hugged the pixie queen of sweet. "We all deserve second chances. But we have to be a lot more careful the second time around," she added, not solely for Jan's sake.

CHAPTER TWELVE

The new Baylander Restaurant overlooked the entrance at the southernmost tip of Piper Cove. Alex and her parents sat on the shaded side of the restaurant overlooking the red-bronze glaze of the sunset on the bay. Below their window was an open deck and Tiki bar, where informal dress was allowed. The reggae strains of a Jimmy Buffett imitator entertaining the customers on the water reached Alex's ear.

As opposed to the informal seating, B. J. leaned toward the more formal British colonial décor of the dining room that Alex had designed to make the inside guests feel royal as they overlooked their subjects cavorting on the lanai.

Although Alex felt anything but. She'd been so on edge, waiting for B. J. to drop the bomb, that she hardly enjoyed her appetizer and now picked at her jerked chicken dinner salad.

Instead, wedding talk had dominated the conversation. To Alex, her mother seemed more animated than she'd been in a long time.

She rattled on about the number of RSVPs she'd received to date and how Lynn had said that she could hardly concentrate on her job with so much going on. The dresses had come in, and they were just lovely. The dark red of Alex's maid-of-honor dress would look stunning on her.

"What is the name of that color again, dear? Not wine ... a Mexican drink—"

"Sangria," Alex told her.

Lenora met Alex's gaze and enveloped her in a smile as only a mother could. It was like basking in sunshine. "One of these days, we'll be planning your wedding, dear."

"Not too soon I hope," Alex quipped.

Simultaneously, B. J. replied with the same exact words.

The three of them broke into spontaneous laughter.

"Listen to you two. I ought to call you Pete and Re-Pete," her mother teased.

B. J. grunted, noncommittal. "I'm just saying that our check-book will only handle one wedding a year. Maybe even every five years."

Alex did a mental jerk. What had happened to *spare no expense*?

"And that's only if someone decent comes along," her father said with a pointed look at her that said *decent* meaning not Josh Turner.

"Did Daddy tell you my good news?" It was a rhetorical question aimed at turning the conversation to a less volatile subject. If B. J. had told her mother about Alex's paying off her loan, Lenora would have ordered champagne by now.

"No, I don't think so." Lenora gave B. J. a searching look. "He's been rather tight-lipped of late."

"I'm sorry, darlin', it slipped my mind," B. J. told her.

Alex cringed inwardly. One of the milestones in her life, and it had slipped her father's mind.

"I've been trying to think of how to tell you . . ." B. J. paused, casting a glance at Alex for help.

Alex tightened her fist around her napkin. It was always about him.

"Tell me what?" her mother asked, suddenly tense. "Are you all right, B. J. Butler? You're not sick, are you?"

"No, now, darlin'—" He reached over and took his wife's hand between his. "You'd be the first to know, if I was . . . even before the doctor."

"Then what is it?" her mother insisted.

"I've decided to retire."

Lenora couldn't have looked more shocked than if he'd told her he was Superman. Pressing her hand against her chest, she sought out Alex with her gaze, looking for confirmation of what she'd just heard.

Alex nodded, groping for a reason. After all, Daddy hadn't exactly been forthcoming with her either. "Mama, he's been there going on forty years. Don't you think it's time the two of you spent more time together?"

From the look on her mother's face, Lenora clearly did not. "That is the most ridiculous thing I have ever heard of. I expect to plant you in the ground before you retire, Benjamin James Butler. Tell me why."

Only one person on earth could make B. J. Butler squirm, and she sat next to him, half his size and tapping a finger on the table like a judge's gavel.

"It's . . . well it's just like Ally said," he blustered, color crawling up from the crisp white collar of the dress shirt she'd ironed for him. No one, not even the local laundry and dry-cleaning service could *do up* B. J.'s shirts to suit Lenora Butler. "I thought we'd spend more time together. You haven't been yourself since Lynny left for college."

Alex groaned. Not the empty nest syndrome again. Mama would fall out of her chair laughing at that. Not the concept, but that Daddy even knew what it was.

"Maybe Daddy's just tired of working ten hours a day, six days a week," Alex suggested. Her father did look tired. Had for a while, now that she thought about it.

"Hmm." When Mama used that tone, it was not acceptance. It was pure challenge. *Is that so?* flashed in neon across her gaze. "Just how long have you been thinking about this, B. J.?"

"Since our baby girl announced she was getting' married. Made me realize how old I was, I guess."

Alex's wounded heart started to melt around the edges. Sheepish looked adorable on her father; and *adorable* and B. J. didn't belong in the same sentence as a rule. That Mama, no bigger than a minute, could make him that way after all these years, made her heart drip even more. That was the thing about Daddy. He wasn't all bad. And around Mama, he turned to mush.

"Whatever will you do at home, B. J.?" Lenora asked. "You don't like golf enough to play it six days a week. Heaven knows you're not exactly handy around the house or yard. Never did like to sweat."

"Maybe we could travel. You always did want to travel."

"You hate airplanes and complain about your back when you have to drive long distances." Suddenly the suspicion on Lenora's face gave way to alarm. "When was the last time you went to a doctor?"

B. J. squirmed in his seat, thinking. "I don't know. I'd have to ask Sheila. She keeps my appointment schedule."

"Don't think I won't, first thing Monday morning," Lenora told him. "There's more to this than you're telling me, B. J."

Alex glanced at her father. His reasons did seem kind of flimsy, at least for him. Her father was born to sit on a throne, and his desk at the bank was it. Not that he didn't do good for the community or have a big heart. He'd have made a good king . . . as long as he didn't have to deal with affairs of the heart. Money made B. J. tick. Love was his Achilles' heel.

At that moment, the waiter approached the table and placed a bucket filled with a bottle and a long-stemmed rose next to them.

"What's this?" her father asked, scowling. "I didn't order any champagne."

"It's Chateau de Fleur," the waiter announced, presenting the bottle to Alex. "One of California's finest nonalcoholic champagnes for the young lady."

Alex's pulse hitched as she looked past the champagne at her father. Was B. J. feigning innocence? Had he had this in mind all along? To surprise her?

"Oh my goodness," her mother exclaimed. "But all that ice can't be good for the rose." She plucked the flower from the ice bucket and sniffed it. Mama loved roses, no matter to whom they belonged. "Look, Alex. There's a card attached."

Alex had seen it, but was in too much shock to do anything except gape like a large-mouthed bass. She took the card from her mother, swallowed hard, and opened its foil-lined envelope.

Aloha and congratulations to my island princess. You look gorgeous tonight. Guess who?

There was no doubt in Alex's mind from the familiar scrawl,

just who it had come from. Alex's spur of hope that B. J. had actually thought enough to recognize her accomplishment died, but a warm bemusement was taking its place. This was sweet, but how did Josh know she'd dressed tropical?

She looked around the room as the waiter set three champagne glasses on the table. "Where is he?" she asked him.

"The order was called in, miss. I just filled it."

"Someone has an admirer," Lenora teased. From the way her eyes danced, one would think she'd received the bubbly. "So what does the card say? Or is it too private?"

Resisting the urge to wave it in her father's face—to show him that someone cared—Alex slipped the card back into the envelope. "It says congratulations . . . I paid off my building loan early."

"Oh, that's right! You were about to tell me some good news when B. J. dropped that bomb of his about retiring," Lenora said. "Although, since this is the first week of the month, I should have known."

Alex nodded, the glow of her pride widening her smile. Of course Mama would know. Lenora might get distracted, but she latched on to anything that might be happening with her family. Alex had told her last month that she had one more payment to go. Even in the wedding-planning frenzy, Mama hadn't forgotten, at least for long.

"Oh, Alex darling, I'm so proud of you. But I always knew you'd do well. You have your daddy's business sense."

Alex leaned into her mother's big hug. For a 110 pounds, Mama could squeeze the breath out of a person when she was enthused. And Lenora was enthused.

"B. J. Butler, you should be ashamed of yourself, keeping this to yourself."

"I figured it was Alex's place to announce the good news, not mine."

Lenora put her hands on her hips. "And just when were you going to tell me, young lady?"

"I was going to earlier, but—"

A rhumba—or rather, her cell phone jingle—interrupted Alex. She retrieved the phone, staring in disbelief at the name on her caller ID.

Josh Turner.

"Hello?"

"Hello, Princess Mahi Mahi. How's it going?"

Alex glanced around the room once more. Where in the devil was he? "Mahi mahi is a fish."

Realizing that her parents were both staring at her—no small wonder—Alex slid out of her chair. "I'm going to take this in the lobby. Can't hear," she explained.

"I'll bet it's your mysterious admirer," Mama ragged, as Alex grabbed the glass of Chateau de Fleur that the waiter poured for her and abandoned the table.

"Whoa, where are you going?"

"Where are you?" Alex demanded, a little annoyed. Josh was nowhere to be found among those seated in the formal dining room.

"You're welcome, too."

Take a deep breath. Exhale. "Thank you, Josh, that was very thoughtful." Josh wasn't hiding behind the columned and arched entrance from the lobby either. "Now where are you?"

"Down here in Margaritaville on the deck."

It made sense. If she could see the clientele on the deck, he could probably see her from there, since she'd sat next to the window.

"Wanna come down here for a while?"

Alex took a drink, a long one. That was not a good idea, no matter how good it sounded. Besides, her parents—

"It'd be a shame to waste that dress when the night is so young."

That man could talk the moon out of the sky.

"And you looked like you might need rescuing."

But not from the frying pan and into the fire. Her parents had picked Alex up on the way to the restaurant. That meant Josh would have to drive her home. And if he'd said what she thought he'd said earlier . . .

Yes was on the tip of Alex's tongue when the strains of an old Bellamy Brothers tune in the background on Josh's end registered. The singer crooned a line asking if he said she had a beautiful body, would she hold it against him. Cute twist of words. Dangerous implications.

"I can't tonight, Josh." She couldn't think of a good reason, not with her heart doing a cha-cha to the blooming song. Not a reason that she'd want to admit to. "I just can't. But thank you so much for the champagne and the rose. It . . . it meant a lot."

"You deserve more than that, Ally."

If the song wasn't disconcerting enough, the velvet rumble of Josh's compliment was devastating. The woman in Alex tried to outscream reason's warning to retreat in all haste.

"I think Mama was as excited over it as I was," she dodged. Sideways was better than no retreat at all. "I had to help Daddy tell her that he was going to retire, in case she got upset, and—"

Her voice faded upon seeing Josh enter the lobby, clad in a Hawaiian print shirt and khakis, his cell phone clasped against his ear. Before she realized what he was up to, Josh dragged her toward the door with his free hand.

"Josh!" It was all Alex could do to put her glass in a planter on the way out.

"One dance." He turned doleful Hush Puppy eyes on her, all the while speaking into his phone. "It's the *least* you can do for the rose."

They were on the sidewalk under the canopied entrance, for heaven's sake. "But—"

"Right here, right now. Then you can go home like it never happened."

Alex groaned, half in dismay and half in delight, as Josh slipped his free arm behind her and started to sway to the music. It was a different tune, something that might inspire a conga or limbo, but he heard the same slow beat that Alex did.

"People are staring," she said. "Bad enough we're dancing slow to a fast song outside the restaurant door, but we're talking to each other on our cell phones."

Josh's lips quirked, then spread into a lazy smile. "Just maintaining a comfortable distance."

Alex couldn't help but return it. This was what she loved about Josh. He was spontaneous. He protected her from herself and her obsessively ordered life.

"So, how'd it go?"

Alex drew a blank.

"Telling your mom about B. J.'s retirement," he prompted.

"I don't think Mama's too keen on the idea, but she didn't come anywhere close to a crumble. She turned him into a sheepish pup with her questions. Daddy was squirming in his seat."

"You gals have a way of doing that to a man." Josh turned her, invading her very being with his searching gaze.

I still love you . . .

He'd lied. This was not a comfortable distance. There was no escaping the electricity that coursed between them, pulling opposites together as they were meant to be.

"And how is Alex? You looked a little stressed from my viewpoint."

It took Alex a moment to wet her mouth enough to speak. "You were watching us?"

"I was watching *you*."

Alex frowned, confused. "How did you know where we'd be?"

"Didn't. Fate decided to smile on me."

Fate. Did she really hear *I still love you*?

It looked real. Felt real. It was all Alex could do to keep from tossing her phone and running her fingers through those bad boy locks that curled in the humidity around his face and ears.

But as she pondered where to put the worrisome phone, her father's voice boomed from the entrance.

"You two look like a pair of colicky calves staggering around in public like that."

Instinct kicking in, Alex stepped away, snapping her cell phone shut. "Oh, Daddy," she chided, regaining her composure, "a little dance was the least I could do for that champagne and rose. It was nice to be thought of."

"Evening, sir," Josh said, extending his hand to B. J.

Instead of taking it, her father focused on Alex. "Are you coming back to join us, or do you want me to take care of the check, so we can go?"

Ignoring B. J.'s bullying, Alex turned to Josh. "Since it's your treat, would you like to join us?"

Josh shook his head. "No thanks. I didn't exactly dress for the occasion." He leaned over and bussed her on the cheek. "See you tomorrow, princess. G'night, B. J."

"What are you two doing tomorrow?" B. J. demanded, as Josh walked away, grinning ear to ear.

Over getting in the last word, no doubt. Darn his handsome, devilish picture.

"He's found some delivery help for me," Alex replied, taking the lead to go back inside. She was so tired of being tugged on like a bone between two dogs. "Why don't you get the check? I'll take the bottle home with me."

Of course, as much as Alex resented B. J.'s interference, it was just as well he had come out when he did. She'd been within a breath of making a big mistake, one that might set her heart back sixteen years.

CHAPTER THIRTEEN

"He's late," Alex told the yellow tabby curled in the sunlit window seat of the dining niche.

She glanced at the pitcher of fresh iced tea that she'd made and the box of cupcakes she'd bought from grocery bakery. They were Josh's favorite—chocolate-frosted devil's food cake.

Alex picked one up, then put it back down, resisting the temptation to reduce the dozen treats to eleven. Instead, she checked the refrigerator to make sure there was enough ice. One with an icemaker was her next purchase.

"Oh, honestly," she exclaimed, slamming the freezer door and giving Riley a start. "It's not like this is a date," she told the cat. "And what's the point of impressing Josh anyway?" Instead of replying, Riley devoted his attention to something outside. Alex looked through the window over the back parking lot in time to see Josh's black truck pull up.

"They're here!"

Still love you . . .

Flying on three words that she might not have heard correctly, Alex rushed toward the steps that led from her apartment to the first floor. By the time she unlocked the double-wide cargo doors, Josh and two teen boys as tall as he stood there.

"So where do we start, boss?" Josh asked. His ratty, paint-stained tee shirt and jeans looked like he'd already worn them out, but what they did for his well-toned physique made up for it.

She forced herself to look at her prospective employees, remembering them from church. "I'm offering minimum wage for tonight," she told them, "but if you two do a good job, I'll give you a raise and more work, how's that?"

The boys nodded eagerly, thrilled to be working at all, and followed Alex to the stepvan. In no time at all, they had it unloaded, except for the armoire, which Alex decided to take directly to the Turner property. The decision was practical, but it meant running her emotions through another wringer, as if they'd not been through enough of late.

Although just having Josh in her home while she served the iced tea and cupcakes had every feminine nerve she possessed screaming *hunk alert.* Even Riley, who was suspicious of men, became Josh's best friend over a cupcake. The guy was born to charm.

As they headed toward the riverfront home. Kyle accompanied Josh in his pickup to the Turner place, while Brandon rode shotgun with Alex in the stepvan. The whole way over, Brandon chatted about their work at the community center. He idolized Ellen, but then what fifteen-year-old wouldn't? She lived on a boat and rode a motorcycle. How cool was that?

Once they arrived, Alex used her key to open the front door. It would be easier to carry the armoire straight in and up the steps.

As she stepped inside, the smell of fresh paint and polyurethane on the gorgeous hardwood floors assailed her. The fumes always threw Sue Ann into an allergy attack, but to Alex, it smelled like renewal . . . a fresh start.

Lynn's fresh start, she reminded herself, following the men upstairs, breath lodged in her chest with every tilt and teeter of the large piece of furniture. Once in place, the armoire was exactly the way Alex had envisioned it, its antiqued white finish contrasting with the soft green walls. When she hung the shades and curtains and the new twin beds were set up, the room would have the bright yet cozy cottage quality she was going for to accommodate future guests.

"Unless there's anything else, we're out of here," Kyle announced, drawing Alex from her vision of the room.

"Not until the other furniture arrives," she answered. "It's due in over the next two weeks, along with the curtains, carpets, and spreads." She'd bring things over and install them as they came in. Otherwise, the project could turn into a last-minute marathon just before the bridal shower, which was to be held here, as an added surprise for her sister. "Are you guys handy with small tools? I could use help putting up curtain rods and some other hardware."

"Sure," Brandon said. "I've helped my dad around the house."

"Me too," Kyle jumped in. "You can call my mom or tell Miss Ellen when you'll need us."

"Yeah, we see Miss Ellen almost every day. Josh, too."

Alex glanced at Josh as she jotted down the boys home phone numbers. He'd really taken the community center project to heart.

"I'll put my cell phone on there, too," Josh volunteered, adding, "Just in case."

What was he saying with that suddenly solemn look that seemed to be speaking in volumes? Maybe it was her imagination—all of it, including the declaration of love that had sounded too real for comfort.

But that embrace on the day of the great crab escape hadn't been her imagination. Nor the kiss he'd given her on the side of the road. Nor had last night's dance, the heady high of being in his arms, the natural way her body gravitated toward his, clinging...

No, she did *not* cling. Ever. Alex clenched her teeth. She hated this limbo of uncertainty. And it was going to end the moment she saw her chance. She couldn't risk going there again ... *just in case.*

⁂

"Wow, you've really done wonders with the place," Josh said, following Alex down the front staircase a short while later after the boys left. Eager to be on their way and with energy to spare, they'd insisted they didn't need a ride to the development next door.

The light colors were a stark contrast to Gran's vibrant wall coverings and made the rooms look larger. But then, Gran's busy wallpaper had to cover cracked plaster walls, not new Sheetrock ones.

"Thanks," Alex said, her demeanor distant.

Aware that she had tensed the moment the boys left, Josh tried to keep the conversation light. "And, man, these floors are mind-blowing. Who'd have thought they'd come up so nice, or that those imperfections"—the result of his playing with metal Tonka toys and, later, moving band equipment in and out of the house—"would actually add character? It'd be a pure shame to cover everything with carpet."

Maybe he'd gone too far last night. But the moment he saw Alex get out of her father's car in the parking lot, his heart rolled like cast dice. And the gamble had been worth the short time he'd held Alex in his arms, watching her face as he spoke to her over the phone. *Yes* had been in her eyes.

"Actually," Alex told him, "I've ordered area rugs for color and to take the heaviest traffic, but the floors will show." Strictly business today, she stopped in the doorway of the front parlor with its hexagonal walls. Her gaze softened, as though taking in more than its barren space.

Josh wondered if she saw the newly refurbished room or the old one with Josh's sound system, stereo, TV, and the threadbare sofa, where Alex used to curl up with a book while he worked on a new song. They'd made more than music in that room.

Whoa, buddy. He should have skeedaddled with the boys. Alex needed time to come around to what the woman within had told Josh. That she needed him as much as he needed her. That they were made for each other.

On the pretense of looking to see what else had been done since the last time he'd been in the house, Josh hurried past Alex and down the wide hallway to the kitchen.

Of all the rooms, it had changed the most. He liked how she'd taken out the wall between Gran's sewing room and the kitchen to extend the latter.

"Hey," he called out, examining a modern gas version of a porcelain Victorian woodstove, complete with little warming ovens overhead. "Where'd you find this stove? It reminds me of the one Gran converted into a roost for her laying hens in the barn."

That was why Alex had bought it. She remembered the stove.

"There are suppliers who carry modernized reproductions," she answered, coming into the room behind him.

"Wow . . . and the sink. It's just like Gran's."

"It *is* Gran's," Alex told him. Warmth infected her gaze. "I had it resurfaced and set in a granite counter."

Josh leaned on the combination work island and breakfast bar in the center of the main part of the kitchen that was once commanded by Gran's red Formica table. "She'd be honored."

He knew he was touched by the obvious thought and love that Alex had put into renovating and restoring the old house, even if it wasn't for him. Memories sprang at him from every direction, taunting him over what might have been.

"Do you always put so much of yourself into your projects?" he asked. It didn't do to dwell on the past. It couldn't be changed.

Alex regarded him warily. Back stiff, shoulders squared, she moved to the opposite side of the island.

"Look, I don't want to start anything," he stipulated. "It was meant as a compliment. I see a lot of your personality here . . . and yet, you've left some of Gran here, too, that's all."

"Why did you come back, Josh?" The question came at him like a shot from nowhere.

"The wed—"

"You know that's not what I mean," she snapped. "Why are you looking to buy a home? Why are you getting involved in the community? It looks to me like you intend to stay in Piper Cove."

Josh narrowed his gaze, wary. "Does that bother you?"

"We're not discussing me, Josh, we are discussing your reason for returning to a place you said you'd never come back to."

Clearly she hadn't heard his spontaneous declaration of love, nor was he speaking to that repressed woman within, the one who'd almost made a fool of him last night. Still, Josh didn't know whether to be relieved that she didn't have a weapon to use against him or disappointed that she had to ask why he wanted to stay.

Granted, he'd come back for other reasons . . . at first. He hadn't realized he still loved Alex until he'd seen her again. Talk about a sucker punch to the heart.

"I can't say it's any one thing, Alex." Although it was rapidly becoming one.

"So name *them*." Exasperation coated the last word and raked at Josh, sending a familiar rush of heat up his neck. If she had to ask, he didn't owe her any explanation.

Yes he did . . . at least a partial one. But two could play the game of denial.

"When I heard about the wedding, I had this urge to rub my success in everyone's face, especially B. J.'s. I know it wasn't very Christian, but I wanted to watch him squirm while the Whitlowes forced him to entertain me."

A smile haunted her lips. "You've certainly had your chance to do that."

"But then, it started to feel good being here . . . I don't know." Josh shrugged, uncertain where this was taking him. "It felt like home . . . but better than before." He shook his head. "I'm not a California kind of guy . . . especially since turning my life around and dedicating my life to God. I'm just not at home with the crowd I used to hang with . . . not that there aren't fine people out there, too, but . . ." He sighed, annoyed at how words failed him when he needed them most. "Do you have any idea what I'm trying to say?"

"Maybe."

But how could she, when Josh wasn't certain himself? How could he feel at home with the people who'd driven him away? Granted, he didn't see himself as ever being comfortable around B. J., but even with regard to his ex-father-in-law, Josh's anger and resentment seemed to have given way to something else. Pity, perhaps.

"And I really am into this community center. I love working with the kids. Maybe if I'd had someone—"

"Your music led you away, Josh," Alex interrupted. "It's a part of you."

Josh knew by the gentleness in Alex's tone that she meant no harm, but her observation was still a truth with gnashing fangs. Music had pulled him away and to the top of the charts . . . then it was gone, snatched from his life by his own foolish behavior. He'd made enough money that he didn't have to work, but making it work for him wasn't enough. Nor was song writing or his work as an occasional spokesperson for alcohol and drug awareness. He'd been bored out of his mind until—

Wonder swept through Josh. God had outslicked him good, and he hadn't even realized it until now. "I can't believe I didn't see this before."

"What?" Alex asked, her face brightening.

"The emptiness left by my inability to play professionally . . . I'd prayed that God would fill it, but everything I'd tried to do for His glory—things I'd felt called to do—didn't work." Excitement drove his every word. "But when I came back here, for reasons that were not so godly," he admitted with a rueful grimace, "I found it."

Alex leaned across the island, resting her hand on his arm, searching him with her gaze. "What did you find?"

"The community center . . . the kids, of course. I'm called to warn others, not just on the national speaking circuit a couple of times a year, but to do so right here in my own hometown. I can make a difference."

"Oh. Well, Ellen, I know, is thrilled." A hint of disappointment in Alex's voice trimmed Josh's elation short. "Look, Alex—" He seized her hands as she straightened to distance herself from him just as he'd bared his soul to her. "I've made a lot of mistakes in my life that I'm not proud of. But God's using my trials and triumphs to help others . . . and, hopefully, to mend fences as well."

He walked around the island, forcing Alex to face him. "And I can't do that unless you forgive me. Or at least give me a chance to show you how sorry I am . . . to see that I'm not the same man who left here."

"I don't believe you are, Josh," Alex replied. "I really don't."

"So I'm forgiven?"

She pulled away. "I don't seem to have as direct a line to God as you do, Josh. I need a little more time." Pivoting, she made a bee-line toward the front door. "Please lock the door when you leave," she called over her shoulder as she hurried outside.

Josh ran his hands through his hair. He'd upset her. How, he didn't know. But she certainly didn't share his excitement over his revelation. And if he'd declared his true feelings, she'd still have run off.

Thawing from his shock, Josh hurried down the hall, lit only by the sunset filtering through the windows on the west side of the house. By the time he made it out to the yard, Alex had started the stepvan and closed the side door. At a loss as to what to do, much less say, he waved as she backed out of the drive, the clutch jerking and engine gasping for gas.

Lord, something tells me that I stand a better chance of understanding You before I'll ever understand women . . . or at least that one.

Josh brushed his perspiration damp hair off his face with his fingers, looking at the beaded-board ceiling overhead as if it held the answer.

Yeah, I know. In Your time, not mine.

CHAPTER FOURTEEN

Time always flew when Alex was busy. But running the hotel project that had set her free financially, while completing her sister's summer home at the same time had made July pass at warp speed. Because of last-minute arrivals, Brandon and Kyle had had all the work they could handle in the past week on both projects, but today, just forty-eight hours away from her sister's wedding shower on Saturday, Alex needed an extra woman's touch to complete the house. Fortunately, Jan was always willing to work an extra job, although her friend would have pitched in for free had Alex needed her to.

Jan stood back inspecting the variegated white-to-green sheers that she'd draped over decorative curtain rods as Alex entered the guest room to check on her progress.

"I give up," her friend complained. "The drapes won't drape for me like they will for you."

The plastic protecting the special-ordered hooked scatter rug rustled under Alex's feet as she walked over to the ladder Jan had abandoned in disgust. "And icing won't *ice* for me like it does for you," she said in consolation.

"We might even finish up today if you let me put up regular curtains that know how to hang themselves, instead of these draping thingies," Jan said wryly. She stooped over to pick up some of the plastic and paper containers that the rods and curtains had come in.

"It's doable, thanks to you and the boys," Alex agreed. With the carpets and furnishings in place, the window treatments and accessorizing were all that remained to complete. She climbed the ladder that Jan had abandoned. "Let's see if we can get this window behind us before the boys get back from the Mini Mart with lunch."

She had the usual mixed feelings as the project wound down. She was anxious for the newly designed home to embrace Lynn and John, for them to fall in love with it. But there was also a reluctance for Alex to let it go. She left a part of herself in every project. For obvious reasons, this particular home practically owned her heart. It was more beautiful, more inviting, than she'd ever imagined when she'd dreamed of doing it over during the time she'd lived there with Josh and Gran. She could only pray that her sister would find the happiness she had dreamed of having for herself.

"How about handing me that garland?" she asked Jan after arranging the curtains just so. The leafy strand of pink-and-green foliage complemented the painting on the antiqued armoire.

"So how's things with you and Josh?" Jan tugged at the curtains.

Alex focused on weaving the silk garland through the draped

sheers. How could she tell Jan how things stood between her and Josh when she wasn't sure herself? All she knew for sure was that whatever they shared wasn't dead, but very much alive and easily roused.

"I owe him big-time for finding the boys to help me." Alex admitted. Not to mention keeping a safe distance. Although that night at the Baylander, she'd thought she was a goner. "I don't think I could have gotten this done without them . . ." Alex reached for the far end of the window, her voice stretching with her. "And you—"

Without warning, Alex lost her balance and the ladder beneath her tipped at a precarious angle. Not wanting to rip or ruin her perfectly placed sheers, Alex fought to stay upright without grabbing on to anything, and ultimately failed. The world plunged into slow motion. One of the twin beds broke her fall and bounced her and the ladder to which she clung off and onto the floor. A splitting crack reverberated through every fiber of her body. Then the marbled color palette turned senseless black.

❧

Josh looked up as the ER physician entered the waiting room and approached him. Josh had met the boys at lunchtime at the Mini Mart and driven them back to Gran's house. Just as they entered the back door with the lunch order, the crash of Alex's fall and Jan's scream met them. A sickening cold seized Josh, the moment he saw Alex lying on the floor, but he'd rushed to her side and checked her head. When his hand came away bloody, he'd ordered Brandon to call 911, even though Alex had begun to stir.

It had taken them a lifetime to get there . . . a lifetime that Josh spent holding Alex in his arms, trying to coax her into staying conscious and seeing that Jan and the boys carried out her slurred orders to keep the blood from getting on the carpet.

"Mr. Turner?"

"Yes, sir," Josh said, rising. Jan had to go to work, but only after he'd promised to call her as soon as he found out anything. Then Josh had followed the ambulance to the hospital in Berlin, trailing its bumper as close as was safe. Time was, he could have ridden with her, but Josh didn't know the paramedics well enough to get them to bend the rules.

"Miss Butler's tests show no brain trauma. Since she'd been unconscious for a while and was somewhat disoriented when she was brought in, I suggested that she stay overnight for observation, but she'll have none of that."

"Now *that* doesn't surprise me." Josh chuckled. "Her head is as hard as walnut."

Despite her pain and wooziness, Alex had started taking charge on the way down the stairs at the house. "Do *not* call my parents," she'd ordered.

Josh promised he wouldn't although, if the test report had been different, he'd be on the phone right now.

"She seems to be in control of her faculties," the doctor replied tactfully.

Josh got the picture. Alex had taken over her own case and, knowing her, the ER staff. "Well, I'll take her out of your hair and keep an eye on her."

As soon as the physician left, Josh used his cell to call Jan at work as promised. By the time he finished the call and retrieved his pickup, Alex was waiting at the patient pickup area, looking a little worse for wear but nonetheless fully collected.

"You can just drop me off at my place," she said, as he pulled into traffic after getting the rundown on Alex's care from the nurse. "And thanks for not calling Mom and Dad."

Josh glanced over to where she held a hospital ice pack on the back of her head. "Look, baldy—"

"Omigosh," Alex exclaimed, "did they shave my head? No, they didn't shave my head. I remember." She shot him an annoyed glance. "They just cleaned it well and did the stitches."

"I was giving you my own test," Josh replied, grinning. "You passed with flying colors. And," he added, "I'm not *dropping you off* anywhere. I'm sticking to you like gum, at least until morning."

Once again, alarm registered in her gaze. "I do not need you to watch me. All I need is for this souped-up Tylenol to start working on my headache, some fresh ice, and a bed."

"Nope, you heard the nurse's orders."

"I won't have it. Don't make my head hurt any more than it does now. Just drop me off and leave me alone."

That chin set of hers belonged next to the word *stubborn* in the dictionary. "Let me put it this way. You have a choice. You either let me stay with you, or I call your parents. Your call, babe."

Alex's long, heavy sigh of resignation became the only communication between them until Josh pulled into the parking lot behind her building. But he'd won . . . at least round one.

"This is entirely unnecessary." She threw open the pickup door and slid out before he cut the engine. Holding the ice pack with one hand, she unlocked the rear door with a ready key.

"Hold up, Ms. Independence." Josh jumped out of the vehicle and hit the autolock button. He hurried after her, catching up as she started up the stairwell. "Hey, you tip backward on these steps, and it's back to the ER, so slow down."

"I'm fine," she declared. The way she took step after step as though she balanced books on her head, white-knuckling the rail, told Josh otherwise.

Hardheaded—Josh batted away the rise of anger nipping at his neck.

"Hey, Riley," he said, greeting the cat perched on the stairwell half wall, watching them with bright amber eyes. Riley nudged into the head-scratching Josh gave him, purring like an engine.

"Two-timer," Alex accused from the kitchen area, where she started going through a drawer near the sink.

"I came here to help, not argue," Josh reminded her. "What do you need?"

"I'll get it," she sniped.

The drawer contained an assortment of bottles, mostly vitamins and a few basic over-the-counter medicines. Then, as though suddenly drained of resistance, her stiff demeanor collapsed.

"I'm sorry, Josh—" Her chin quivered, registering ten on the emotional Richter scale. "It's just that my head aches, and I—"

Josh's annoyance crumbled in the aftershock. "Tell me what you are looking for, and I'll get it. You"—he took her by the shoulders, his hands gentle, but firm—"come sit down in this recliner and let me wait on you."

"Aspirin, the one with caffeine," she mumbled, settling into the plump chair like an obedient child. "And more ice."

"You already took pain medicine."

"Oh."

Oh yeah, she really needed to be alone.

"But the ice is coming right up." Josh scooped up Riley, who'd followed them out of curiosity, and placed him in Alex's lap. "You keep your mama company until I get back, boy."

As though he understood Josh completely, the cat settled, its paws resting on Alex's breastbone, and watched her face with the intensity of the Sphinx.

Alex giggled. "I can't believe he's doing this. Riley never sits in my lap. He usually curls on the back of my chair and swats at my hair."

"Cats know when something's not right," Josh answered. After emptying the ice from trays into the rectangular holder, he wrapped several cubes in a towel and crushed them on the counter with a meat tenderizer.

"Do you have to be so noisy?"

Dimwit. "Sorry, babe. Wasn't thinking." *Maybe I should call her mom after all.*

Upon refilling her ice bag with the crushed ice, he carried it over to Alex.

"The way Riley's watching me, I might not need you," she teased, a welcome hint of a smile tugging at the corner of her mouth.

"Guess he is quieter. But, man, I never thought I'd be replaced by a four-legged furball . . . no offense, Riley," Josh added, when the cat glanced at him, ears laid back. "How about a little something to eat? You didn't get lunch."

"Maybe some chicken noodle soup. There's some in the pantry cabinet near the stove."

"Gran's cure-all, coming right up."

Aware that Alex watched him, Josh found the soup and prepared it in the microwave. Was she thinking of the time she'd been sick with a cold, and he'd made her canned soup? Then the two of them had curled up on the sofa, her in his arms, and fallen asleep watching some black-and-white movie on a minor channel.

Funny how the past shoved the bad times to the rear, letting the good times obscure them. But the bad was there. Most of it his fault. All of it he wanted to make up for . . . if she'd let him.

"I need to change this top," Alex announced, pulling him back to the present. "There's a little blood on it." Concern entered her voice. "Did I mess up the room? Oh, I hope I didn't get any blood on the carpets—"

"Nope. Don't you remember ordering everyone to clean up before the paramedics got there?"

"Oh."

Josh rushed to her side as she set Riley aside to get up. "How about if I get a top and bring it to you. I promise I'll keep my back turned while you change."

"You can't go to the potty for me, too," she said. "I'll be fine. Put the soup on the table, and I'll be back in a jiff."

Make that putting her entire bio next to the word *stubborn* in the dictionary. Alex was probably born telling the doctors what to do next. "At least leave the door unlocked," he called after her. "I'd hate to have to kick it in if I hear you fall. I mean it, Ally."

Alex paused at the bedroom door, her penetrating look enough to make Josh want to roll over and show her his belly like the attention-hungry Riley was doing at his feet. "You would, wouldn't you?"

"Oh yeah," Josh managed to answer through the sudden dryness in his throat.

Thankfully, Alex went inside before he said—or did—anything else foolish. But the time he'd purposely spent keeping his distance had been an utter waste. What he felt for Alex had grown stronger than ever. He'd known it the minute he'd heard the crash back at the farmhouse and Jan crying out Alex's name in alarm. His reaction couldn't have been more telling—the sense of panic, the sudden fear of loss, the absolute certainty of knowing if she hurt, so would he.

If only God would give him the right words to tell her . . . to convince her that he'd changed. That he'd never leave her again.

CHAPTER FIFTEEN

The beep-beep backup warning of the garbage truck that serviced the Dumpsters behind Alex's building gradually invaded her sleep, forcing her to open her eyes to the morning. Her senses cleared.

Josh!

Where was he? Careful not to upset the delicate balance of ache and bliss knotted on the back of her head, she scrambled out of bed as fast as she could and headed for the bedroom door. That was funny, she thought, glancing back at the unmade bed. Usually, the moment she stirred, Riley was in her face for his morning attention.

On peeking out into the living room, she saw the reason why. The big yellow tabby was sprawled on a sleeping Josh, who, in turn, was sprawled out on her sofa. Both were adorable. A yawn caught up with her as Alex turned toward her private bathroom to freshen up. Not that Josh was going to kiss her, but her teeth could use a brushing, and a shower would make her feel like a new person.

While Alex bathed and dressed, memory by memory came back to her of awakening in the night to featherlight kisses and opening her eyes in time to see Riley batting Josh's head away gently with his paw, as if to say, *That's close enough.*

Then came the questions. Did she know where she was? What happened to her? What year was it? Who was the president? After the first couple of times, they became more personal.

What was Gran's dessert specialty? Bread pudding with hot vanilla sauce. What was her nickname for him? Cuddlebud. What was the first meal Alex ever cooked for him? Swiss steak. And no one could eat it because, not knowing what a clove of garlic was, Alex had put in cloves *and* garlic.

A half an hour later, Alex emerged from the bedroom with her hair pulled gingerly into a loose ponytail. The shorter layer around her face fell according to its own will, too tender to move, much less comb. Not quite as fresh as the embroidered daisies on her red, lounge-length tee-shirt dress, she made her way to the kitchen with Riley in her wake.

Alex quietly fed the hungry kitty and made coffee for two. Two, she thought, mindful of how nice it felt—as wonderful as it had every time she awakened to those concerned blue eyes and that tummy-tugging smile of his. And as sweet as his kisses. Swept by a surge of tenderness, she meandered over to the sofa and straightened the afghan her mother had made her, covering Josh's feet.

Josh cracked one sandy-lashed eye at her and stretched, his bare feet once again losing their cover. "You don't look a day over sixteen."

Although she knew better, Alex answered with a smile.

He grabbed her hand. "C'mon, have a seat," he said, shifting so that she could sit on the sofa next to him. "How's the head this morning?"

This wasn't wise, she told herself, as she perched on the edge of the overstuffed cushion. How come bedhead looked so good on a guy?

"I could get used to this," he said, inching upright against a pile of oversized accent pillows. The humor in his gaze danced around something else, something more serious.

Or was it because she wanted it to be more than it was? Alex recoiled against the admission, but Josh tightened his hold, not as much with force as with reassurance. It might as well have been her heart in his hands, the way she felt.

"What?" she evaded, Ellen style. "Playing nursemaid to a klutz on a ladder?"

"No, *you* . . . *me*—" He broke off with a grunt as Riley leapt onto his lap and continued in a strained voice. "Although kids may be out of the question now."

Alex giggled. She couldn't help it. When she was nervous, really nervous, she went beyond laughter to outright giggling. Better that than let him see the emotions that had been gaining weight and depth with every minute since he'd returned to Piper Cove.

He'd mentioned kids. He'd said he could get used to this. The memory of *I still love you, Alex* came back to haunt her—or taunt her—she wasn't sure which.

"I mean it, Alex," Josh said, the probe of his gaze halting her in midgiggle. "This is good . . . being with you. It's ri—"

"Josh, we can't go back," Alex interrupted, wishing she sounded more convincing, that the spark of hope negating her statement wasn't there.

"I don't want to go back, Ally. There's a lot of baggage best left back there." He eased her closer, so that Riley was edged out, and cupped her face with one hand. "I'm talking about who we are now, not who we were. I want to be here when you need me and know you're close by when you don't."

Unlike before. It had been the other way around as she recalled. But like Josh said, they were both different now. *Oh God, dare I hope? Is it possible to have the same dream twice?*

Alex didn't draw away when he moved but a breath away, searching her gaze with his own. This is what she wanted . . . at least a part of her did. The protesting part fell silent the moment their lips touched and melded as if it were meant to be. The contact set Alex's senses afloat, each one on its own flyaway balloon of pleasure.

"Alex," a voice boomed from the back stairwell. "Are you all right up here?"

Her balloons popped, a machine gun burst that sent her falling back to the reality that her father was coming up the steps.

Startled, Alex disengaged from Josh's arms and slid off her half perch on the sofa onto the floor with a thud. She gasped from the painful jar of the impact.

"Are you okay?" Josh asked, on his feet in an instant. He reached under her arms and scooped her upright.

Her father must have used the spare key she'd given him for emergencies, she thought as B. J. emerged from the stairs and froze at the sight of Alex trying to struggle upright in Josh's grasp.

"What in tarnation is going on here?" he demanded, so loudly that Riley dove behind the couch.

"Daddy—" Alex started. Dear God, her head hurt.

"Not a thing that's any of your business, B. J.," Josh told him in an even voice. But Alex knew it was precariously balanced. "For heaven's sake, Alex, you're a grown woman," he reminded her. "You don't have to answer—"

"It *is* my business, *boy*," B. J. shot back, "when her mother sends me over in a panic because her daughter's phone has been busy since last night."

Alex groaned. "Riley must have knocked the receiver off in the bedroom. Why didn't Mama try my cell . . . oh wait," she broke off. "I called in the lunch order yesterday and left the phone in the kitchen at the Turner place."

"Well, you've got a business to open in a half an hour, young lady," her father reminded her, eyeing Josh with blatant accusation, "and call your mama."

To her astonishment, B. J. turned and started back down the steps. No ranting about how she should have better sense than to let Josh close again, for it was obvious that the two of them had been intimate. Not real intimate, but intimate enough to make her hot skin compete with her dress for best shade of red and her lips swell with a passion that shouted to the world, *What a kiss!*

"Now *that* was odd," Josh remarked, as the back door slammed to below. "B. J. must be mellowing out in his old age."

Old. The description shook Alex from her embarrassment. Josh was right. Her father had looked old—too tired and haggard to rant. Alex went to the back window and looked out at the parking lot in time to see B. J. spin his Mercedes sedan out of the lot. But it didn't take a clairvoyant to know this wasn't over.

"I haven't heard the last of this." With a heavy sigh, she turned away and started for the kitchenette, where the coffee had finished brewing.

"I'm sorry for my part in causing you grief with your dad"—Josh came up behind her and turned her into his arms—"but not for anything else."

Alex shook her head, wincing from the warning of her injury to be still. "It's not just you, Josh. Nothing I've ever done measures up in his eyes. Sometimes I think I disappointed him from the get-go for not being born a boy, and it's gone downhill ever since."

"Ally, Ally," Josh chided, drawing her against him like old times. "When are you going to realize that God made you who you are, and that makes you unique *and* special, whether you're the way B. J. expects you to be or not? God gave you your gifts and talents and has a plan for you to succeed according to His will, not B. J. Butler's. And that's not my BS, that's a promise from the Bible." He cupped her chin with a tenderness that made her tremble. "And you've done well for yourself, Alexandra Butler. Only a fool would fail to see that . . . and just how special you are."

Alex knew that Josh was right . . . at least to some degree. "He's my dad, Josh, and I want him to be proud of me," she said with a sigh. "And knowing the truth and feeling it's real don't always go hand in hand."

"Hah," Josh laughed without humor. "Don't I know *that*. I didn't feel like I had any life ahead of me after the accident . . . without music."

"I know, Josh. I was sorry it happened." The kindred anguish tingeing Josh's confession had two edges. Even though Josh had put his music ahead of her, she'd been devastated for him when she'd read about the debilitating accident.

"That's where faith comes in, babe." Josh brushed her lips with his. "We have to let go and trust in Him. Why don't we both try that . . . not just with B. J., but with each other?"

Alex's beleaguered heart shuddered, fear and hope assailing it at once.

Fear that it was too late and that dreams came around only once before they died. Hope that speared through her with the realization that she wanted this. That the dream had always been a part of her . . . waiting to be fulfilled . . . or destroyed once and for all.

"We had something great together . . . still do, if that kiss was any indication."

The grin. Alex dug her toes into her slippers. He had to use the grin. And she *wanted* to believe him. "But a relationship based on kisses and chemistry alone doesn't last, Josh. It didn't back then, and it won't now." Alex turned back to the counter and grabbed the coffeepot. "As much as I want things for us to work out, I can't let it. Not based on kisses alone."

"Fine then. No more kisses."

Alex held the pot poised over a stoneware mug. "What?"

Josh peeked around her shoulder, looking like a kid who'd just caught Santa. "I'm going to win you over without kisses. No chemistry allowed."

"Right." She shoved the mug his way with a skeptical arch of her brow. "Like that's going to happen." Even now, there was a part of her that wanted to continue what had been kindled there on the couch, to fly in reason's face.

"No matter how those beautiful brown eyes beg for it."

Sheesh, was he reading her mind now? "My eyes do not beg for kisses."

Josh moon-danced away, his own full of mischief. "You're right. They just *dare* a guy to kiss you."

Alex suppressed a smile at his antics. "Now you're being silly because you know I'm right."

"I am going to woo you with my nobility of character and charm," he announced, taking a seat at the table. "Starting by taking you as my date to all the wedding functions."

Presumptuous. Now that was old Josh. "How do you know I don't have a date already?"

"Because word is, Willie has popped the question to Barbara Carrington."

Such was the curse of small communities. News, good or bad, traveled fast.

"Not that I believed for a moment there was anything serious between you two."

He didn't have to be so smug. "And how do you know that?"

"I heard you and your buddies talking through the bathroom wall at Clamdiggers," he admitted with a sheepish twist of his lips. "Barely made it out ahead of you."

Alex didn't know whether to hug him, slap him, or drop dead from embarrassment. "Fine then, have your way. I'll go with you." She glanced at the clock on the stove, hoping she didn't betray her excitement too much. The rascal had cared enough to eavesdrop. She'd forgotten how thin the walls were at the old hangout. "Meanwhile, help yourself to more coffee, if you want. I've got to call Mama and dress for work."

"Just trust, babe," Josh called after her. "It's all going to work out."

Alex entered the bedroom, immediately spying the telephone cord draped over the bedside table. She didn't know how it had escaped notice, but the handset had been knocked down between the stand and the bed. After making sure the door was secured against further feline mischief, she headed for the nightstand, her fickle heart all but begging her to dance.

Okay, God, I trust You. And I even trust Josh a little . . . now. It's me that I don't trust. Alex fished the handset from under the bed and reseated it in its cradle, staring at it. *Make that me and Riley.*

CHAPTER SIXTEEN

Another milestone, Alex thought, two days later as she paid the caterer in the midst of the after–bridal shower chaos. The affair had gone smoothly, thanks to her buddies' pitching in yesterday for the final touches that had been interrupted by Alex's accident. Alex hadn't laughed so much in ages. It had been worth the bump on the noggin just to see Sue Ann, the fashion maven, wearing jeans and one of Martin's old shirts.

"What in creation is this for?" Josh called from the dining room, where the presents had been stored and inventoried by Ellen after opening.

Alex caught herself in midsigh as she returned her checkbook to her purse. She was getting as besotted as Jan.

But he and the groom-to-be had been Johnnies-on-the-spot for last-minute details. Despite their macho protests that there was too much concentrated estrogen for them to stick around, the two men seemed very interested in the event, almost to the point of being in the way.

"Josh Turner, I'm going to fry your grits if you don't stop opening those boxes," Sue Ann warned. "You're supposed to be loading them in your truck, not looking at the goods."

"Now Suzie Q," Josh chided, giving it right back, "you never know when I'll have to deal with the same kind of shenanigans, and I like to know what I'm in for."

Was Josh talking about marriage? Alex leaned against counter, her heart bouncing around in her chest like a lottery ball—up, down, over, around.

Surely, he was making conversation, giving her buddies a hard time. He was good at that. Besides, she was in no way even ready to contemplate a future with Josh. The present was all she could handle.

Pulling out of her daze, Alex hastened to the back door and held it open for the caterer to carry out the last of her supplies. The dish set, completely contemporary in black and white, didn't go with the summer home at all. Very little on the wedding registry did, she thought, going back into the kitchen. It was all so modern and sleek, the tastes that had dictated Lynn's choices casting doubt that Lynn would truly enjoy this house as it was meant to be enjoyed, and more—loved.

The cloud of doubt that Lynn's enthused reaction to the unveiling of the Turner home that morning was an act was so obvious to Alex that it smothered the remnants of her earlier elation.

Or maybe Lynn simply wanted the summer home to be a contrast to her contemporary habitat in the city.

Lord, why can't I just go with the flow? Are You even listening? Of course He was. Alex knew that. But she sure didn't feel that way. He knew best. But Alex always had trouble letting go of control.

Lenora Butler swept into the room looking radiant. "Everything is almost packed up, and the parlor looks like a parlor again."

While B. J. seemed to be failing, Mama had been more her old self than Alex had seen her in a long while. "Darling, you did it again," her mother continued. "Everyone raved about the house and the shower. I'm so proud of you. Daddy and I both are."

Alex's doubt swayed beneath the compliment, but held fast. While Mama was sincere, the emotion meter in Alex's brain broached SOS level.

"And the entertainment center you had converted from a linen press—"

Was something Alex had reworked three years ago, but she'd never been able to bring herself to use it on a project. Somehow, like the guest room armoire, it belonged here.

And so did she.

"Not now, Mama." Her fragile defense crumbling, Alex turned away from her mother and raced up the back stairwell.

God, not now, she prayed, entering the master bedroom's walk-in closet. *Lord, please let me hold on until everyone leaves. I can't break down in front of them.*

"Alex." Her mother entered the closet and embraced her. "I know, honey, I know."

Feelings that had been bottled up inside Alex from the moment she'd heard B. J.'s announcement that the house was to be her sister's spilled out in tears and words. Yes, she knew it was just a house, but her heart and soul were in it. It could never mean to Lynn and John what it meant to her. No, it shouldn't mean so much to her, because of all the pain and anger she'd experienced here, but there'd also been love.

Maybe it hadn't been strong enough, but it had been real and precious to her. And it was still alive . . . and maybe it would bloom again. She and Josh were taking it slow this time.

"D . . . did Daddy tell you about Josh and me?" she sniffed, when her heart and tear ducts had bled dry.

Actually, Alex had told her mother that Josh spent the night watching her after the concussion and that it was as a friend. But her mother understood what Alex meant by her question.

"Actually, he did grumble something about it," Lenora replied. "But that was about it. Your daddy is mellowing in his old age."

Alex drew away, taking in her mother's features. In spite of Lenora's small attempt at humor, her face was drawn in concern. Alex put away her tumble-dried heart. As her father always told Alex when she'd become distraught as a child, time to *buck up*. Mama needed her to be strong.

"Mama, what do you think is really going on with Daddy?" she asked. "Do you think it's just the idea of retiring or what?"

Lenora shook her head. "I wish I knew, dear. I've tried to get him to talk, but you know how protective he is of me." A smirk formed on her lips. "I'm not as delicate as you all believe, you know. Not when it comes to my family."

Alex couldn't help but smile at the irony. "Strange, isn't it? You are becoming more like yourself while Daddy is weirding out on us."

"He's been so preoccupied these days," her mother agreed. "But I don't know what I'll do if B. J. stays home all the time," her mother said with a soft chuckle. "He's not the kind to sit still or while away more than two days a week with golf or fishing. And while his temper could use tempering, it seems as if the fight has totally gone out of him."

"When was his last medical checkup?"

"December 15, two years ago." At Alex's surprise, Lenora explained, "I told you I'd call his doctor's office and check." Her chin took on a stubborn set. "So I put my foot down and made an appointment for him right after the wedding."

Now that was the Mama Alex remembered. "Maybe it should be a head doctor instead of his GP." She chuckled. "I expected him to fly into Josh at my apartment, but he just glared and left."

"Maybe that's a good sign."

"What's a good sign?" Josh asked, peeking around the door and catching Lenora in midwink. "That the two of you are hiding in a closet?"

Lenora stepped away from Alex. "That love is in the air." A mysterious tilt to her lips, she walked past Josh. "I'd better get back to Marilyn," she said, referring to Lynn's future mother-in-law. "She'll think I've abandoned her."

"Miz W's out on the porch swing with Aunt Rose, unwinding, I think," Josh called after her. He glanced back in the closet at Alex. "So . . . mind if I join you?"

Alex inhaled deeply and nodded, so ready, but so scared.

"Of course I won't kiss you, no matter how much I want to, but . . ." He hesitated, blue eyes twinkling. "Is hugging okay?"

"Hugging is great. I could use a hug." Especially a Josh hug. "Then I'd better pull myself together and join the others before they come looking for me."

"Lynn and John already left with the goods in my truck, and everything is all tidied up," he told her, taking her into his arms.

The male sweat and laundry detergent in his tee shirt assailed her nostrils, drawing her even closer. Her head fit perfectly beneath his chin.

It was good. He was good.

"Don't look back, babe. It'll turn you bitter as salt," he said, voice rumbling in his chest. "You ... me ... we're going to be just fine. It's just a house."

Alex's heart smiled. She didn't have to say a word. Josh knew what she was thinking and feeling. He absorbed the pain, so that she was left cradled, comforted, and something that she'd not felt in a long, long time. Loved, warts and all.

"I have something I'd like to show you, if you're not booked tonight," he whispered after a space of time where words were not required.

Alex reluctantly gave up the moment. "What's that?"

"I've been working on some blueprints for a place on a canal lot. I'd like your expert take on them."

"You mean you're not going out with the others?" Alex had been invited, but she had so little in common with her younger sister and her friends. She'd used her recovering head injury as an excuse to opt out.

"Not my thing," Josh answered. "Looks like you and me are the old couple in the bunch."

Who knew a few years would make so much difference?

"Sure." She hoped she didn't sound too eager, but she didn't have immediate plans, or any plans until tomorrow afternoon. Josh was taking members of the wedding party out on his boat after church. As for tonight, returning to her apartment alone was the last thing she wanted to do.

Besides, Josh was right. Dwelling on the past, what might have been, could only lead to heartache and bitterness. And it wasn't her style . . . usually.

It was hopeless to try to hide from the others that she'd been upset. Nonetheless, Alex splashed cold water on her face in the master bath and headed downstairs with Josh, a bright smile pasted on her lips.

"There's the diva of design and entertainment," Jan exclaimed, as Alex and Josh joined her friends and the mothers of the bride and groom, now gathered on the large screened porch overlooking the river.

"Thanks to you all," Alex said, her appreciative gaze traveling to each of her friends. In addition to help with the house, Sue Ann had handled the invitations, Jan had made her sweet concoctions, including a two-flavored cake that looked like a wrapped present, and Ellen had surprised her with flower arrangements. "We could go into wedding planning, if all else fails."

"Even if Ellen doesn't know squat about cross-stitch," Jan teased.

Ellen glared at her petite friend. "That," she said, referring to her shower gift—a beautiful counted cross-stitch kit—"has nothing to do with wedding planning."

"But it *was* the highlight of the shower, sugar." Sue Ann laughed. "The look on your face when you saw that box was full of thread and fabric and charts, instead of the finished item on the cover."

"What?" Jan mimicked Ellen's Brooklyn-shaded accent. "I bought a box of *string*?"

"Look, I'll hear enough about it from Ma, without you all reminding me how domestic-challenged I am," Ellen declared. "But you try grafting a tree or tuning your own engines." She shrugged.

"Besides, it was just a little something to go with the linens I gave her."

"It was the thought that counts," Alex consoled. The decorative poem was about a successful marriage taking three—man, woman, and God.

Although, she thought that she and Josh had had God with them the last time. They got married and went to church, but their relationship still fell apart. So much anger . . . the arguments over money and Josh finding a respectable job, over the pursuit of his self-destructive dreams. So much pain from hurtful words. Then there were no words at all.

Lord, what would make this time different? If there was to be a *this time.*

⊗

Lord, help me make it different this time. Amen.

Freshly shaved and showered after leaving Alex's bridal soiree, Josh closed the Bible he'd been studying.

All things are possible. The words that crossed his mind gave Josh a sense of peace because he knew them to be true. God had taken his broken life and mended it. If it was His will, He'd take Josh's broken relationship and restore it, too.

In the meantime, it would be nice if there was a home in which that relationship could grow. He considered the canal beyond the yard of his temporary living quarters. It was little more than big enough to have a small speedboat tied off, but the lot he'd chosen to hold back from the development for his own had sufficient dock space for his Sportfisherman. What was once a wayward teen's daydream was becoming a reality. A house on the water, a boat . . . and Alex. Even now, it was hard to get his mind around it.

The *who* of his good fortune brought him back to the disconcerting study at hand. Josh focused on the Bible in his lap. His hands were fisted around it, bending it out of shape, just like he'd been wrestling with bending the Word to suit the turmoil stirred in him by Alex's earlier despair. He made a conscious effort to relax his hold.

Okay, God, I get your drift. Prayer and fight mode don't go together.

But unfisting his hand was a lot easier than letting go of his anger with B. J. Butler, both past and present. Yes, Josh should hate the sin and not the sinner, but it was hard to separate the man from the way B. J. manipulated people, even those he loved, without thought to their feelings.

There was no doubt in Josh's mind that B. J. bought the Turner home and gave it to John and Lynn just to get at Josh. And, just like in the past, Alex had been caught in the cross fire.

Not that Josh blamed B. J. entirely for his part in making Josh leave Piper Cove. Josh had made the final decision to follow his dream rather than fight for his marriage. He'd run from it and from God. But what was their life going to be like if he and Alex got back together, and the war between him and B. J. continued?

When Josh left Alex after the shower, he'd wanted to go straight to B. J. Butler and strangle the man for tearing her apart like that. Instead, he'd gone home and sought comfort, release—*something*—in Scripture.

Maybe he should take Alex far enough away that they were beyond B. J.'s reach. Except Josh was tired of running. And Alex had worked hard to build her business. No, God had led him back to Piper Cove, and He'd given him the courage to come back and face up to it. God would see him through this.

But, God, You know I can't stand the man.

Yet, Josh loved his daughter, and Alex loved her father. Worse, she longed for his approval.

So I'm gonna need your help big-time if I'm going to love my enemy. I don't want to put Alex in the middle again ... and that man is my enemy.

His soul seesawing between confidence and despair, Josh looked down at Luke 17: 3 and 4. Besides, it said right there that he was to forgive, but only if his transgressor repented. And there was a snowball's chance in July that that was going to happen with B. J.

Frustrated, Josh ran his fingers through his hair and glanced at his watch. Alex would be here anytime for the cookout he'd suggested when they'd left earlier. As he put the Bible aside, the sight of the cross that he'd had tattooed on his forearm after he'd rededicated his life to Christ caught his eye.

Forgive them for they know not what they do.

Josh groaned. In his heart of hearts, he knew that Christ's forgiveness trumped that of the law of Moses and of man. That truth was a vital part of Josh's witness in the rehab programs. But the yoke wasn't as easy to put on when it was his.

The chime of the frontdoor bell tore Josh from the conflict between his emotions and his conviction.

I'll try, God. He laid the Bible aside and went inside the house.

"Hey, beautiful," he said, upon opening the door for a weary-looking Alex. Even in that state, she was beautiful to him. He wanted to forget the cookout and hold her in his arms, kiss all her cares away. What in heaven's name had possessed him to swear off kissing Alex when that was all he thought about? Well, almost all.

"I brought some dessert," she said, handing him a Food Mart bag.

"Spent the whole day in the kitchen, eh?" he teased, peeking into the bag. "Jell-O parfait. Cool."

"I hear there's always room for Jell-O," she shot back, forcing brightness in an otherwise cautious demeanor.

Now he remembered the why-for of the no-kissing declaration. Slow and easy, lest he scare her off.

"So where are your plans?"

"Huh?" Josh blinked. "Oh, the *plans*. Boy, you don't waste time, do you?"

That got a smile, such as it was. But he knew her heart wasn't in this.

"Tell you what," he said. "I'll start the grill while you look at them. It's just a basic story and a half blueprint that I like, but I want to tweak it to our"—her gaze flinched—"*my* specs."

He led her through the combination living/dining room area to the kitchen and got the plans off the built-in desk by the phone. Since the model home's kitchen was basically for cooking only, with a small breakfast bar, he unrolled the plans on the counter and pulled out a swivel barstool for Alex.

"Can I get you something to drink?"

"A cold can of soda would be great—diet, if you have it."

"Got your favorite brand," Josh announced, heading for the refrigerator. He took out the soda and the hot dogs he'd purchased.

"Hey, you're going all out," Alex teased. "Are you trying to impress me?"

"I have citronella candles, too," he told her, brow quirking up and down with mischief.

"Hot dogs *and* citronella candles?"

"Don't forget the Jell-O." Josh said with a snobbish sniff.

Alex's low chuckle tripped warning signals on every system in his body.

"I'm going to have to watch my step with you, buster," she said.

Josh grabbed a set of barbecue tongs and a tray for the franks. "And I was trying to be subtle. That's why I didn't do filet mignon." That and the fact that the meat case at Food Mart on a Saturday night had been picked over. "Besides, nothing beats a good, barbecued hot dog loaded with mustard, ketchup, and . . ." He closed his eyes for effect. "Onions," he finished dreamily. "Chopped raw onions."

Alex wrinkled her nose . . . what there was of it. "*Raw* onions?"

With a wicked grin, Josh headed for the kitchen door. "No worries, babe. Remember, this is a no-kiss zone."

He didn't look back. It was time to get out of Dodge. That purr of a chuckle and nose thing she did told him that if anyone was going to have to watch his or her step, it was he.

CHAPTER SEVENTEEN

Alex had never eaten baked potatoes with hot dogs. She scrubbed the raw potatoes while Josh wrapped the already grilled hot dogs in foil to keep them warm in the oven. No one ever told him that he could cook more than one item at a time. "I don't see what's so funny. You eat french fries with hot dogs, and they're potatoes," he complained, giving her a roguish nudge as he passed by to put the wieners in the stove.

"I'm sure everything will be delicious," she told him. "I just said that I'd never seen baked potatoes served with hot dogs." The wounded look he pulled tugged at her heart, even though she suspected it was feigned. "Just be glad you don't have to rely on your cooking to make a living."

She placed the two potatoes in a dish. As she reached up to put them in the microwave, Josh circled her waist with his arms.

"We could just go out . . . or order in."

"Nonsense. This is just fine . . . or it will be in fifteen minutes."

Too fine, she thought, resisting the urge to lean against him. It was hard to take things slow when the chemistry between them was so volatile. Alex unhooked his hands and went to the refrigerator to take out butter to soften.

"So . . . o," he drawled, taking the hint. "What do you think of the plans?"

The blueprints were for a simple four-bedroom story and a half. Locally, it was called a Tidewater home. Farther north, a Cape Cod.

"They look good. I can see that you put a lot of thought into it." Alex checked the drawers. No sign of butter, although there was a half-used block of cream cheese. Typical bachelor refrigerator. "Although four bedrooms is a bit much for a bachelor, don't you think?"

"I won't be a bachelor forever."

Ka-thump. Alex closed the refrigerator door to cover the noise of her heart slamming against her chest.

"I figure two kids and a guest room . . . when the time's right, that is."

Kids? She never thought about kids. Marriage had been a far reach for her.

Lord, I'm freaking out. Alex threw herself into tossing the salad she'd made, but she knew Josh was watching her. When he was around, she felt him. His was a presence that made itself known to her senses, setting off Josh alerts from tip to toe.

"The room over the garage will make a perfect studio. I didn't realize you still played that much." Picking up a jar of dressing before she tossed the salad into a puree, Alex pretended to read the nutritional content.

Josh moved to the barstool across the counter from her. No

avoiding those blues of his now. "Just for writing mostly. My songs still sell pretty well. If the band doesn't pick them up, the studio does for one of its other performers."

His songs. She didn't know he was still writing songs. Like the music, they possessed a part of him that she'd never been able to hold.

He spread his hands on the counter, staring at them. There was no resentment in his appraisal. If anything, it was filled with wonder. But the sight of the scarring on his left hand in particular began to pry loose the emotions she'd kept under close guard. The physical pain had surely been bad, but it must have paled to the emotional pain of that loss. Medicine could ease the one, but not the other.

"I'm glad you still have your music."

Alex meant it. Josh without music, without song, would be a vacant-souled stranger. She picked up his left hand, a patchwork of skin and bone, and folded it between her palms. Closing her eyes, she brushed the thick flesh of his thumb with her lips.

At Josh's sharp intake of breath, she looked at him. To her astonishment, his eyes were glazed, fathomless pools opening the depths of all that Josh was. All that he'd been. And, oh, the pain she saw. It couldn't be missed. It seized upon that within her, embracing it, wrenching it . . . pleading. Thousands of sentiments flowed back and forth without so much as a sound. Time passed.

Alex had no idea how much when Josh broke the charged silence.

"I didn't think . . ." He stopped, concentrating as if what he had to say was vital to his next breath. "I needed that sweet compassion . . . for my music." His fingers entwined with hers. "But I want . . . no, I *need* your forgiveness even more, Ally. I don't deserve it, but I need it."

Was that what she'd given? Forgiveness for the music that had taken him away from her? Forgiveness that she'd sworn she'd never part with. Alex wasn't sure. All she knew was that she couldn't bear the sight of his scarred hands and not be moved to the core of her being. And if it was her soul reaching out to Josh—

"I forgive you, Josh."

The words just rolled out, freed from the fists of fear that had held them for so long. And they continued to unfurl, releasing a peace like she'd never known before. It wasn't cloaked in chemistry. It was far more powerful, pouring pure joy through her until she surely glowed like a neon light.

But Josh had grown statue-still, staring at her as if she really was emitting Day-Glo colors.

"Josh?"

He moved his jaw from side to side, as if checking to be sure it was still in working order, his emotion-packed gaze never leaving hers.

"What's wrong?" she asked. Why wasn't he as happy as she was? As free?

"Nothing." He bit his lip, as though to hold back the wild love song swimming in his gaze.

Josh would write this moment, Alex knew. But if he shared those lyrics now, she'd be lost.

Instead, he cleared his throat, erasing them with mischief. "I just wish I'd served you hot dogs and baked potatoes before now."

Alex laughed, releasing the breath she'd inadvertently held. It was just as well. What had just happened was too precious to lose in the heat of the moment.

⨺

A sea of masts, flying bridges, antennas, and fishing poles defied the Sunday afternoon breeze that rattled cables and banners on the fleet of pleasure and work craft docked in the marina near the inlet. It promised to be a perfect day for an outing. Already Lynn and her two bridesmaids had staked out sunning spots on the bow of the Sportfisherman with John's groomsmen.

In the cabin of the *Lazy Daze*, Alex held her container of Waldorf salad, while Josh and John tried to figure out how to fit it in the yacht's refrigerator. It was already filled to the brim with her mother's homemade deviled eggs, potato salad, and a jelled fruit salad, Lynn's raw veggies and spinach dip, and the Whitlowes' fried chicken. Meanwhile, the galley counter was afloat with sweet potato rolls, crackers, chips, home-canned pickles, and anything else the ladies could think of to complete the menu.

"Man, if we eat all this, my boat'll sink," Josh observed, overwhelmed by too much food and not enough refrigerator. "I'm going to have to put this in the cooler in the cockpit."

"With the bait?" Alex exclaimed, mortified.

Josh in the kitchen was something she could get used to, even if he was like a fish out of water.

"Just because I serve baked potatoes with hot dogs doesn't mean I'd put bait in with our food."

But a sensitive fish, she thought. Last night, he'd acted as though he, too, sensed how fragile this new relationship was. As if he knew as well that if they got too close, too fast, that the spiritual side so vital to its survival might be lost in the physical.

Josh started up the steps to the salon. "We're going to need another bag of ice for the spare cooler though."

"I'll get it," Alex offered, following him. "I wanted to get some sunblock for my lips at the store anyway."

"We want to protect them," Josh said, casting a devilish look over his shoulder at her. "I plan on testing them . . . *someday*."

Back to Chemistry 101. It riddled her with an awareness that made Alex's nerves stand on end. Thank goodness they couldn't be seen waving shamelessly at him.

They'd settled by the time she purchased the sunscreen and ice at the small dockside market. As she returned to the yacht, Alex caught sight of Will Warren helping Barbara Carrington off the *Carrington Seas* and recalled Jan's mention of possible wedding bells. Not wanting to become entangled in a conversation, Alex hastened down the pier, hands stinging from the bag of ice. In the ninety-something temperature, it had begun to drip all over her knit tee shirt and capris.

Josh had the diesel engines running when she climbed aboard the *Lazy Daze*. In no time at all, the gangway was taken up, the lines cast off, and the boat was headed out into the sun-silvered bay. Once they cleared the choppy, narrow, rock-lined inlet, where the currents of the Atlantic Ocean met those of the bay, Josh headed out to sea at twenty knots.

Leaving the older folks to chat in the shade of the open salon, Alex climbed the ladder to the bridge to join Josh, John, and one of the groomsmen by the name of Ryan.

"Come into my web, said the spider to the fly," Josh shouted over the engines in his best Dracula imitation. He slid over on the captain's bench to make room for her and patted it. "Wanna drive?"

"No women drivers, *please!*" John protested from behind them on the wraparound, white-cushioned seat.

"No worries, gents," Alex assured them. "I intend to relax and enjoy today, not captain the boat."

Alex leaned against the bronzed arm the captain slipped around her, reveling in more than the day. It was good . . . good to have someone who understood her, whom she could lean on for a change. Alex checked the direction of her thoughts. For someone who prided herself on her independence, she was really slipping. No, make that *falling . . .* as in *head over heels*.

⊷

Thirty minutes later, Josh cut the engines at the Jackspot, a favorite offshore fishing spot for locals, which offered a variety of fish. Josh had chosen it for its proximity, since they'd gotten such a late start in the day. The sight of a half a dozen other boats in the area was a sign that bringing along twenty pounds of butterfish and tackle wouldn't be a waste of his time and money. Although Josh would enjoy an afternoon at sea with friends and good food, whether they caught fish or not.

More enjoyable still was watching B. J. forced to enjoy his hospitality. It almost made up for the times B. J. rubbed it in Josh's face that he'd never be able to afford more than his sixteen-foot skiff and outboard. If he couldn't strangle the man, Josh could at least kill him with kindness. Nothing to feel guilty about there.

"B. J., let me get you some bait," he offered, as his ex-father-in-law got out his own custom-made rod and reel.

"Get it for Whitlowe here. I don't need a guppy like you baitin' me up yet," B. J. responded with a gruff snort.

"No, I think I've got the hang of it now," the senior Whitlowe declined. "You're a good teacher, Josh." He jerked his head to where the two groomsmen, brokers in John Jr.'s firm, outfitted their rods. "But I imagine that Bill and Ryan could use some help."

"I'll take one. You take the other," Alex volunteered.

"Uh-oh, now we're in for some competition if she puts a line over, boys," her father warned everyone. "Takes after her aunt Rose . . . born to fight a fish."

Or anything else, man or beast, that got in her way, Josh thought, watching the way Alex's cheeks blossomed pink from the compliment. But it was that spunk that first drew him to her. And she didn't mind getting her hair wet like a lot of the bathing beauties. She reminded him of a veteran charter boat first mate, setting Bill up, while Josh rigged up Ryan with bait and showed him where to put his line over.

That was the cool thing about Alexandra Butler. She could be anything she wanted to be and was everything he wanted. And it had nothing to do with the passion she stirred in him. It drove him up a wall with his dumb—really dumb—*no-kiss* declaration.

Last night had been a real test of willpower. He'd wanted to forget dinner, forget the plans, and show Alex how much he loved her. How grateful he was for those four words. *I forgive you, Josh.* But Alex had become more than that to him, and it was the only way he knew to prove it.

"What about the ladies?" Josh asked.

A selfish part of him hoped the women would be content with sunning because he didn't like to have more than six lines in the water at a time. With the four men fitted up, that left two for John and him.

"Not us," Lenora Butler replied. "Marilyn and I are going to start getting the food out. "You kids have fun."

"Even you old kids," Amanda said, nailing her husband with a loud smackeroo on the cheek.

Josh glanced toward Alex. Their gazes met and held. Was she thinking what he was? That in the years to come, they might still have a little fire going beneath the snow of age.

"I'm going to read topside," she told him, nodding to a paperback she'd placed on ladder to the bridge.

And he was going sappy, he thought, watching her climb topside. Meltdown, simpleminded sappy.

Once the lines were in the water, Josh opened the bait cooler and took out some of the butterfish, cutting them in half for what was called chunking or chumming. Tuna loved it and he'd like nothing better than to see Ryan or Bill hook his first big fish.

"Okay, folks, grab a couple of these and toss them over the side. When they sink just so you can't see them, toss more over. That'll get the fish's attention. The trick is to keep the chum coming so they'll gather around here and won't scatter."

Josh did the same from topside, where he joined John and Alex, her nose buried in a Carol Higgins Clark novel. She'd shed down to a Hawaiian print swimsuit, its tank top far more modest than the bikini she'd worn years ago, but there was no doubt in Josh's mind that she'd retained all those delicious curves.

He focused on his fish finder, a poor substitute for watching Alex. Definitely activity going on below, so something should happen soon. "It'd help if you jerk your lines to discourage shark or skate," he shouted to those below.

"Sharks?"

"Like in *Jaws*?"

Two feminine heads popped up above the bench seat on the bow where bridesmaids Chrissy and Ashley had been chatting, lost in their own world. "Relax, ladies. No *Jaws*, just nuisances," Josh assured them. Although some whoppers had been caught off the coast. If anyone hooked one of those babies, Josh would cut the line and let it go rather than try to bring it in with a boatload of mostly novices.

Turning his attention back to the stern, he spied a threesome of yellowfins near the surface. At least a hundred pounds each, they divided and streaked past the boat. "Tuna!" he shouted, watching as they regrouped beyond the bow and shot back, headed for the chum-laden waters and the lures trailing astern.

Within seconds, it looked like miniexplosions in the water behind the boat, and Whitlowe Sr. shouted. "By George, I've got one!"

"Me too," B. J. bellowed.

"Yo!" Ryan chimed in.

Talk about feast or famine. Josh handed his rod over to Alex. "Everyone else reel in. We're in for a tangle of a fight."

And it would have been a tangle, except that B. J.'s fish missed the hook on the strike, and Ryan's pulled the hook and got away. But a red-faced John Sr. dug into the fighting chair, watching stunned as his Penn 1050W spooled out its fifty-pound line at smoking speed. There wasn't much that pulled meaner or faster than a yellowfin. Marlin danced on the water, but tuna were brawlers, diving for the bottom. And judging from the glimpse Josh got from topside, this one was a heavyweight.

"Reel him back, John, he's headed for the bottom."

"I got a blasted whale on here," John Sr. exclaimed. Already, sweat beaded on his face as he struggled to reel the angry fish back in.

So began the struggle. Everyone aboard gathered at the back, coaching and cheering, but not touching Whitlowe's pole. To do that would negate the catch as his. The fish fought valiantly for its life. A couple of times, Josh thought the line would snap, but John Sr. was relentless and listened to Josh's and B. J.'s advice.

Soon the leader, the heavier-duty length of line designed to withstand the cut of sharp fins during a fight, came up on the stern. "You've got yourself a prize," Josh said, reaching, for the leader, gaff ready, to manually haul the fish in.

But just as his fingers brushed the line, the tuna—at least 150 pounds—caught sight of the boat and bolted.

"Let her out!" Josh shouted, but it was too late. Before John Sr. could let out line for the fish's one last rally, it snapped. Leader and fish disappeared into the blue-green water.

"I have never seen anything like that," Amanda Whitlowe marveled, wiping her husband's brow with a paper towel. "Although I'm glad it got away." At her husband's scowl, she pulled a sympathetic face. "It fought so hard, dear."

"I'm with you, Mrs. W," Chrissy, the literally bouncing blond nurse colleague of Lynn's agreed. "It would be a shame just to take it out of the water and hang it on a wall, Mr. Whitlowe."

"Yeah," Ashley said, "although tuna steak is delicious on the grill."

"My thoughts exactly," John Sr. snorted. "That monster would have gone in my freezer. His picture would have gone on the wall."

"B. J.?"

Josh turned at the alarm in Lenora Butler's voice to see her husband slumped over in one of the deck chairs, his reeled-in rod propped on the rail.

"B. J.!" Lenora gave him a shake that elicited a grunt, nothing more.

"Daddy!" Lynn rushed to her father's side. Despite the alarm in her eyes, her professional training kicked in. "Daddy, are you in any pain? Are you nauseated?"

"My chest," he managed, struggling to speak. "Feels like a whale is sittin' on it."

"Any aspirin aboard?" Ashley asked. "Or does Mr. Butler have nitroglycerin pills?"

"Aspirin is in the head's medicine cabinet," Josh told John. "You get them. I'll start the engines. Bill, Ryan, man the anchor."

B. J.'s perspiration-dotted pallor sent Josh scurrying past a stone-still Alex to the bridge. As much as he wanted to hold her and tell her it was going to be okay, time was of the essence. Instead, a hasty hug had to do.

"Hang in there, babe." Josh raised his voice for the men making their way to the bow. They were green, but could do the job. "Okay, guys. I'm going to work the anchor. You check it in between engine thrusts and let me know when it's loose from the bottom."

Josh started the engines and tuned the radio to the emergency channel. He hadn't thought B. J. was acting right, quieter than usual and not nearly as prickly. Now Josh knew why.

"Mayday, Mayday, Mayday. This is the *Lazy Daze*—" He rattled off the call sign. "—twenty-one miles east of Ocean City, Maryland. We have a fifty-nine-year-old man, suspected heart attack. Semiconscious. Twelve people aboard, including nurses. *Lazy Daze* is a forty-foot Hatteras Sportfisherman, white hull, black trim. Keep watching on Channel 16. Over."

While he awaited a reply, he maneuvered the boat, alternating between forward and reverse, watching for the men's signal from the bow that the anchor had broken free of its hold on the seabed. The moment he got the signal, he started the automatic winch.

They were better than a half an hour away from shore. Either paramedics would meet them at the docks or the Coast Guard would initiate a MEDEVAC air/sea rescue. Either way, it was time. Time Josh prayed that B. J. Butler had.

CHAPTER EIGHTEEN

Although the designers had done all they could to make the waiting room for the Cardiac Care Unit warm and comfortable, warm and comfortable was the last thing Alex felt. The last hours had been surreal. Since it would have taken as much time to send a chopper for a sea rescue as it would to make it back to landfall, Josh had been instructed to proceed to the nearest dock at full speed. There, paramedics waited to transport B. J. by ambulance to the nearest hospital, fifteen miles away.

Meanwhile, the three nurses aboard gave her father the immediate attention he needed. While they'd had no nitroglycerin, the aspirin they administered bought the time they needed to reach landfall. But as the paramedics transported B. J. in the ambulance, he went into cardiac arrest. If it had happened on the boat—

Alex shuddered. She didn't even want to think about that. According to the ER physician, it was the quick action on everyone's part that had saved B. J.'s life, but Alex's mother credited God with the timing. Now, B. J. was in the CCU, with a staff working to stabilize him.

The irony of the situation was that her mother, whom everyone considered fragile, stood like a trouper at B. J.'s side, in command, talking to her husband, praying, but not interfering with the medical help. To Alex's shame, it was *she* who'd watched in helpless tears . . . until she'd heard her mother's declaration that they had to trust God.

Now, after a great deal of insisting and a reminder of her statement about Who was in charge, Mama was in the hospital cafeteria having dinner with Lynn, John, and the Whitlowes. Of course, Alex had sworn she'd go get them if she heard any news. The others, having to be back at work the following morning in the Baltimore–Washington area, had left for home.

"Want some more coffee?" Josh asked.

Alex shook her head. "No thanks. I'm tired of being the middleman between the coffeepot and the ladies' room," she told him. "I may never sleep again either." Whenever she was nervous, she either ate or drank her way through the crisis—coffee, sodas, water . . .

Maybe there was something to the theory of oral fixation, and it was her substitute for a baby bottle. Alex's half laugh at the direction of her musings was another sign that she was losing it.

Arm around her, Josh pulled her closer. "That's my girl," he said, misreading it for strength. "You were starting to worry me."

She appreciated it though. That and Josh's genuine concern and determination to get B. J. to help as if it were his own life depending on his effort. "You know, you are really growing on me," she confessed. "I know you and Daddy are born enemies, but you've been so sweet about this." She laid her head against his shoulder.

Yes, Alex admitted, her mother was right. God *was* in charge.

But Josh had pushed the engines of the *Lazy Daze* for all they were worth. And Lynn and her friends had given him immediate care.

"Your willingness to risk blowing your engines saved Daddy's life."

Josh shook his head with vehement objection. "Oh no, that was all God's doing. I was just an instrument He put me in place, same as the fact that we just happened to have nurses aboard."

"But if everyone hadn't pitched in, Daddy wouldn't be here," Alex objected. "I mean, it's not like I'm not giving God His due. I've thanked Him a gazillion times in the last few hours in between prayers to save Daddy. But in my opinion, the saying that *God helps those who help themselves* should have been in Scripture."

God had smoothed the way for her in business, but she'd had to work her tush off for it. And now the doctors were doing their best to do the same thing for B. J.

"But He doesn't need us. He just—"

"Mrs. Butler?" Clad in surgical greens, the doctor stood in the entrance of the waiting room, looking around at all the expectant faces of those whose loved ones were in peril.

Alex bolted to her feet. "I'm B. J. Butler's daughter Alex. Mama's in the cafeteria. Should I call her? Can you wait? I promised—"

The doctor held up his hand, stopping Alex's verbal floodtide. "Let her finish her meal. The nurse will give her a number where she can reach me, if she has any questions." He extended his hand. "I'm Dr. Stephens, your father's cardiologist."

The doctor proceeded to explain that B. J. had a blockage in the LAD—left anterial descending—artery. At the moment, he was serious, but stable and very lucky that they had transported him to the hospital within the golden hour. They expected to do an angioplasty if he remained stable, and hoped to get his fluid down, regulate his medication, and start him on a low-fat, low-salt diet in the days to follow.

The coils of anxiety in her neck and shoulders started unwinding with relief, although B. J. wouldn't be thrilled about the diet, especially the low-salt part.

"So he'll be out of the hospital and okay for the wedding?"

"That was the first thing he asked me when he came to." The doctor chuckled, his robotic demeanor cracking for a moment. "I told him yes, but he needs to take it easy."

"Can he have visitors now?"

"Yes, immediate family only," the doctor replied, the flatline of his tone never changing. "In fact, he's asking for you."

Surprise seized Alex's neck and shoulder muscles again. "*Me?*" If her father wanted to see anyone, shouldn't it be her mother?

"You can go in now if you'd like."

Beside her, Josh gave her hand an encouraging squeeze. "I'll go tell your mother what's happening."

"Can Mama see him when she comes back?" It didn't seem right usurping her mother's place. "I mean, visiting hours are set, aren't they?"

"Your mother can visit with Mr. Butler when she comes back even though it's after hours. I'll leave permission with the nurse. He's in bed nine."

"Thank you, Dr. Stephens."

"I'd go in with you," Josh offered after the physician walked away, "but I don't want B. J. to have another spell." He leaned over but checked the kiss that almost reached her cheek. With a sly grin, he backed away with an accusing, but impish look. "Almost got me."

Instead Alex kissed him, a hasty peck on the lips. "You made the pledge, not me," she replied to the surprised lift of his brow. She wanted more than anything for Josh to go with her, for moral support, for ... *just because*. With him at her side, she could face anything. That's how it had been before, until she had to square off against him and his irresponsibility.

But this was a new and improved Josh; and, for now, she had to go into the Cardiac Care Unit alone. Bracing herself with a deep breath, Alex entered the ward, past a number of cubicles until she reached the one marked NINE. B. J. lay on the hospital bed, his gown pulled off his shoulders to accommodate the electrodes glued to his chest to monitor his heart. The wires were hooked to machines, while the blood pressure cuff on his arm was connected to an automatic recorder on the IV pole.

B. J. was a strapping six-foot-three, but, in that bed, surrounded by machines and monitors, her father looked almost fragile ... vulnerable. Alex reeled against a rise of alarm, stepping up to his bedside. At least some of the color had come back to his face. Not much, but some. She covered his IV-free hand with her own. His eyes fluttered open, heavy-lidded.

"Hey, Daddy. What were you trying to do, scare *us* into having heart problems?" she said in an effort to lighten the emotional impact of the situation.

"I should'a seen it coming, I guess." It was an obvious effort for him to speak. He was still short of breath. "With the wedding and all, I just ..." He heaved a sigh and pulled a down-to-business look.

Her breath caught. It was a reflex, although Alex couldn't think what she had to be worried about. Hadn't she done everything he'd asked her to?

"I'm proud of you, gal."

Wonder knocked the wind from Alex's lungs, but alarm put it back. Did B. J. think he was dying? Tears—there was no end to them—blurred her father's face in front of her. "I hope to make you proud for a long, long time."

"You will." B. J. closed his eyes for a moment. "I just hope you'll have the good sense not to do it with that Turner boy."

That Turner boy. How many times had she heard those words, in that tone? "That's a possibility," she admitted, cautious. "But there's a lot of past hurt to deal with first."

She held back telling him that it had faded so fast in the wake of Josh's attentions that she had to keep reminding herself of it. Hope had settled in Alex's heart and being with Josh watered it. Who was she kidding? He had it floating in Miracle-Gro.

B. J. nodded, his lips pressed together, bloodless. "I figured," he admitted, "but I got to tell you, no matter how much it grieves me, that it wasn't all his fault, Ally. You need to know that."

"What do you mean, Daddy?" In B. J.'s eyes, everything was Josh's fault, from their broken marriage to global warming.

"I . . . I bribed him to go away."

Bribed? Alex stepped back, as if to dodge this out-of-the-blue— make that out-of-this-reality—confession. No. No way. Josh would never have taken money to leave. He'd followed his dream, the one that caused nothing but conflict between them.

God, please tell me this is a bad dream. Make that nightmare. Blood drained from her face at ten times the rate of the IV drip, making her light-headed. She leaned on the printer cart monitoring the activity in her father's heart. Hers would have shown nothing.

"And now *I'm* being blackmailed."

If her father kept this up, she'd need to hook herself up to these machines surrounding him. Alex staggered over her father's revelations.

He was proud of her.

He'd bribed Josh.

He was being blackmailed.

Not by Josh. Not the Josh of the past, nor the Josh of today. Certainty was a steel rod, helping her to straighten, to calm down and understand what her father was saying. He'd bribed Josh.

The betrayal curdled in her mind amidst protests that it wasn't true.

"But why . . . how—" She couldn't even form an intelligible question.

"Though I got to say, that Turner boy is a prince compared to Will Warren."

She had to sit down with that one. With no chair in sight, Alex sidled onto the edge of the bed. Even if it was against hospital rules, it was better than having someone come into the curtained cubicle and finding her sprawled on the floor, taken out by jellied knees and an emotion-razed heart.

Wait. Had Daddy said Will Warren?

"Is Will blackmailing you?" That was more in character for Will than Josh, although Josh had taken a bribe—

"I'll tell you," B. J. said, his words jumbled by his struggle to breathe.

Alex's overloaded mind, having scattered in a dozen directions at once, froze as he continued. Although how her father would tie this all together was beyond her.

"Josh's uncle needed a loan to save his store . . . didn't have the collateral to qualify without . . . without using Amanda Turner's farm."

But Joe Turner didn't want to jeopardize his mother's farm, even though Amanda was willing. "Was a matter of pride," B. J. told Alex. "I admired that . . . and I knew Joe'd make it good, so . . . so I went to Josh. Killed two birds with one stone." Her father shifted his brown gaze from the ceiling to Alex, unrepentant. "Maybe I shouldn't have, but I can't say I'm sorry. The boy's better off for it. You are, too."

Alex wasn't so certain. It didn't take a genius to fill in the blanks, even though her thoughts seesawed from condemnation to consideration.

A payoff.

To save his family.

But a payoff.

For an already broken marriage.

Still, a payoff.

Bitterness seeped into her voice. "So you're saying that we are better off that Josh took a payoff to leave me and save his family store?"

"You two were miserable," B. J. reminded her. "Think, girl. If you'd gone with him, you'd have been into his drugs and booze . . . and if he'd stayed, he'd have hated you for holding him back."

As usual, B. J. had worked it all out for her, behind her back. Hurt, both past and present, tortured Alex with the same ruthlessness that her father's illness did his breath. Emotions conflicted on every front. She wanted to hurt B. J. like she was hurting now, like she'd hurt back then. But she couldn't.

Not with him lying there fighting for his every breath . . . certain he'd done the right thing for her.

"Funny, isn't it? Now Will's puttin' the screws to me."

And not when someone else was threatening him.

"But what could Will possibly threaten you with? I thought as president of the bank that you had discretion to make that kind of loan, based on your knowledge of the borrowers. I mean, that's not criminal, or even grounds for dismissal."

"All started with old Steve Jackson's . . ." B. J.'s voice faded. With a labored breath, he finished, "credit report."

Steve Jackson? Alex's mind reeled in another direction. She had trouble imagining that Piper Cove's late resident drunk—and handyman, when he was reasonably sober—even had a credit report. Good-hearted, Steve had lived hand to mouth on the little cash he earned and borrowed.

Seeing that B. J.'s forehead was dotted with perspiration, Alex instinctively dampened a paper towel in a nearby lab sink and wiped it. She might be upset with him, but he was still her father. She loved him, even if she didn't always like him. "Daddy, do you want to talk about this now?"

The blips and beeps on the monitors seemed normal, but he looked so pale and wan. Besides, Alex wasn't certain she was up to any more shocks.

But, after a few minutes of silence, B. J. insisted on telling her the rest of the story.

In the settlement of Jackson's meager estate—a rusted trailer in a patch of woods—a large loan had shown up on a credit report that had been requested by his brother. The man had been floored to find that Steve had borrowed more money than he'd ever seen in his lifetime; and more shocked to see that the loan had been paid off. So he'd called the bank about it.

"Will took the call." B. J. said it like a death sentence. "But my first development was in need of more liquid capital. I'd borrowed to the max, so I took a big loan out in Steve's name and used the money for the investment."

"Did he know?"

"We had a little deal, but it was mostly paperwork, shifting money around. I paid it off. No one was the wiser."

"Until Steve died." Alex said it as much to herself as to B. J. She knew her father had approved loans in the good old boy fashion, the I'll-scratch-your-back-and-you-scratch-mine dealings. But this was something else. This could cost her father his career.

"Will was like a dog with a new bone, even though I honored every last cent owed, interest included." He snorted, lifting the hand Alex held. "What Will Warren knows about honor could be etched on the point of this needle in my hand. To think, I helped that boy up from a wet-nosed clerk at the drive-thru."

Honor. It seemed to Alex that everyone had their own version of what that was.

Exhausted by the toll of his confession, B. J. drifted off. Alex stared at her father's drawn face, at a loss as to what to say. Her brain had gone into a TMI freeze—too much information. Before she could recover from one confession, her father had dumped another on her just as disconcerting.

"But I'm not going to let that little sneak ruin Lynn's wedding," he rallied, opening his eyes. "I didn't spend all that money to see my baby girl's heart broken."

Alex's thoughts careened in yet another direction. Her father hadn't blinked an eye when she'd presented him with the bills to date for all the wedding-related expenses and renovating the Turner place. Heavenly Father, had the bank financed them with a bogus loan?

"Daddy, the wedding and the house . . . did the bank—"

"No!" B. J. gasped for the breath his vehement denial had taken. "Just that one time . . . an' I paid more than interest for it in conscience."

"What does that social-climbing little sneak want?" she asked, focusing her anger on Will. It couldn't be money. If B. J. had that kind of money, he'd never have resorted to the fraudulent loan. Besides, if Will landed Barbara Carrington as a bride—

"My resignation and recommendation that he take my place as president of the bank." The reply seemed to drain her father of his last ounce of strength.

Now it all made sense, at least this talk about retirement. Daddy was going to give in to Will's demand, rather than be exposed and ruin, not only Lynn's wedding, but relations with her future in-laws.

It would kill her father if the latter happened, more than his reputation falling into ruin. But then, giving in to Will Warren and retiring with his blackmailer in B. J.'s former place of power would as well. It would simply take longer.

"It's in my top desk drawer," B. J. said, opening his eyes again. "Just in case."

Before Alex could ponder B. J.'s meaning, footsteps alerted her to someone's approach.

"This is between us, darlin'." He grabbed her arm, his whisper urgent. "If I don't go home, you hand over that letter to Whitlowe."

Alex went cold. Her father didn't think he was going home? She felt as if the weight of two worlds had dropped on her shoulders.

"No one else . . . promise."

Alex bent over to plant a kiss on her father's damp forehead. "Don't worry, Daddy." She'd take care of this . . . somehow. "Why, look," Alex added more audibly as Lenora peeped around the curtain. "Mama's here . . . Lynny, too. Did Josh fill you all in?"

Lenora nodded and stepped up to the bed, taking B. J.'s hand. "Your daddy is going to have to start taking orders from me," she said in no uncertain terms. "You hear me, B. J. Butler?"

"I hear ya, darlin'."

Alex watched her parents' gazes connect. Love flowed back and forth, a love that had grown and matured over thirty-six years of marriage. One that the monitor blipping with her father's heartbeats couldn't measure.

Alex's fists clenched as she left them behind and headed for the waiting room. She had to do something. And to do something, she had to sort this all out. But what?

At the punch of her fist on the stainless flat square on the wall, the heavy wooden door to the waiting room opened, revealing more people had arrived on her father's behalf. In addition to the Whitlowes and Josh, Sue Ann, Jan, and Ellen were also there. Upon seeing her, the Bosom Buddies rushed to surround Alex with hugs.

They'd come as soon as they heard about B. J. and brought food with them. Alex's beleaguered heart swelled, pushing yet more waterworks to her eyes. When her world turned upside down, she could always count on her friends for food, hugs, prayers, and, above all, support . . . just when she needed them most.

"How'd he seem to you?" Josh asked, looking over and through her circle of friends to make eye contact.

Alex's gaze sharpened through her tears. "Better than he was." And she was worse. Alex didn't know what to trust anymore. Certainly not her instincts. Not where Josh was concerned. Not until she had time sort out her emotions about what she'd just learned—something she could not do around Josh Turner.

CHAPTER NINETEEN

Alex couldn't help herself. Back at her apartment with her dearest friends, she'd told them what B. J. had shared with her. It was too much for her to bear alone. And what was said between her friends stayed with her friends. Besides, she really hadn't promised in so many words not to tell anyone else. And heaven knew, four heads had to be better than her aching one.

"I can't believe Will Warren is blackmailing your father!" Sue Ann's blue eyes bulged with incredulity as she moved back and forth in the rocker that Grandmother Butler had given Alex.

"I can't believe that Josh took a bribe to leave Alex," Ellen said from the overstuffed chair opposite the sofa where Alex and Jan sat.

Josh. Alex knew he was confused by her sudden cold shoulder, but she'd had to get away from him to clear her head and think rationally. When her buddies picked up on her distress vibes, they closed ranks. Their insistence that they go home with her, since

B. J. was stable, and established visiting hours were over for the evening, was nonnegotiable and Alex had grabbed at it as a lifeline.

After making certain that Lynn was staying with Mama. Not that Alex had to worry about Mama. Lenora was weathering all this like a trouper, considering how fragile she'd been just a few months ago. She'd invited John and his parents back to the Butler home. No doubt by now, they were all being fed again with the leftovers from this afternoon's foiled picnic. Alex supposed Josh was with them as well.

Ellen forced the plastic pastry container open, drawing Alex back to present. They'd already had sandwiches from Jan's party tray, and dessert would wait no more.

"You *had* to open it, didn't you." Sue Ann glared at Ellen as though her obligatory sampling of the pastry tray were the tomboy's fault. She picked out a sugar-dusted lemon tartlet and took a bite. "And the real shame of it is, you eat like a horse and never gain an ounce, and that little wisp of a thing," she mumbled, pointing to Jan, "won't eat a single goodie she brought."

Janet rarely ate her own creations. She claimed that she was usually too miserable from tasting as she prepared them.

"But honestly . . ." Finishing-school training shot to the dickens, Sue Ann brushed off the powdered sugar that fell from the treat to her bosom. "Did your daddy do anything really wrong? I mean, he paid back the money."

Alex wanted to believe what Sue Ann said, but she couldn't. "The loan was fraudulent. What if something had gone wrong?"

"His butt would have been in a sling . . . Jackson's, too." Ellen licked chocolate from one of Jan's éclairs off her fingers.

"And now it is." Alex sighed. "Worse, Daddy is going to give in to Will without a fight."

Sue Ann looked up from scooping the vanilla cream out of a second pastry with a fingernail painted fire-engine red. *Sweet tooth* should have been her middle name. "Well, that's just not right. His own daughter's father-in-law will have to fire him. Imagine how that would make Lynny feel."

"Not to mention ruin his career and reputation," Ellen agreed. "Definitely a wedding downer."

"Some help you guys are," Alex grumbled.

She eyed the tray of pastries that Janet had made, her earlier determination to abstain from sweet indulgence wavering in the hopeless tide engulfing her. She picked up a sinful-looking chocolate-sprinkled delicacy filled with—she stuck her finger in it, Sue Ann style—Bavarian cream. Even though it was her favorite combo, she could hardly get excited about it.

"I don't think Daddy is as worried about his reputation around here as he is ruining Lynn's life and his image with her in-laws." Alex bit into the delicacy, thinking aloud. "Yes, he took out a bogus loan, but he honored it. I don't think that would change Piper Cove's opinion of him."

"Not among the folks he's helped," Sue Ann agreed. "Except you and Josh. Seems to me he hurt both of you."

Although this pickle did serve B. J. right. He'd abused his position at the bank to manipulate her and Josh. But his motives were good . . . from a fatherly point of view. And Josh hadn't been bribed so much as coerced. B. J. had caught him well and truly between a rock and a hard place.

Oh God, I don't know what to think . . . my feelings are all over the place.

"Josh should have at least told you why he left," Sue Ann continued.

Josh. Just his name made her ache, even though he had put money, music, and his family ahead of their love. And while she understood why he did it, Alex couldn't fathom how he could have hurt her like that. Why couldn't he have trusted her enough to tell her about it so they could work it out together? Back then, she'd have chosen Josh over life.

Just as my father feared. And she could have been in Josh's accident and hooked on drugs and alcohol, though she'd like to think she had better sense. She might have been a good influence on Josh. Yet, she hadn't been enough of one to keep him from getting hooked in the first place.

If I'd believed in him. But she hadn't believed in his dream.

"Maybe it's for the best if your dad did retire," Ellen speculated, drawing Alex back to the topic at hand. "I mean, his health might demand it, you know . . . and everything would be cool with the wedding and all." She shoved a shock of limp brown hair behind her ear, her tanned brow furrowed as she searched her idea for flaws.

"No!" Jan's miniexplosion startled the lot of them. "Will Warren deserves to be punished more than Alex's dad."

Three pairs of eyes shot to where the usually quiet Jan fumed like a fury.

"Hey, what gives?" Ellen asked, echoing Alex's thoughts.

Sue Ann cocked her head at the smaller girl. "My word, you look like a mad pit bull with a grudge." She leaned forward. "What is it?"

Sue Ann was right. Gone was the duchess of sweet. Jan sat, fist clenched in fight mode, nostrils flaring with each breath.

"Jan?" Alex inquired gently, lest her friend implode with the watery rage filling her eyes. Jan loved everyone, even those who didn't deserve it.

Jan hesitated. "Oh, I don't suppose it matters anymore, now that both our daddies are gone." She leaned forward. "Let's just say that arm-twisting runs in the family."

❧

It wasn't exactly blackmail. It was bribery. Every native of Piper Cove remembered the hunting accident that sent Jan's father to jail on involuntary manslaughter charges. Cal Kudrow worked for Will's father as a handyman and, knowing the area as well as he did, took the senior Warren and his son deer hunting.

"It was really Will who shot that Baltimore hunter," Jan told them. "Daddy had told Will to hold his fire till he was sure of his shot, but he didn't. So Mr. Warren paid Daddy to take the blame for the accident, and no one was the wiser."

"But Will was just a kid. He wouldn't have gone to prison," Ellen objected in disbelief.

Jan gave her a dour look. "Mr. Warren didn't want his golden boy's reputation or chances of moving up in the world tarnished."

"Children learn what they live," Ellen said to no one in particular.

Jan folded her arms across her chest. "That time in jail changed Daddy. I mean, he always did like his liquor; but when he got out, he'd turned mean with it." She grunted, bitter. "No wonder Mama ran off. And it was all for enough money to buy us a new trailer. Two years of a man's life for a double-wide." She shook herself and threw up her hands, trying to force humor into her voice. "Girls, I have a bigger selection of skeletons in my closet than Saks has clothes."

She wasn't successful. Alex saw her pain. If anyone knew how the past could haunt and hurt, she did. "That's horrible, Jan," Alex told her. "I'm so sorry."

"Looks like our Willie didn't have to leave home to learn how to manipulate people, did he?" Sue Ann smirked over a powdered donut hole. "Like father, like son."

"And now Will's taking *my* father down." Alex grabbed another confection and bit into it as if it were Will's leg.

"That wimpy little—" Ellen finished with an unladylike name that summed up Alex's opinion of Will Warren perfectly—the advantage of hanging out in a garage with a bunch of guys. But the moment she heard herself, she filled with remorse. "Aw, shine, he's made me lose my religion."

"Oh no," Sue Ann declared. "He's not getting away with piddly." She raised her arm in a battle cry. "This is war." Although it kind of lost something when *war* came out like *war-ah*. Even Susie Q's temper—and she did have a doozy, when riled—had a sugar coating.

"What do you have in mind, General?" Alex asked, as their drama queen began marching back and forth in front of the sofa, huffing like she was gearing up for Stonewall Jackson's march through the Shenandoah.

"Dirty *gets* as dirty does." Sue Ann smacked her lips in satisfaction as she spun around. "I say we confront the coward. And that's what Will is . . . a coward."

"Confront." Alex wasn't exactly carried away by her friend's genius.

"You pull Will aside and confront him. Ask him how he expects to get away with blackmailing your father. Shoot, you can even throw in that you know he shot that hunter years ago. That'd shake him in his Italian leathers. Can he still be prosecuted for that?" Sue Ann looked askance at the ceiling as if the answer were there.

"I don't know, but I'll find out." Alex could look it up on the Internet. If not, she'd ask Tony Richardson on the sly.

"Anyway," Sue Ann went on, "if you can just get Will to talk about what he's doing on tape—"

"You mean wear a wire like on TV?" Jan warmed instantly to the idea. "You could even get him to admit to shooting that hunter."

"Hey, Perry Mason, she's not."

"Thank you, Ellen," Alex said.

"But if anyone of us could wring a confession out of Will," Ellen added, "you could. All you have to do is get him to talk about it . . . lead the conversation."

"For your daddy and your family," Sue Ann reminded her.

For her father and family. Alex's spine stiffened as she polished off the rest of the donut. "Okay. But we've got work to do to set this thing up. Time is wasting."

It was nuts, but she saw no other way. She had to do something. Her family needed her. Her *father* needed her.

"Atta girl." Ellen slapped her on the back. "We'll be right there with you."

Jan launched into applause. "You go, Alex."

Sue Ann slowly dusted off the powdered sugar from her fingers before slipping an arm around Alex's shoulder. Pure devilment twitched on her lips.

"All for one and one for all, sugar, remember?"

Not exactly bowled over with the same enthusiasm, Alex nodded. That meant if she went down, her friends would go down with her. She smiled. At least she was in good company.

CHAPTER TWENTY

The courthouse clock, a block from Alex's apartment, rang 7:00 A.M. as Josh turned on the coffeemaker. Yes, he could be arrested for breaking and entering, he conceded as he put the frozen precooked sausage that he'd picked up on the way over in the microwave. But he was counting on the chocolate chip pancakes he'd stirred up to exonerate him for using Alex's spare key to get in.

Besides, this was an emergency of the heart. He had to know what B. J. told Alex last night that had turned her as cold as a side of beef toward him. When her friends closed ranks around her, it had been impossible for Josh to get through. And much as he liked all the ladies, they could be exasperating.

Surprised that Alex had yet to stir on a business day, Josh cleared the coffee table of glasses and empty pastry containers. Definitely the aftermath of a girls' night, but not in character for Alex to leave the mess until morning. He couldn't count the number of times she'd shamed him into doing dishes that he'd as soon as left for later.

Josh carried the glasses to the dishwasher. Of course she was upset over her father's heart attack, and on top of all the stress she'd been under—who wouldn't be upset? As much as B. J. annoyed him, Josh had prayed for the man. The woman Josh loved loved her dad. Having been raised by his grandmother after the death of his parents in a car crash, Josh couldn't relate to fatherly love—at least not the earthly kind.

But if Alex was to be a part of his life, B. J. came with her. Josh didn't know how they'd manage, except that God would be in the picture now. Like that string kit that Ellen had given Lynn at the bridal shower said, marriage takes three.

Marriage. Josh stopped short. He hadn't thought marriage specifically, but that's the way his heart was heading, downhill fast. If only Alex's was on the same road.

Dishes taken care of, Josh checked the heat on the electric frying pan. Perfect. Too nervous simply to sit and wait for Alex to awake on her own, he started cooking the pancakes, silver dollar size . . . just the way she liked them.

Face it, he told himself. B. J. had told her about the money Josh had taken to leave town and probably left out the mitigating factors regarding his aunt and uncle. That had to be the reason she'd shut him out so suddenly. Maybe he should have told her the entire story early on, even if doing so made her father look as bad as he. The old Josh would have done so in a heartbeat. But he wasn't that man anymore. And blaming her father wouldn't exactly ingratiate himself with Alex.

God, I don't know what to do.

Except be honest with whatever questions she threw at him.

Josh flipped the tiny pancakes one by one as the coffeepot alarm signaled that it was done—

"What are *you* doing here?" Alex stood in the bedroom door, disheveled in a tee shirt and cranky humor. The large circles under her eyes told Josh that she'd had as restless a night as he had. "Better yet, how did you get in?"

"I saw you get your spare key the other day. I hope you don't give your secret away with all your dates," he chided gently. "Anyway, I figured after the rough day we had yesterday, you could use a little pampering." He scooped up one of the pancakes, holding it like a peace offering. "Chocolate chip . . . your favorite."

"You usually made those when you felt guilty over something," Alex observed wryly. "But everything smells yummy." She reached behind the bedroom door and retrieved a lightweight robe. "So what's up?" she asked, putting it on as she shuffled barefoot to the coffeepot.

Not to be upstaged, Riley immediately intercepted her, weaving in, out and around her feet. At his plaintive mew, Alex sidetracked to the cabinet under the sink and got out a container of cat food. "Men!" she swore at the pushy feline. "Always wanting what they want when they want it."

Ordinarily, Josh would have taken up that gender gauntlet, but the diversion gave him time to assemble his thoughts. The only way to deal with Alex was to be direct. "So what did B. J. have to say that chilled what you and I had going?"

Instead of answering, Alex fed the cat and carried her coffee to the table, where she sat down and rested her head in her hands.

"Headache?" he asked, concerned.

"Brain crash."

"Or was it sugar? I found the empty pastry container."

"Both."

"How many eggs?"

"One. I need protein more than chocolate chips . . . although you really don't have to do this. I'm fine." She didn't sound too convincing. Alex picked up her coffee and took a sip.

Black, Josh observed. When she was in a good or playful mood, she used milk and half a diet sugar pack. Black meant she was gearing up for business. Or confrontation.

Past guilt collided with reason in Josh's mind. He'd hurt her . . . horribly. But he'd had good reason. Their marriage had turned into an ongoing argument over his music and refusal to let Alex plan out his life for him, trying to box him into a job at B. J.'s bank. Taking the money had saved his uncle's store and his grandmother's home.

Lord, just give me the words. Don't let me blow it. Help me convince her that past is past, and it's our future that counts.

"You want to talk about it now or wait till after we eat?" he asked, clarifying more tentatively. "About us."

"I don't want to talk about us at all right now, Josh . . . please. It's Daddy and—" She broke off. "It's *Daddy* I'm worried about."

Josh didn't argue. He could fill in the blanks without Alex spelling it out. *His bribery.* At that moment, Josh wanted more than anything to tell B. J. Butler where to go. Just because Josh had forgiven the man didn't mean unchristian thoughts didn't pop up. What he did with those thoughts was what mattered. There was no way to separate B. J. from their relationship, and that was a thorn in his side he'd have to learn to live with.

Lord, I'm waiting on You.

In the meantime, the best plan was to be still and listen. Even if it was driving him crazy.

The remnant of last night's headache floated about in a numb fog that cast doubt on Alex's ability even to discuss what she'd learned yesterday. She'd hoped to have a little time before facing either one of her adversaries. If Josh could be called that, his champion voice reminded her. If one could be put away for voices in their heads, Alex would be first in the line. She had a football stadium full of them with divided loyalties. And the game had been an all-nighter.

A yawn sneaked up on her as she watched Josh break two eggs simultaneously, one in each hand.

"Over easy, right?" he asked, back to her.

"Great." He remembered. Before she savored the sweetness too much, the visiting team in her brain protested the call. Josh could be so charming when he wanted to, but he'd betrayed her.

But lack of trust cut both ways, and she wasn't innocent in that regard.

"Look, Ally, I know I was no saint in the past," Josh said, "nor am I now, but at least I'm trying. I've learned from my mistakes."

"By breaking and entering?"

"And cooking, don't forget, cooking." He flipped the eggs.

Alex fought the temptation to let her smirk melt into a smile. She wanted to be angry with Josh. She'd argued with him all night long in her mind, mounting offense and defense, venting all her hurt and anger at the way he'd left her. Today, she was too tired to do so. And not sure she wanted to anymore. "You are so obvious, you know."

"Oh?"

"Don't think that I don't know why you're here pulling a Mr. Mom to stay in my good graces."

Josh's shoulders took an exaggerated plunge. "Busted." He took up the eggs, put each on a plate, and carried them to the table. "Not mad, are you?"

Alex hesitated. Who'd won last night's head game? Had she gotten it all out of her system, or was she just too tired to fight right now? *God?*

"Hurt," she replied, when no great revelation came to her. Unless she counted the one that warned her Josh was not going to go away as easily this time. "I . . . I just wish you'd come to me . . . explained it all. I understand how you felt obligated to help your family." That part had been admirable. But it didn't lessen the pain of abandonment. "I—"

"Ally," Josh interrupted. "You'd not have let me go without the mother of all fights. You wanted me to become a banker, remember? You didn't believe in me enough to take the risk my music required."

As much as she wanted to argue, Josh was right. That's what he'd told her in their imaginary scramble. "I know."

But it still hurt. Her eyes stung as she looked at the plate he'd set in front of her.

"If you think I was happy, Ally, think again. My music wasn't enough. It was like I—" In the periphery of her vision, Josh propped his hands on his hips, looking at the ceiling as though searching for words. "Like I had this big hole inside and . . . and there weren't enough drugs and alcohol to fill it."

Alex knew exactly what he meant. She'd tried to fill hers with work. Thought that if she could just have her own business, be Ms. Independence, that she'd be happy. Thought she'd succeeded . . . until she saw Josh again.

"I needed God," he said.

Nice, but that wasn't what her wounded heart wanted to hear. "And *you.*"

That was. Playing Josh in person was a whole other game.

Josh retreated to the stove to get the sausage and pancakes.

And you. Little words, but their impact bowled through the doubt in Alex's mind, dividing the urge to melt into a heap of happy tears from the one to run for fear that this wasn't real. She did neither. There was such a thing as time-out.

Josh returned to the table with the rest of the meal. "Our love alone wasn't enough, but it was real, Alex," he said. "Neither of us, if we're honest, can deny that."

"But not real enough to keep you here." How many times was her heart going to be tackled and dragged through this hurt? One would think it would have toughened up by now.

"Real enough to bring me back."

He reached for her hand, but she drew it away, fisting it in her lap.

The wedding had brought him back. It wouldn't keep him here.

"I was miserable with you, Alex, but I was more miserable without you."

Scars this deep didn't go away with a few words. It took more. Alex wasn't even sure what *more* was, or that she had any of it.

"I just need time to deal with this, Josh, so let's drop the subject for now . . . *please.*"

"Sure."

Alex ignored the disappointment in Josh's reply. She was doing what she had to do, prioritizing her woes, protecting herself.

In the silence that ensued, she poked at her egg, arranging the sausage and pancakes just so on her plate. Segments of her conversation with B. J. plodded through her mind.

I'm proud of you, gal.

I bribed him to go away.

And now I'm being blackmailed.

Her problem with Josh had to wait. Daddy wasn't able to take care of himself. Daddy needed her . . . for the first time in her life. Mama and Lynn would fall apart. Mama was doing great so far, but this might send her back into that awful, joyless hibernation from life and her loved ones. The scrape of Alex's fork as she went after a stray chocolate chip on the plate brought her back to the present and the fact that she'd practically inhaled the hearty meal Josh had prepared.

"That good, huh?"

"Too good."

Why couldn't she be like Jan, who couldn't eat when she was upset? At this rate, Alex wouldn't fit into the dress she'd bought for her sister's wedding. *If* there'd be a wedding. She buried her face in her hands. *Get a grip, Alex.*

Josh got up to clear the table, taking away her plate before she had the chance to stir. With his back to her, Alex parted her fingers, watching him. Even scarred, his hands were more than capable. And those arms, wiry with muscle and bronzed. Just the right amount of sun-bleached, manly bristle. In them, she'd felt safe from the world at large. She wanted them, no, *needed* those arms around her. Needed him more than her hurt and fear combined could discourage.

"I need you, Josh."

The clatter of dishes in the sink stopped. Josh shut off the running water as he turned. "What?"

He wasn't the only one astonished. Alex's thoughts scattered, but her heart knew its own mind. She rose and closed the distance between them.

"I *need* you," she repeated. It wasn't a matter of reason or choice, but of raw survival instinct.

She took the dripping dishrag from his hand and tossed it into the sink along with the anger and bitterness that had clouded the truth. Slipping her arms around his waist, she pressed her face against his crisp blue oxford shirt; felt the warmth of his body through it; heard the hammering of his heart; inhaled the lingering mix of detergent with a hint of sausage and pancake syrup.

Whether she melted in Josh's arms or the reverse, heaven descended to earth. Last night she'd tried imagining God's arms around her, holding her as she cried in uncertainty and anguish over past and present. Only then had sleep come, but it had been tortured.

Lord, I'm not comparing Josh to You by any stretch of the imagination, but this feels so good, so safe, so right. I believe that You sent Josh back to me, just when I'd need him most.

With a moan, Josh hooked a finger under Alex's chin, lifting her face to his. "If I ever make a no-kissing declaration again, just shoot—"

Alex rose on tiptoe and silenced him with her lips, sweetly at first, then with more meaning. "The pact is broken," she told him a few thunderclaps later as she pulled way. The way her body tingled and glowed with warmth, she wasn't sure there hadn't been lightning flashes as well.

"You . . . are . . . amazing." Josh breathed each word against her forehead. "I left a hotheaded girl behind and came home to a . . . a grace-filled woman." He swallowed the emotion thickening his voice. "I've prayed for this . . . for your forgiveness."

Forgiveness? Is this what it was? What forgiveness felt like? A heart spreading its wings like a wounded bird, healed, taking flight, singing?

Outside, the courthouse bell rang the turn of the eighth hour.

"I have to go," she whined, pulling away, but reluctant to let go of Josh's hands. "I told Mama last night that we'd go to the hospital together this morning. I have to pick them up at nine."

Josh nodded. "I love you, Alexandra Butler."

Alex saw it in those blue, blue eyes that wouldn't leave her, even as he tucked his shirt into dress khakis.

"I love you, Joshua Turner." If a moment could be captured forever, this was it. "Still," she added softly. That word had made a difference. It implied consistency, permanence . . . till death us do part.

That slow, knowing grin crept onto his lips—the one that ought to annoy her, but made her feel wicked instead. "You'd better get moving."

"You, too." This wasn't sixteen years ago.

"I'll finish the dishes."

"I'll grab a quick shower and dress." They were more mature now.

"Want me to pick up your mom and swing back by for you?"

"That would be great."

"Well . . ."

"Well . . ." she echoed.

"One of us has got to move."

Alex snickered. So much for being more mature. "Okay, the count of three. One . . . two . . . three!"

She bolted for the bedroom at the same time Josh spun back to the sink. Riley, who'd settled onto one of the companion chairs shoved under the kitchen table, leapt from napping onto all fours.

By the time Alex reached the bedroom door, the cat had disappeared behind the sofa.

Alex's silly grin faded, giving way to guilt as she closed the bedroom door. How could she be so giddy with happiness? Yes, she'd forgiven Josh, but she hadn't exactly confided in him that her father's career and the wedding were about to crash and burn. The two were still like tinder and flint. And her heart was the kindling.

CHAPTER TWENTY-ONE

Alex's sports car clung to the curve of Cove Road as she left her parents' home in Waterview Village that Wednesday and headed for Wiltbank Manor. Thankfully, Josh had gone to Annapolis to be fitted with one of the designer tuxes that Lynn had picked out for the groomsmen and spend a couple of days with *the boys*, so Alex didn't have the temptation to tell him what was going on with B. J. Not that she thought Josh would think harder of her father than he already did, but why add fuel to what she hoped was a dying fire?

As for her father, B. J. had come home after a successful procedure with medication, a diet, and strict orders to take it easy, at least till after the wedding. Taking it easy to B. J. meant running his office from home, although Lenora kept an eagle eye on him and made certain that doctor's orders were followed to the letter. And because of Mama's eagle eye, there hadn't been a chance to discuss the letter of resignation in her father's desk or Will's blackmail any further.

From what Alex picked up, B. J. planned to go ahead with his resignation. And given his weakened state, Lenora was now a hundred percent behind his decision. So was Alex, but only *if* Will Warren got what he deserved without hurting her father. Like Suzie Q said, this was *war-ah*.

As she turned into the long tree-lined drive approaching Sue Ann's house, she spied Ellen's bike parked in front. What should be a last-minute check of wedding arrangements was going to double as a strategy-planning event. Alex was going to confront Will Warren, and the ideal time and place would be at the country club's annual dinner dance, where new officers were installed, and the old guard took their leave.

"Hello, I'm here," Alex announced as she let herself into the marble-tiled foyer of Sue Ann's home.

"In the dining room," Sue Ann answered in a singsong voice.

Ellen looked up from toying with a battery to a funnel-shaped contraption. It was about the size of a dinner platter with a headset attached. "How's your dad?"

"Like a Timex. He takes a licking and keeps on ticking . . . just a little slower than usual." Who was Alex kidding? "But he looks like death warmed over."

"Poor thing," Jan commiserated over a cup of coffee from the Food Mart where she worked. "I wouldn't be surprised if Will's blackmail wasn't the cause of your father's heart attack."

"I don't know," Alex said. "B. J. burns the candle at both ends."

"Like someone else I know?" Sue Ann gave Alex a pointed look.

"Ready to get down to business?" Ellen turned on the power and pointed the wide end of the funnel at her. "Speak, oh wise one."

"What *is* that thing?" Alex asked, stepping back.

"You don't want to know," Sue Ann warned her. "Ms. I Spy really went overboard."

"It's a parabolic listening device," Ellen replied, shaking the contraption. "I just point this . . ." She held up the funnel-like part. "And I can hear everything you and Will say to each other. Except it doesn't seem to be working."

"It amplifies *nature* sounds," Sue Ann said, branding it with disdain. "Like for bird-watchers or hunters . . . not eavesdropping. It records a whole minute or so of chirping, so you'll have to talk fast."

"Just give me some time to read up on it. I might be able to put a recorder up to it."

Sue Ann's hands flew to her hips. "Well, it can't be much if that hunter left it behind in a deer stand. How do you know it even works?"

"Must need a new battery," Ellen murmured as she probed the cover off again with a tiny screwdriver from a glasses repair kit. "Unless you have something better."

"As a matter of fact, sugar, I do." Strutting smug, Sue Ann opened a drawer of her burled-walnut sideboard and withdrew a FedEx envelope. "I talked to that weird kid at the electronics store about how I wanted to tape a conversation without the other person's knowledge, and he ordered me this overnight."

Sue Ann pulled out a shrink-wrapped package labeled SPY-MASTER WIRELESS LISTENING DEVICE AND RECORDER. "We just tape this sending box under Alex's blouse, and we can receive and record everything that's being said."

"Omigosh," Jan gasped. "That's just like on *Law and Order*."

Ellen picked it up, skeptical. "How much did you pay for this?"

Sue Ann's gaze sparkled with triumph. "Thirty-nine, ninety-five plus fifteen bucks for shipping."

"You went all out, Suzie Q," Alex drawled. *God, please help us get what we need to shut Will up.*

"The range is only—" Ellen squinted at the small print. "Fifty-feet, max. So you've got to get Will near one of the tall hedges surrounding the club grounds so we can have receive and record that close."

Jan chugged the remainder of her coffee and slapped it down on the table so hard, the plastic lid popped. "Just so we get him. He's had it coming a long time."

Alex exchanged a quick look with Sue Ann and Ellen. This saddle-up and hang 'em high demeanor was not their Jan. One would think she held more than grudges against Will for ruining her father's life.

"For ruining *everyone's* lives," Jan added, picking up on the suspicious vibes circulating around her.

Alex sighed. For a moment, she'd thought Jan might tell them more about Will. "I talked to Tony this morning about a hypothetical case involving an accidental shooting, by the way. Basically he said that, unless there were eyewitnesses, meaning yours or Will's dad, or evidence, the case wouldn't stand a chance of being reopened on hearsay. And with legal reason, if the perpetrator in question was a juvenile at the time, it wasn't likely he'd have been charged."

Alex didn't add that she thought Tony had guessed that she was talking about Will. At least his specific questions led her to think so. Being a local, he'd have heard about the case even though he was a kid at the time.

"So his daddy was just protecting a future blackmailer's reputation and future from smears," Ellen said wryly.

"But you're still going to stop Will, aren't you?" Jan's switch to little girl lost tugged at Alex's heart.

"Sure. I just can't use the shooting for any leverage." She put her arm around her petite friend. "Don't worry, Tink, we'll get him."

Alex wished she was as sure of herself as she sounded. But Jan's anger was infectious. To think, Alex had tolerated Will's unsolicited flirtations, all the while suffering from her father's apparent opinion of how he was a far better choice for Alex than the one she'd made. "So . . . let's figure out how to use this thing because we won't get a second chance."

⤬

Saturday evening Alex entered the club dining room with her parents late, although, with B. J. on the board, their places were assured near the head table where the Piper Cove Golf and Country Club's incoming and outgoing officers sat. Friends immediately surrounded her father, inquiring about his health, but Lenora ran interference so that B. J. was seated as soon as possible. Mama hadn't wanted him to attend the affair, but stubborn was and stubborn did.

As soon as her parents were settled, Alex joined Ellen and Sue Ann's table, a smaller one near the entrance and ladies' room access. "Are we all set?"

"All systems go," Sue Ann told her. Jan gave Alex a thumbs-up from a nearby table where she sat with Scott Phillips and his entourage from the Baylander group.

"Josh didn't get home in time either, eh?" Ellen observed.

"Some of John's work buddies had a preliminary bachelor party thing this weekend, thank goodness." This was hard enough to do without juggling Josh in the mix as well. "Martin still in Belize?"

"No, he's laid over in Miami . . . canceled flight. Won't be home till Monday." Sue Ann sighed. "At least I won't have to worry about what to do with him while we *work* tonight."

Ellen fingered a silk flower arrangement with a disapproving grimace. "This time next week, I'll have fresh rose globes in pink and red on every table to contrast with the tablecloths Sue Ann ordered."

"Carnation pink and Sangria," Sue Ann reminded her.

"Of course I'm using calla lillies and dendrobium orchids for the bouquets and boutonnieres. Can you believe Jan can make lilies out of icing? Or just about any flower. I mean, you can hardly tell the difference."

Sue Ann stiffened full alert. "Look, there's Will and Barbara."

For a moment Alex's full-speed-ahead momentum wavered. Barbara looked ten years younger than her fiftysomething years on Will's arm. No botox or face-lift could create the glow of love.

"I wish for Barbara's sake that this wasn't real," Sue Ann said, voicing Alex's concern. "She turned into such a hermit after Phil died."

"Hey, we are doing her the biggest favor of her life," Ellen reminded them.

"Not if this information doesn't come out," Alex said. "It'll stop Will from ruining Daddy's life, not hers."

In the midst of seeing to her parents, preparing for her confrontation with Will, and running down the home stretch of wedding planning, she hadn't thought about Barbara in all this. She didn't know the woman well, but still—

"Let's just think about this a minute." Sue Ann narrowed her gaze in fevered calculation. "There has to be a way to save her . . . if not tonight, maybe later."

If the dinner of chicken cordon bleu and blackened tuna fillet seemed to take hours, the program afterward lasted an eternity. It reminded Alex of why she avoided these affairs as much as possible. She didn't mind the work involved in community projects, but she'd rather watch paint dry than deal with the social side. She wasn't like Sue Ann and Ellen, who seemed at home at these affairs, with or without escort. Alex had always felt like the half that Josh had taken with him glowed neon, drawing attention to the fact that she was alone. Tonight, at least, she felt whole again. Josh wasn't here in person, but he was back, filling that void so that it ached no more.

Finally, the last bad joke was told, and the emcee for the evening turned the entertainment over to a DJ. On cue, Alex and her friends headed for the ladies' room—not the one closest to the dining room, which would be filled with the after-dinner rush, but the one just off the coffee shop, now closed for the evening.

"The way I figure it, Ally, you have to get Will over by the tall hedge bordering the parking lot," Ellen said, digging into, of all things, a rhinestone-studded backpack.

"Here's the tape," Sue Ann said, dangling it from a jewel-bedecked finger.

Ellen took it and pulled a strip out. "Okay, *Ms. Phelps*," she said to Alex, "time to suit up."

Although they'd already tried out the unit at Sue Ann's home, Ellen insisted on trying it one more time outside. With the transceiver taped to her midriff beneath the empire waist of her dress, Alex spoke normally to Jan, although she had to prompt her nervous counterpart to reply louder to achieve a normal voice range.

Surprisingly, for $39.95 plus overnight shipping charges, the unit worked.

If their plan worked half as well, they'd have Will Warren exactly where they wanted him. If it didn't—

Alex didn't have a contingency plan. She closed her eyes in short prayer. *God, this has to work.*

CHAPTER TWENTY-TWO

Alex forced brightness into her voice and expression as she leaned over the Carrington table. "Will, I hate to interrupt, but could I borrow you for a few minutes? It's about Daddy." Caught the weasel off guard, Alex thought, noting the check in Will's spreading smile. "Banking business never stops, although we're trying to convince B. J. that it does," she added for Barbara's sake.

"Anything I can do to help." Will turned to his companion. "Would you mind, darling? Things have been hectic since B. J.'s unfortunate turn of health."

"Don't be silly, Will. I was married to a businessman for thirty years. I know the ropes. You go ahead. I don't need a sitter."

Will gave her hand a squeeze. "Of course not. I'm more concerned about someone sweeping you off your feet while I'm gone."

Alex watched the fiftysomething woman dissolve into a schoolgirl giggle. It was enough to curdle what little she'd eaten for dinner in her stomach. Not Barbara's reaction. That was real. It was Will's tin charm that nearly tripped Alex's gag reflex.

"Where would you like to talk, Alex?"

At the touch of Will's hand at her back, Alex stiffened. Thank goodness the wire was taped to her front. She'd almost forgotten how hands-on the man was. "It's quieter outside, if you don't mind."

Rather than let Will take the lead, Alex walked briskly out the front entrance and around to where a large hedge separated the parking lot from the tennis courts on the building's left.

"What's wrong with here?" Will asked, slowing at the edge of the parking lot.

"I'd prefer no one see us, if you don't mind." She slipped through the gate to the lawns on the other side of the hedge where the courts were located before he could answer. "It's kind of awkward," she called over her shoulder.

"Don't tell me you're afraid Josh might see us."

Oh, puh-leez. "Josh is out of town." Alex moved to one of the concrete patio tables situated between the courts and parking area. Even though the courts were closed, a pole light illuminated the area, so she felt relatively secure. For a woman wearing a wire with a known blackmailer, capable of who knew what if he was cornered. And she intended to do just that.

❧

Josh parked his Ram near B. J. Butler's Mercedes sedan in the club parking lot and rolled the electric windows up, leaving a crack for ventilation. He'd hoped to get home early enough to surprise Alex and take her to the dinner dance, but the Chesapeake Bay Bridge traffic had been bumper-to-bumper. She'd sounded so distracted when he spoke to her earlier in the day that he'd decided to come home a day early.

"Who are you fooling?" he told his grinning reflection in the rearview mirror.

He picked up the small velvet box on the seat beside him and opened it. Even in the dim light of the parking lot, the Signature diamond mounted on a band of platinum and yellow gold shone like a spotlight. This costly bauble had been burning a hole in his hide since he'd bought it two days ago.

While accompanying John to pick up the wedding rings, Josh spotted the ring in the glass display case. It was practically a dead ringer for the cheap one he'd given Alex sixteen years ago. Except that this was the real deal, not cubic zirconia and ten-carat gold inlay on sterling.

Josh couldn't wait to see her face when she saw it, although the time had to be right. He took the ring from the box and slipped it into his pocket. But who knew? That time could be tonight, if—

If the woman he was about to propose to wasn't heading behind the hedges bordering the parking lot with Will Turner in tow.

Josh blinked in disbelief, as Alex and Will had disappeared from sight. What in the name of—

The clubhouse double doors opened, drawing Josh's attention to where Ellen Brittingham and Jan Kudrow emerged and took off in a kind of Pink Panther trot in the same direction. But instead of ducking through the gate to the tennis greens, Ellen and Jan made their way between the tall hedge and the parked cars, where they stopped and busied themselves with something. He couldn't see what.

Something was definitely going on here. What, Josh had no idea. But it couldn't have anything to do with Alex and Will . . . in a romantic sense, that is. That was just plain stupid. He wouldn't even think it. Besides, no way Alex would do something like that with Britt and Tink on her heels unless she was . . .

Nothing. Josh couldn't think of a reason any of this was happening. But there was only one way to find out. He cut the internal lights of his truck cab and slid out the door. Whatever was going on, secrecy seemed to be a part of it. A juvenile tingle of excitement tripped up his spine as he moved to the line of cars parked parallel to the tall hedge. A guy had to admit, Alex and her friends were never bor—

"Come on, sugar. You may hate me now, but you will thank me later." Sue Ann Wiltbank's barroom whisper stopped Josh in his tracks as Piper Cove's Southern belle emerged from the club entrance with another woman. Like all the others, they were clad in fancy evening attire.

Josh wasn't certain who Sue Ann's companion was, but she was skeptical of accompanying her into cover of the hedges.

"I do not like spying on people, Sue Ann."

"You *need* to hear this, Barbara Jean. I cross my heart and hope to die you do."

Alex, the Bosom buddies, Will Warren, and Barbara Carrington. Talk about a mixed bag of folks. Josh hunkered down a few cars away, watching as Ellen and Jan shushed and hissed at the approach of the debating ladies. What were they doing . . . eavesdropping on Will and Alex? Did he even want to know?

No-brainer, dude. Josh tiptoed to where the four women hovered in a group over the front fender of a Volvo. Mischief spurring him on, he tapped Ellen on the back.

"Hey, what's going—"

Before Josh could figure out what was happening, he was

sprawled facedown on the white hood of the Volvo, legs spread, arm twisted behind his back, and perfumed hands clamped over his mouth, nose, and eyes with a warning chorus of hisses and shushes echoing in his ears.

"Got it?" Ellen asked, easing off her hold.

Still in shock at being so swiftly, not to mention, effectively taken out, Josh nodded. Of course, he hadn't expected his friends to turn on him. And he really couldn't defend himself without hurting them, he thought, sucking in a little pride and air as Sue Ann removed her hands from his airways.

"Not a peep," she whispered, wagging a polished nail at him in warning.

"Oh my God, what *are* you people doing?"

Barbara Carrington's strangled gasp brought Josh's attention to where she and Jan listened to a box the size of an old transistor radio. Alex's voice crackled from it.

"The statute of limitations is up on Daddy's crime, but not on what you're doing, Will Warren . . . not to mention what you've done."

❧

"I'm not aware of any crime that B. J. Butler has committed, Alex," Will declared, unruffled by Alex's accusation. "Furthermore, I can't believe that you think your daddy has done any such thing. Your father is a pillar of the community."

Alex couldn't believe it. The man would not admit to blackmailing her father. He didn't even acknowledge that B. J. had done anything criminally wrong. He insisted that this was all a product of B. J.'s imagination, blaming the heart attack for her father's state of mind.

"As for what I've done . . ." Will's mocking laugh added the heat of embarrassment to Alex's anger. "Again, I have no idea what you're talking about. Blackmail indeed," he snorted, indignant. "And I don't want to hear any more. I'm going back to the dance and to my lovely companion."

"You're not listening, Will." Alex caught his sleeve as he turned away. One way or the other, he was going to hear her out. "We also know the truth about your hunting accident. How your father paid Cal Kudrow to take the blame and do time when you were the one who'd fired the weapon and killed that other hunter. You certainly don't want that getting out, do you?" There. Her last card, such as it was, was on the table.

Except he wasn't squirming like she'd envisioned during one of her many imaginary practice runs. Instead, he stared down at Alex as if he could make her wither and disappear. "I don't know what you're talking about, Alex, but I'm beginning to think that delusion not only runs in the family, but has spilled over into your friends." His gaze narrowed with wariness. "What else did the Kudrow woman tell you?"

That stopped Alex for a second. Was there more to Will and Jan's past? She bluffed.

"Enough that we can scatter your dirty laundry about for everyone to see . . . Barbara included. How do you think she'd feel if she knew the truth about you?"

Alex caught her breath as Will grabbed her arm, a velvet warning in his voice.

"You are a desperate, pitiful soul, Alex Butler. As pitiful as your father and that trailer park trash friend of yours to suggest I'm such a villain."

Trailer park trash. Alex hated that term, even though she'd used it before befriending Jan. "You make trailer park trash look like royalty, Will." She snorted in disdain. "Talk about losers. You were a loser even as a kid. Your father had to buy you out of trouble. I wonder, if he were alive, what he'd think of your methods now? Probably that he'd wasted his money early on . . . that you still weren't worth much."

When she got home, Alex promised herself to wash out her mouth. This was so not her. But she was desperate now, and Will's smooth veneer seemed to be cracking. He grabbed her arm. "That is *not*—" His fingers bit into her flesh. "—true. My father believed in me."

Bingo. She'd struck a sore spot. And if there had been any doubt in Alex's mind that Will was a fiend, his expression abolished it once and for all. Had this been a movie, his fair features would have shriveled away, leaving the pure . . . What was that in his eyes? Anger? Hatred? Evil? All of the above?

But fiendish looks were not proof. She had to get him to talk about it. Making him angry seemed to be the best route.

"I'm sure you'd have made him proud with your stellar climb to success." She filled her voice with disdain. "Especially since it was by hook *and* crook."

Alex kept his fisted hand in the periphery of her gaze, ready to dodge it if the aroused fury turned physical. This was a side of Will Warren she'd never seen and hoped never to see again. Rather than acknowledge the cold fear pinpricking its way up her spine, she pressed on.

"Or was he the one who taught you that you didn't have to make that climb on your own merit? The big rich man forcing the little man to take the rap for daddy's not-so-fair-haired lad . . . maybe your father climbed to the top the same way."

"Shut up! That's not true, and you know it."

Alex tried to pull away from Will, but his hold on her was stronger than that of his slipping self-control. "And you're just like him. You like this, don't you? Picking on someone smaller than you. What are going to do? Hit me. Force me into silence?"

She stared at the hand bruising her arm, hoping he was not susceptible to suggestion.

Will followed her gaze, a startled look grazing his face. Then it was back. The control. The mask. He let her go.

"Wait a minute." A slow, cold, collected smile formed on his lips as he flexed the offending hand. "Now I know what you are up to."

Alex didn't answer. Her heart stopped. Did he suspect she was taping him? She stepped back as he moved toward her, but instead of grabbing her, Will crossed his arms, once again smug with confidence.

"You believe that I am blackmailing your father, and you and your friend are making up these stories to stop my alleged blackmail."

"What?" No, no, no. This was not how this was supposed to go down. Granted, they were trying to stop him, but not with lies.

"In the first place, why would I blackmail your father over a crime that can't be prosecuted? And if I were, do you really think that anyone will believe that trailer trash's lies. Both my late father and I have impeccable reputations in this community."

Will laughed, without humor.

"Delusions, Alex. All delusions. Go home. Get some sleep. The past week has been hard on all of us."

The growing gloat in Will's demeanor made Alex felt almost as sick at how reasonable he sounded.

"Now I'm going back inside to join Barbara. And I will not say a word of this to anyone because I have too much respect for your father and family to see them hurt by this lunacy you've been running on about." He gave her a parting nod, military sharp. "Good night, Alex."

Will was a monster, but a very slick one. Smarter than Alex had ever given him credit for. Certainly smarter than she'd been, she thought, as he walked away. And their recording wasn't even worth $39.95 plus shipping.

CHAPTER TWENTY-THREE

"I can't believe you four did something that stupid," Josh said as he got out of his truck in the back lot of Alex's building. It was not the first time that night he'd told Alex that, nor did she expect it to be the last.

Alex had seen Josh this mad before, and he was approaching full steam. His anger had been coming out in little spurts throughout the evening, starting with telling the buddies how lame their plan had been. As it turned out, he was right.

Barbara had simply walked off when Alex had attacked Will's father's reputation; which was just as well, considering how smoothly Will had turned their accusations back on them, making the tape more incriminating of Alex than of him. Just saying those things had sickened Alex, so she could imagine what Barbara thought of her now. What she thought of all of them. What *ever* was Sue Ann thinking when she took it in her head to insist Barbara join them?

It had been all Alex could do to walk back into the dance with head held high and see if her parents, who were only going to stay for the ceremonies anyway, were ready to leave.

And Jan had been so upset that she sent word to Scott that she wasn't well and went home with Sue Ann. Although, if there was more than Jan said to her history with Will, her friend wasn't talking, even to her best buddies.

The only thing that would have made things worse was if Josh had actually gotten past the Bosom Buddies' body blockade when he thought Will was threatening Alex. He'd been within a microsecond of vaulting over the car hood when he heard the conversation proceed in a nonviolent fashion according to Ellen, who still had his shoe in her hand when Alex joined them.

"Taking him down a second time would have been a lot harder," Ellen had admitted with a sheepish glance in his direction.

The scene might have been funny had it not been so serious. And Josh was the last one Alex had expected to see when she joined her friends.

"A blackmailer, and you meet him on an abandoned green at night to corner him into admitting his guilt," Josh said, still fuming as Alex locked her car to go into her apartment. "How dumb is that?"

Dealing with him, explaining everything, was the last thing she wanted to do, but he was not giving her a choice. "I had backup behind the hedge and Will is too much of a coward to pull anything with me." Although Will's eyes when she'd taunted him . . .

"Oh yeah, you're real tough. Look at your arm."

The first time he'd pointed it out it was an ugly rug-burn red. That was after she'd driven her parents back to their home and climbed into her own vehicle. Now it was starting to get a darker cast to it. *Good thing my maid-of-honor dress has sleeves,* she thought, exhausted.

"I mean it, Ally," Josh said, as she held up her keys to the light to make out the right one for the back door. "How could you do something like this?"

Alex shoved a likely key into the lock. It didn't fit. "Like what, Josh?" she snapped. "Like trying to save my father's reputation and family relations, not to mention Lynn's wedding?" A second key failed. Why did these keys have to look so much alike? Mental note. Color code. Although she usually didn't have this much trouble.

Josh reached into the cage of the outside lantern and got her spare. Dropping her key ring into her purse, Alex stepped aside for him to open the lock, resigned. What was one more skirmish?

"What are you doing back home anyway? I thought you guys were going to the Inner Harbor tonight in Baltimore for a big-screen sport night and seafood."

Allowing her to enter first, Josh returned the key to its not-so-secret hiding place and followed her up the back stairwell. "It wasn't to get home in time for this, I can tell you that much."

Alex spun at the top of the steps. "Okay, Josh, I get it. You think it was stupid. And frankly . . ." She passed Riley, who'd abandoned his window seat to greet them. "I don't care enough to argue right now."

"You don't *care*?"

The thunder of the last word sent Riley scampering for cover. Josh shoved his hands in his pockets and looked up at the ceiling as if something up there would keep his clenched jaw from popping out of joint. Alex felt a pang of regret, but she'd at least silenced him for a moment.

She didn't want to hurt Josh. She just wanted to be left alone to curl up in a fetal position until this was over. In the ensuing silence, Riley ventured out from under the table and rubbed against Alex's leg, his appetite overriding his anxiety. Without her usual cooing and fawning, Alex got the cat food out from under the sink and filled his dish.

"This isn't a relationship on demand, Alex."

Alex straightened. "What does that mean?"

"It means we're the same, even if things get bad. We don't keep secrets from each other. We share our burdens together."

"So that's what this is about? Not that I was at risk, but that I didn't tell you what was going on?" Alex laughed, short and without humor. "And I thought you cared."

Josh held up a stopping hand. "Oh no, you're not going to make this about me. I'm upset because I do care about you . . . obviously more than you do about me. Why didn't you come to me about B. J., Alex? Why'd you take this on yourself to handle alone . . . with your friends," he added, as she opened her mouth to refute the *alone* part of the accusation.

Alex put the cat food away and took a seat at the kitchen table. "I didn't want to upset the applecart between you and Daddy . . . between us." Alex kicked off her heels. That didn't come out right.

"You mean you didn't trust me," Josh said flatly.

Definitely didn't come out right. "Of course I trust you. I just didn't want . . ." Want to give Josh something else to hold against her father? Their history was so volatile. "I was embarrassed . . . upset . . . I wanted to protect Daddy. He . . . he was so vulnerable."

"And you thought I'd tighten the screws on him a bit more?"

Alex shook her head. "I just wanted to make it go away."

"I suppose it didn't occur to you that I might want to help you help your father?"

Darn his picture, Josh was twisting her motives so that she hardly knew them. She wasn't the villain here.

"Okay," Alex conceded. "I'm sorry. I'm sorry I didn't consult you about this whole mess. I don't know what you could do to make it better, but I'm sorry. I don't know why you'd even want to help B. J. after all he did to you . . . to *us*."

Josh slowly stiffened, as if she'd crossed some unseen line. A mask cold as stone settling on his face, he turned and walked to the top of the back stairwell. Upon reaching it, he looked over his shoulder.

"Try love, Alex."

Love. The word thrust through Alex like a blade, twisting with each retreating footstep on the stairs, then withdrew, as abrupt as the slam of the door below. Tears seeped from her eyes, stinging, then tickling as they trickled down her cheek.

Dear God, what have I done?

❧

The following morning, Alex sat in her car in the driveway of the model home where Josh had taken up temporary residence. Her entire world as she had known it had spun out of control. Will was still in control, threatening her father and the wedding. And now Josh was avoiding her. He'd come to church late that morning, sat in the back, and slipped out before she could catch up with him.

Not once during the sermon on storing treasures in heaven had he so much as glanced her way. At least so that she could catch him. And by the time she got to his house, it was locked up with a sign posted on the front door that read in his familiar scrawl, *Gone fishing.* The footnote he'd added for those who had a key to make themselves at home implied it wasn't an afternoon jaunt.

Well, isn't that just fine and dandy? she thought, blowing her nose on one of the handful of a tissues she'd snatched from the box in the foyer on the way out of the church.

God, I do not need this cold. Not now. Not on top of everything else.

The entire wedding party planned to come down a few days before the wedding. The guys were going to stay at the house with Josh, and Ashley and Chrissy planned to spend Wednesday through the wedding at the summer house.

It was going to be one freaking happy love-dizzy week. One she'd envisioned spending with Josh, looking toward the future. Not wallowing in guilt because she'd blown it again. After tossing and turning all night, battered by her failure and Josh's parting words, she'd finally admitted that he was right. If she thought that he'd add B. J.'s crime to his list of grievances against the man, then she hadn't trusted him. For better or worse couldn't possibly work when she'd held back the worst.

Alex took another tissue, this time to wipe away the tears blurring her eyes. Then she blew her nose. Where were all these body fluids coming from?

So instead of sharing her burden, she'd hidden it. Instead of leaning on Josh, accepting his loving support, she'd leaned on her friends.

Take your burdens to the Lord and leave them there.

The last line of the service's closing hymn blindsided Alex. She'd sung it with half a heart, all the while planning what she was going to say to Josh, how she was going to apologize and yet convince him that her motives had been good.

And I prayed, she argued against a rising cloud of guilt. *I prayed that my plan would . . .*

My plan.

The old eye for an eye thing went out with the New Testament.

Fight fire with fire.

How about fight fire with faith?

Alex leaned her head on the steering wheel.

God, is this You, the cold medicine, or am I praying myself in circles where I'm wrong, no matter how right I mean to be?

A nasal-sounding horn bleated behind her as Ellen pulled up on her motorcycle.

"Yo, what's up?" her friend shouted, cutting back the engine. Ellen took off her helmet, squinting in the sunlight. "Are you crying? Did you and Josh have a fight? What gives here?"

"I've got medicine that could help that horn," Alex quipped.

"Cute," Ellen shot back. "So what gives?"

Alex's smart aleck demeanor broke with her voice. "He . . . he's not here."

"He did cut out of church in a hurry." Ellen spied the note on the front door. "What'd that say?"

"G . . . gone fishing." This was ridiculous. It wasn't like she'd never see Josh again. But she needed him now.

"Weird." Something in Ellen's tone distracted Alex.

"What's weird? That Josh went fishing on Sunday afternoon?"

Ellen shrugged. "Nah, this morning was weird. When I came by to pick up one of the boys for Sunday school this morning, Josh was walking around in the front yard with one of those metal detectors like you see guys using on the beach. I hollered and asked him if he was looking for sunken treasure, but he just waved me on." She snorted. "Like he'd find something here after all the excavation that went on."

That tidbit of information fit about like everything else Alex knew. It didn't.

"He was mad at me because I didn't tell him about Will blackmailing Daddy. We had a fight."

Ellen winced. "Sorry. Wanna come over to my boat and have a cup of coffee?"

"Wonder if Sue Ann's civil yet?" A buddy gathering always helped.

"It was a late night," Ellen admitted. "We picked up three pints of ice cream on the way to Sue Ann's from the club."

Sundaes were for celebration. Ice cream by the pint was shock trauma treatment. And Alex had missed it. She'd spent the night alone. Without Josh. Without her friends. Without God, for all intents and purposes. Sure, she'd cried out to Him to fix everything . . .

"I personally think Jan was more upset than ticked that Will had called her a trailer trash liar. Something isn't kosher there if you ask me," Ellen puzzled aloud. "Of course, Sue Ann doubts Barbara will speak to any of us again. She'll be sorry, I'm afraid."

Had God been talking to her all along, just like Ellen was now? Just like the preacher had in church? Words, important ones, words that weren't really sinking in because of her distraction?

"You know, Ellen, I think I'll pass on the coffee today. But thanks . . . I mean it. I just need some quiet time to think."

Actually, it was to be still for a change and listen.

CHAPTER TWENTY-FOUR

Standing at the front door of the Butler home, ringing the bell, gave Josh an unpleasant sense of *déjà vu*. He'd come a long way from the screwup he'd been that morning B. J. had summoned him to make an offer he couldn't refuse. Okay, he could have, but he hadn't. Man, it was hard to the keep the past guilt down, even though he'd confessed it, asked for and received forgiveness.

Fran opened the door. The housekeeper's face brightened upon seeing Josh. "Well, hello sunshine. I'll bet you smelled those cookies I just took out of the oven."

He hadn't, but he did now. "Aw, Fran, you've got my tummy doing backflips." It was. No one could bake like Fran, unless it was Gran.

Fran winked. "Come on in. I was making them to take down to the summerhouse for them skinny girls," she said, referring to Lynn and the bridesmaids, "but I s'pose I can spare a few for my boy. Got some chicken soup, too; making it for Alex."

"Alex?" Josh's heart did a turnabout in his chest. He should never have walked out on her, but as angry as he was, as hurt, he'd needed time to try to see things through her eyes. "Is she okay?"

"Got herself a cold." Fran shook her head in disapproval. "I keep telling her if she burns her candle at both ends, she's gonna run out of candle sooner or later."

Josh could hear Fran saying it. "If you want, I can run it over to her when I'm through here," he offered.

Fran narrowed her gaze at him. "You sound like somebody needin' a makeup excuse."

That was another thing Fran and Amanda Turner had in common. They could read his mind and see things he didn't even know he was thinking. Thank goodness neither of them could have seen him at daybreak Sunday morning scouring the front yard for the expensive ring he'd thrown out there in a fit of anger the night before. Talk about a humbling experience.

"Might help," Josh admitted. He'd take all the help he could get. "But don't forget the cookies."

Fran burst out laughing. "Lands, boy, some things never change."

Josh found himself agreeing as he stepped into the large, marbled foyer. He remembered the coolness, the formal, subtle sense of unshakeable power B. J. liked to project and that Lenora Butler tried to soften with a giant oriental vase of flowers on a table of rich mahogany. A family antique, if Josh remembered correctly. "Is B. J. up and about yet?"

"Had breakfast and is just about dressed for work."

Josh lifted his brow in surprise. "Work?"

"You know B. J.," Lenora Butler said emerging from the hall leading to the bedrooms. "He thinks he knows better than the doctors." She motioned him farther into the house.

"Do you think he could spare me a few minutes?" Josh asked. As far as he'd come, and he still felt like a ragamuffin with his hat in his hand. But the shoe was on the other foot this time. This time Josh had something to offer the older man.

Lenora glanced at her watch, a frown grazing her forehead for just a second. "If you make it quick, I'm sure he'd be delighted."

Josh doubted that.

"He has a ten o'clock appointment," Mrs. Butler explained. "You go on into his office, and I'll tell him you're here."

"And I'll get that soup and cookies ready," Fran told him, taking her leave.

B. J. Butler's office was another example of power projection. His massive cherry desk was topped with granite gray. Matching bookshelves reached from floor to ceiling behind his desk, standing like mastiffs of knowledge that reminded Josh how paltry his formal education had been compared to that evidenced in the framed certificates hanging on the other three walls.

Josh eased into one of the smaller chairs that matched B. J.'s throne-sized leather desk chair. This wasn't sixteen years ago. This was now. They were both different. Well, at least Josh and their circumstances were different.

"What brings you here this early?"

B. J. came in behind Josh and marched straight to his desk as if ready do battle.

No sense in beating around the bush. "I know about your trouble and—"

"Alex." B. J. grimaced. "I should have known—"

"Don't use that tone about your daughter, B. J. She risked her neck to get you out of this mess."

If Josh didn't know any better, he'd have sworn B. J. blanched. Between summer fishing and his permanently red-faced disposition, it was hard to tell.

"What did she do?" B. J. sank into his chair behind the desk.

"She tried to bluff Will into backing off with his threat to expose your fraudulent loan with a little blackmail of her own."

The almost continuous bush of B. J.'s brow tilted up on one side, prompting Josh to go on.

"Will's got a past he's not too proud of either." Josh held up his hands. "That's all I'm at liberty to say except that he's one guilty SOB." He was certain Jan didn't want her family name bandied about needlessly. If she did, it was up to her to let the story out. "Alex recorded her confrontation with him with a mic taped to her ribs."

A hint of pride pulled at B. J.'s lips. "Alex did that, did she?"

Josh hoped B. J. would show a little of that to his daughter. "She loves her daddy . . . enough to fight for him."

It faded. "Is that what you came to tell me?"

"No. I came to offer to speak to John Sr. on your behalf . . . and to assure you that he's a good man. He won't let this ruin your children's marriage or the family relations."

B. J. leaned back against his chair, looking over his folded hands with suspicion.

"Why, what's in it for you?"

Our Father Who art in Heaven. Josh opened his fists and breathed deeply. How could such an unlikeable man like B. J. sire an angel like Alex?

"Because I love your daughter, and your daughter, for some godly reason, loves you. Even though you put her down at every opportunity. Even though—"

"I do not put my daughter down, boy!" B. J. slammed his fist on the desk. "I love that girl more than you ever will."

Josh struck the desk on his side, rising on two fists. "Then stop hurting her, you cantankerous old goat!"

Not to be outdone, B. J. rose as well till they stood nose to nose.

But Josh was on a roll and couldn't stop. "And stop using me to hurt her. If you have a problem with me, you come to me from now on. Because I'm going to be around, like it or not."

B. J.'s catlike smile gave Josh an uneasy pause in his rant. "Just wait till you have a beautiful, headstrong little girl, who won't march to everyone else's drum. And because she's so bullheaded, you have to be harder on her, because life will be, and you want her to be strong enough to live with her choices. You just wait till you have to let her fall, when you want to hold her and pull her out of harm's way. She'll wriggle out of your arms anyway, hollering how she can do it on her own."

"Just like her daddy."

B. J. nodded. "Just like her daddy. It's how I survived, and Alex is a survivor, too."

"You have to have a heart to survive, B. J.," Josh accused. "Where's your heart when it comes to Alex?"

B. J. thumped his chest. "Right here, boy. Right where she tosses it back every time."

Josh straightened. Just like she'd done with him Saturday night. And he'd grabbed it and run.

"And while I appreciate your offer," B. J. continued, "I don't need it. I made this mess. I'll clean it up." B. J. stiffened and adjusted the watch on his wrist, squinting. "Thank you for coming. You know your way out. I have to go."

Thank you for coming. You know your way out. I have to go.

Just like that, B. J. left.

As Josh turned to follow, Lenora Butler came into the room with a bag. "It takes a leather glove and gentle heart to enjoy the sweetness of such prickly pears," she sighed, not bothering to hide the fact that she'd overheard the end of their conversation, if not eavesdropped. "But I can tell you from experience, Josh, that they are worth it. Both Alex and her daddy."

Josh took the bag, staring at it, lost in the conversation that had just taken place, trying to make sense of it. Finally, he came to Lenora's advice. If he were honest, there was some prickly pear in everyone at one time or another.

"You tell Alex that if she needs me, I'll be right here by the phone. She needs to rest and get well for the wedding."

Josh nodded and met her gaze. Compassion, sweetness, love. They were all there along with something else. Encouragement.

He cocked his head at her, grinning. "Leather gloves, huh? Guess I'd better stock up."

❧

Alex had coughed until she was convinced that vital organs were in jeopardy. Chest aching and exhausted from the most recent bout, she stopped at the park swings to rest on her walk back to her apartment from the local drugstore. Feeling a bit like Steve Jackson, Piper Cove's late resident drunk, she took the lid off her bagged prescription cough syrup and took a sip. Couldn't tell if it was cherry or grape. More like *chrape*. Not bad, but—

"Not very good is it?"

Startled, Alex turned to see a little dark-haired girl cautiously take the swing two down from Alex. The kid must have heard Alex coughing earlier or been warned about people drinking from bottles hidden in paper bags.

"*Cowld* medicine," Alex replied, holding up the bag so that the PIPER COVE DRUG AND SUNDRIES imprint could be seen. Great, the kid had better diction than she did.

"I can't go to the playground when I have a cold." The little girl kicked off, bow-tied ponytails swinging back and forth on either side of her head as she rocked to gather momentum.

But Alex didn't answer right away. She could have sworn she'd just seen her father drive by in his Mercedes sedan. What on earth was he doing going to Clamdiggers when he'd been told to rest and diet?

"Mommy makes me stay home so I won't spread germs to everyone else."

Alex met the kid's accusing look. Diplomacy was not in her future.

"That is exactly where *I'mb* heading, as soon as I rest *upb*," Alex told her. "In the *meantimbe*, I'll try not to cough in your direction."

Was B. J. going to give Will his payoff? The very idea made Alex even sicker.

God, make it right, please. And now the hard part. *But Thy will be done.*

Alex wondered if there was any bottom to this pit she'd fallen into. She knew God was with her. With her father. But all she felt was hopelessness and misery. Of course, the cold didn't help.

And this, too, shall pass. That's what Mama said this morning when she called and informed her that Fran was making chicken soup. Alex's empty stomach quivered in anticipation. Or was it from fear of another bout of coughing?

"Need a push?"

Was this really Josh or wishful thinking? Alex turned to see the real deal standing behind her with that tummy-warming, toe-curling grin.

"Hey, be careful, she has a cold," Little Ms. Tactless warned. "I like to be pushed," she added.

The pint-sized vixen.

"What brings you here?" Alex asked.

"A little birdy told me you were sick and sent some chicken soup and cookies. They're in the truck." Josh jerked his head to where his pickup was parked in the nearby picnic area parking lot. "I was on my way to your place when I spotted you on the swings."

"Mommy doesn't give me cookies with my noodle soup."

Eat your heart out, kid, Alex said with a glance. Okay, the kid was cute, but Alex was too miserable to appreciate cute today.

"Maybe you don't eat all your soup," Josh suggested.

Bingo. Ms. Tactless focused on swinging higher.

"Need a ride home, Rudolph?" He pinched Alex's red nose.

"God sent you," Alex replied as he gave her a little shove on the swing. She just didn't feel like that last walk . . . although Josh here at the swing where they'd shared their first kiss . . .

"No, your mom and Fran sent me . . . with the soup and cookies."

Alex grinned. "And I'd thought you'd taken *upb* shaking and baking." She let him push a little more.

"Aren't you afraid you'll make her sicker?"

Where did this kid come from? Alex was almost flying, stuffy head and all. In fact, her head felt like it was flying higher than the rest of her.

"Whoa," she said, with more reluctance than she wanted Ms. Tactless to hear. "I am a little dizzy. Must be inner ear."

Josh grabbed the heavy chain links attached to the rubber seats—

long since changed from the wood planks Alex remembered—and stopped her. "I'm the only one who wants to make you dizzy." He walked in front of her and raised her out of the clingy seat.

"Be careful. Germs," their pint-sized companion reminded him.

"I don't mind . . . what's your name?" he asked her.

"Missy. It's short for Melissa."

"You know, Missy, you remind me of someone I know. Bossy, knows it all, but cute." He lifted Alex's chin. "Hey, *Missy*," he teased, "remember this same swing some . . . oh, eighteen years ago, give or take?"

Okay, so he'd pointed out that she, too, was bossy and a know-it-all. But who could hold it against those dancing, blue, blue eyes?

Alex nodded.

"What happened?" the real Missy asked.

"I kissed this pretty lady for the first time right here back then, Missy."

"Did she have a cold?"

This kid's mother had created a *germophobic*, Alex mused, swaying in Josh's gaze. Or was that the cold medicine?

"Even if she had, I was so in love with her that I would have kissed her anyway." He cut a roguish glance at the little girl, wriggling his eyebrows. "In fact, I think I have to do it again . . . cold or no cold."

"Don't say I didn't warn you," Missy told him, smug as she swung faster.

"I do have a cold, Josh," Alex admitted. "We don't need both of us sick at the wedding."

"No worries." Josh chuckled and withdrew something from his back pocket. "I have leather gloves . . . or close to them."

Alex watched, as mystified as Missy, while Josh pulled on a pair of heavy-duty rubber-palmed gardening gloves. But who could argue when he took her in his arms, and lowered his lips to hers?

This was the best medicine yet. Her battered heart and emotions went back for a second dose, so needy of this unconditional love. And it had to be unconditional love, because her lips tasted like *chrape*.

CHAPTER TWENTY-FIVE

"I ho'be you don't get this." Alex sighed when Josh released her to arm's length.

"We share, for better or worse." He pressed his forehead next to hers.

Oh rats. She had to cough. Alex covered her mouth and turned away, doing her best not to sound too gross, considering she'd just had the kiss of a lifetime. God had one perverse sense of humor.

Cough over, she leaned against Josh. Tired, so tired. And happy. Delirious. If it was the medicine, she didn't care. It was good stuff.

"I *hope* you two are married." Missy had coasted to a stop and stared at them with the full judgment of her seven or so years.

"Nope," Josh told the girl, "but we're going to work on that."

Alex perked up. "What?" Through the stuffiness in her ears, she could have sworn he was referring to the M word.

Josh glanced at Missy. "What do you think? Is the time right?"

Not sure where this was going, Missy crossed her arms around the swing chains. "I have no idea what you're talking about."

Josh coaxed Alex back into the swing seat and began to dig in his front pants pocket. To Alex's astonishment, he produced a diamond ring, the size of which caused even Missy to catch her breath.

"I *know* the place is right, so I'm at least fifty percent to the good," he said, kneeling in front of Alex. "I'm counting on God for the rest."

"Is this for *real*?" Alex couldn't think of anything else to say.

She looked at the ring, then at the bag of cough medicine, dubious. After all, Josh now knelt on his knees in the sand in front of her, holding a ring with a stone the size of candy-coated gum between the fingers of rubber gardening gloves.

"It looks real," Missy volunteered. By now, she'd abandoned her swing altogether and looked at the ring as though her future rested on it.

Josh cleared his throat. "Alexandra Butler, will you marry me . . . *again*?"

Alex couldn't answer. What she felt was too wonderful for words. Nor could she see Josh or the ring clearly through the haze in her eyes. But she could hear his soul . . . his beautiful, forgiving, loving soul. She held out her hand, baring her heart and soul to receive the ring—that endless circle of love ministers always talked about in weddings. She was going to have a wedding.

As her giddy delirium cleared, Alex made out the look of confusion on Josh's face and wriggled her ring finger. "Well, go ahead. We're not getting any younger."

"I think that's a yes," Missy said, with all the authority her four feet or so would allow.

Alex nodded. If she said what was on her heart and mind, it would come out in a babble of emotion . . . and coughing.

Josh slipped the ring on her finger. A perfect fit. Alex held it up. The sunlight caught the many facets of the emerald-cut stone, so that she nearly missed the platinum-and-gold inlay. Nearly.

She gasped. "Josh!" After wiping her eyes on her arm, she looked closer at the ring. It couldn't be, but it was. At least it looked like the ring he'd first given her years ago. She still had it in her jewelry drawer. But this was no cheap imitation. Not the way it glittered and shone. "It's *our* ring."

Alex thought Josh's delighted grin would consume him. "Well . . ." His voice had grown husky. "It cost a tad more than the first one . . . real diamond this time and platinum and yellow gold, no silver."

"And grass." Missy, who'd overcome her fear of germs, reached over and plucked a brown blade of grass from the setting.

Josh laughed and gathered Alex in his arms. "The grass is a long story. One you'll have the rest of our lives to razz me about." He looked into her eyes. "Just stay still for a minute. I want to look in those beautiful brown eyes and at that cute little red nose and remember this moment forever."

She must look a sight. She'd just pulled on a tee shirt and cutoffs to go to the drugstore, barely brushed her hair. But he thought she was beautiful.

Alex's heart was already mush, but it melted even more. "I love you, Josh."

"I love you, Ally. I always have. I always will." Josh bathed her in tender-sweet kisses that spread to her nose and eyes, her forehead . . .

Alex reveled in them, the crush of his arms around her, the feel of his perspiration damp body against hers. Nearby, Missy sighed heavily, a witness along with the stillness of time to the declarations of their hearts.

God was so good. Alex had been lower than low, and He'd sent Josh to lift her up. To share everything with her. Together they could face whatever lay in store with their love and faith.

We can do it this time, God. With You, we can handle anything.

A tug on her shirt pulled Alex from her quiet exaltation to where Missy stood.

"Can I be in the wedding?" the little girl asked boldly. "I have a very nice dress."

Alex was on the verge of asking just to whom this child belonged when a loud siren split the balmy summer silence of the cove. One of the town deputy cars raced past the park and skidded into the parking lot of Clamdiggers, red and blue lights flashing.

"Looks like something big's going on," Josh observed as a state police car followed it.

"I'll bet it's a robbery," Missy exclaimed. "Cool!"

"Oh my God," Alex exclaimed, grabbing Josh's arm. "That's Daddy's car."

"And Mr. Whitlowe is climbing out of that van," he said, taking off with her in tow. "Let's go."

By the time they reached the salt-treated ramp leading into the restaurant, Alex was clammy. The air-conditioning inside enveloped her in cool, feeling good and chilling her at the same time.

"William Warren, you are under arrest for extortion . . ."

Sheriff Matkins cuffed Will while his deputy continued reading him his rights.

". . . have the right to remain silent . . ."

B. J. sat at a table looking a little spent. Behind him, his hand on

B. J.'s shoulder, was John Whitlowe, Sr. It looked like a reassuring hand. And supervising the whole scene was Tony Richardson, their local assistant district attorney. But was Alex's former high school upperclassman friend or foe?

"Daddy, are you all right? What's happening? Tony?"

"I'm fine, Ally. Everything is just fine, right, Tony?" B. J. asked the lawyer.

Alex was more accustomed to seeing the short, stocky Tony at the club or here at the bar in shorts and a polo. In a suit, he looked so formal. But it didn't suppress his easygoing, good old boy demeanor for long.

"Fine and dandy, Alex. Your daddy just helped us get the evidence we needed"—he held up a large manila envelope—"to build our case against Will."

"But Daddy isn't in trouble, is he?" Alex held her breath. "I mean, isn't there a statute of limitations—"

Tony's warning shake of his head silenced her. "Why don't we discuss this at my office?"

Dear God, no. Feeling as though her knees were about to give way, Alex preempted them, sidling into a chair across from her father. Behind her, Josh squeezed her shoulders. Just his presence kept her heart from skittering out of her chest in panic.

"It's all just fine, girl," B. J. said, reaching across the table and covering her hand with his. "You should have trusted your daddy to take care of his own—" Her father removed his hand, narrowing his gaze on the large diamond glittering on Alex's hand. "What's this mean?"

"It means," Josh said in a steely voice behind her, "that I asked Alex to marry me, and she said yes."

Alex closed her eyes wearily. *God give me strength—*

B. J. harrumphed. "Thought so." Nothing. No barbed words. Nothing else.

Her eyes flew open to see her father locked, gaze to gaze with Josh. But she'd had enough. She—she and Josh—would not, could not go through this again.

"I said yes, Daddy. And I do not need your blessing, nor will I tolerate your interference."

"Now why doesn't that surprise me?" B. J. said, his hawklike attention still fixed beyond her at Josh.

If Alex didn't know any better, she'd have sworn there was a smile trying to pull at the fixed line of his mouth, driven by an elusive twinkle in his dark brown gaze. There was definitely something else going on here.

"You see what you're getting yourself into, boy?"

"Indeed I do, sir."

As stiff as Josh's reply was, Alex knew him well enough to catch that shade of amusement in his voice.

B. J.'s gaze narrowed. "You know, after our little chat this morning, I think you just might."

Suddenly, he laughed. Big and boisterous as only her father could when his funny bone had really been tickled. He turned to John Whitlowe. Alex had nearly forgotten Lynn's future father-in-law in this bizarre tug-of-war between the two men she loved more than life.

"John, you'd best count your lucky stars that your boy got the sweet one, 'cause this one here is going to have his hands full with *my*—"

Alex couldn't believe how much pride her father packed into those two little letters.

"—Ally. She's her *daddy's girl.*"

Or how much love came through in the latter. Daddy's girl. Her. Alex. Not Lynn. Not in the way her father meant it today. It was more than bone of my bone, or flesh of my flesh. This was spirit of my spirit.

You are your father's child.

The echo of mother's words, doled out to Alex so many times, some in frustration and others in affection, didn't stick like a barb in Alex's ribs as they had in the past. This time, they pumped her full of the love and pride she'd longed for for so long. And it all came bundled in two little words from her father's heart. *Daddy's girl.*

Alex unclenched hands that had been fisted for a fight, opening them to receive this totally unexpected blessing.

"Come here, daddy's girl." Josh knelt beside her, sharing her elation, shouting it out in silence with his little hugs.

Joy flooded Alex's being as she basked in the love of the two most important men in her life. And as she did so, her dancing soul raised her elation in grateful song to that faithful, patient, forgiving One Who loved her even more.

EPILOGUE

❧

Considering what Alex and her family had been through, the wedding of the summer itself was all downhill. Lynn was beautiful in her designer gown. Although the styles of the dresses were different, Alex thought that her baby sister could well have been the youthful, golden-haired, blue-eyed Lenora in the thirty-nine-year-old wedding picture in the Butler living room curio case. Her baby sister walked on clouds of love as she mingled with the guests in the club dining room.

But she wasn't the only one. Alex floated on Josh's arm as he wheeled her around the dance floor with more finesse that she ever dreamed he'd have. Not only had Josh's soul come a long way, his feet had as well. Gone were the days of slow dances only, where even then it was a matter of hugging and rocking from one foot to the other. This guy had had lessons, the result of making the videos in his White Lightning days.

God, you are so good, she thought for the umpteenth time that day as he walked her over to the table assigned to the Bosom Buddies and Aunt Rose, who was showing off a picture of her and her prizewinning catch from the White Marlin Open.

"By golly, I love a man in a tux," Aunt Rose said, putting the framed photo down as Alex took a seat next to Sue Ann. "How about taking this old lady for a spin?" she asked Josh.

"I'd be delighted. But take it easy on me," he teased, as Rose tweaked his cummerbund. "Any woman who can wrestle in a five-hundred-pound blue marlin can take me any day."

Two hours into the reception, Rose was feeling no pain from the pumps she'd been complaining about on arrival. Not the way she boogied out to the dance floor.

"Let me see that ring again," Sue Ann demanded, snatching up Alex's left hand.

"Heck, I could see it from across the room." Ellen put her second helping of wedding cake on the table and took a seat. "I thought that crystal ball thing overhead had fallen and landed on Alex's hand." She sat down, not bothering to straighten the wrinkled dress that her mother had bought her just for *their Lynny's* wedding. Which was why it was wrinkled. That and the way she'd wadded it under her while riding her bike to the country club. Taffeta and Ellen did not mix well.

"It's the most beautiful thing I've ever seen." Jan sighed, in full Cinderella mode. Although the ragged, flowing skirt of her pink dress combined with her short, impish haircut made her look more like Tinkerbell. "I just love happy endings."

And it was a happy ending. For Alex and for B. J. ADA Tony Richardson had explained in his office after Will's arrest that Maryland law did allow for B. J. to be prosecuted, but the state had granted B. J. immunity for his cooperation in helping build its case against

Will. The criminality of B. J.'s conduct was dubious at best, since the signature on the loan that had been in Steve Jackson's name was really Steve Jackson's. B. J. had brought Jackson into a silent partnership on the Waterview Estates project. In exchange for his taking out the loan, Steve received his home, a trailer on a wooded lot. It had been the only home the alcoholic had ever owned.

Steve's family had been among the first to call and offer B. J. their support when the news hit the *Piper Cove Sentinel* the next day. And John Whitlowe, Sr., who'd taken over at the bank after B. J. officially resigned, had been inundated with phone call after phone call and letter after letter from local citizens who told how much they owed B. J. Butler for his role as bank president and a leader in the community.

In fact, the Rotary was putting together a retirement party for her father. It was the first time that Alex had ever seen her father cry—when Ellen told the family about it at the rehearsal dinner last night. For all their help in pulling the wedding off, it was only natural for Lenora to include Alex's friends in the wedding party. Ellen had told B. J. not to get too comfy in retirement, because a little bird had told her that he was going to have a new job soon.

While B. J. didn't know it yet, the county businessmen were setting up a free consultation service for new business owners and wanted B. J. to run it. It was the answer to the family's prayers as to what to do with Alex's driven father. Mama would be ecstatic.

Alex sought out Lenora Butler. Ever the gracious hostess, she was making her rounds, making it a point to speak to everyone, encouraging them to eat plenty and take pictures with the complimentary cameras, and showing them the best of her genteel hospitality. It was ironic how in her family's trial, she'd forgotten her own. Grown even stronger. Maybe the doctor had been right about her fear of no longer being needed. Alex couldn't imagine why Mama thought that, but she'd certainly come out swinging for B. J.

Suspicious that her husband was trying to protect her from something, she'd finagled it out of B. J. what was going on and started the wheels of justice moving. Lenora invited the DA to the house for tea and, as the daughter of a judge, served Will's blackmail case to him on a platter. And Alex had nearly ruined the setup.

God and Mama truly worked in mysterious ways, she thought.

"Okay, folks," the DJ announced, as the current song ended. "It's time for the bride to toss the bouquet, so all you single ladies, step out onto the floor."

"Yeah," Ellen snorted. "Right." She focused on licking the icing off her fingers.

Jan shot to her feet. "Come on, Ellen. We're not getting any younger."

"I'm happy. Take her." Ellen pointed to Alex.

Horror claimed Jan's face. "No way. That ring disqualifies her."

"I hope so," Josh said as he escorted Rose to her seat. He walked around, pulled Alex from her chair and into his lap as he sat down. "I'm not taking any risks," he said, tightening his arms around her.

"C'mon, Ellen," Jan pleaded.

"Ellen, your mother's going to come over there if you don't get your tush out on that dance floor," Bea Brittingham called from a nearby table.

"Aw, Ma. Oy!" Ellen smacked her forehead with her fist and moved, feet dragging onto the dance floor and far to the rear of the gathering singles.

"Don't be a *meshugeneh*," her mother chided. "Move up."

"Look who's calling *me* the crazy lady," Ellen shot back, taking two baby steps forward.

Alex watched, so happy she was drunk with it, as Lynn waited for the countdown while two dozen or so women, including Aunt Rose, watched her throwing arm. At the count of three, Lynn tossed the bouquet—lovingly made of white lilies by Ellen's mother—over the heads of the clamoring wannabe brides for a direct landing at Ellen's feet. Between them actually, since she'd been standing as if ready to block a soccer ball. The flowers were incontrovertibly Ellen's. Not even Jan was going to stoop to yanking them out from between her low-heeled slippers.

But Ellen's mom had no problem fetching them and handing them to her stunned daughter. "A *mitzvah* to be sure."

Ellen looked like catching the bouquet was anything but a blessing as Tony Richardson, who'd caught the garter, danced toward her, swirling it around his finger to the stripper music.

"Man,"—Josh laughed—"Brit will never live this down."

"Wow, you got legs, Brit," Tony teased, more himself than the lawyer who'd explained the ins and outs of B. J.'s case to Alex earlier that week. He slipped the garter over Ellen's ankle and danced it upward.

Ellen leaned forward, arms crossed. "Go any farther, and your bike will never run the same again," she said in a stage whisper.

"Life is so unfair," Jan complained at Alex's side.

Tony took the hint.

"Have you two lovebirds got a minute? We need to have a little family meeting," Lenora Butler whispered.

Alex looked up into her mother's face, zeroing in on that *I know something you don't* smile and tone.

≈

Bewildered, Josh accompanied Alex out onto the patio, where wedding pictures had been taken earlier. He'd been sweating before from keeping up with Rose Butler McMann, but the sight of John, Lynn, and B. J. waiting in the fan-cooled shade of the gazebo kicked up his inner thermostat even more.

"Feel like a mushroom?" Alex whispered under her breath.

"Totally in the dark," he replied. One with a big shoe poised over his head, ready to squash him.

Although John and Lynn wouldn't be part of anything bad, reason reminded him. Old habits or expectations were hard to kick, even though B. J. had been on good behavior. He still called Josh *boy,* but the venom of the past was no longer there.

Lynn, her golden tan set off by the white of her dress, picked up champagne glasses and handed them to Josh and Alex before taking one up for herself. "John and I feel so bad that we've robbed you two of the attention your engagement deserves—"

"And we're grateful," Josh said, lifting his glass of sparkling water. "We like small and cozy." And cool, he thought, putting his arm around Alex. As in khakis and a loose cotton shirt.

They'd already talked about a small tropical wedding, immediate family only. Or maybe Ireland. Alex had always dreamed of going there and meeting her distant Butler relatives. Josh didn't care if it was Timbuktu, as long as it was with his auburn-haired lady in red. Sangria, he remembered from an earlier conversation prior to the wedding that morning.

"Still," John spoke up, drawing Josh in from his admiration. "I want to toast the engagement of my best friend, soon to become my brother-in—" John wrestled with the branches of the growing family tree. "In-in-law?"

Josh chuckled, raising his glass. "That'll do."

"You've come a long way, boy," B. J. said, joining in the toast.

"*Finally.*" Lenora added her glass to the sweet ringing chorus of the lead-crystal flutes. "I've waited so long for this."

Josh's throat was so tight with emotion, it took two attempts to swallow his sip of the bubbly water. He hoped Alex had some of those supersized tissues left, because he thought it might partly be due to the sore throat he'd awakened with that morning. He'd had to smile at himself in the mirror. That was just the way he wanted it to be—sharing everything, good, bad, or ugly.

"I . . . I don't think I could bear any more happiness than I'm feeling right now," Alex sniffled beside him. Her problem wasn't a cold. She was better by midweek. It was heart, beautiful and magnified by the tears glazing her eyes.

"I wouldn't go that far, dear," Lenora cautioned. But her blue eyes belied her words with mischief.

Josh really loved Lenora. If he'd had his druthers, she was the kind of mother he'd have wished for as a kid. Pretty, elegant, and filled to overflowing with love and compassion.

"B. J.?"

At the lady's prompt, B. J. coughed behind his hand gruffly. "I've made two mistakes in my life."

Lenora rolled her eyes.

"Maybe more," he amended with a wink that deepened the color of his wife's face. "Some I could fix. Some I couldn't. But this one, I can." He withdrew a large, unsealed envelope from his tuxedo jacket pocket and handed it to Alex. "Go on, open it."

Josh gave Alex a reassuring hug at her furtive glance. "You do the honors."

With nervous fingers, she removed a blue-covered document marked DEED.

Josh's heart stumbled in his chest. He knew instinctively what was in that deed, but he couldn't quite believe it. Even when Alex gasped in astonishment and showed him the address of his grandmother's home and their names listed as owners, he had trouble grasping that it was real.

"Oh, Daddy!" Alex gushed. Then she caught herself and glanced at Lynn. "But—"

Lynn pulled a similar document out of her new husband's jacket. "I have one, too. It's a condo, just like I always wanted . . . on the oceanfront. There's three bedrooms and everything is new. I just love it. Although we loved what you did with the Turner place, too," she said hastily. Her face fell.

"But it wasn't you," Alex assured her. "I knew it."

"And I figure I can keep my boat at your place on the river," John said to Josh as though it were a given.

It was. Josh nodded, but he couldn't take his eyes from B. J., who watched him like a dog did a choice cut of steak . . . with delighted anticipation.

"I hope you'll forgive me for snatchin' the place away from you, boy. And you, Alex, for makin' you fix it up." He shook his head. "I know I'm a mite insensitive when it comes to business, but—"

"We love you anyway," Alex said, rushing up to her father and wrapping her arms around him.

Josh held back. Lord, this was going to take time. But when Alex let her father go, Josh offered his hand, hoping he hid the fact that he wrestled with feeling grateful to B. J. Butler. "Thank you, sir. I appreciate it more than you can know." He really did, but this whole scenario with B. J. felt straight from the Twilight Zone.

"That's what family is all about, boy," B. J. told him. "Helping one another out. But you already know that."

Boy. Josh never thought he'd hear that used as a term of endearment, but it sure sounded like one. The squeeze of B. J.'s hand backed it up. Josh was in. And his offer of help had not been dismissed without a second thought.

When Josh had left B. J. after offering to speak to John Sr., he'd had his doubts that the Golden Rule would really work on B. J. Butler. Guess it was all about timing.

"And you're gonna need a lot of help with Ally here. Don't know where she gets that stubborn, independent streak."

"Daddy," Alex chided halfheartedly.

"I do wonder." Lenora's elbow jabbed her husband, exacting a grunt of surprise. "Now, we'd best get back to our guests. It wouldn't do to be gone too long." She hooked arms with B. J.'s. "Come along, now." She gave Josh a motherly pinch on the cheek as she passed him. "You two needn't hurry."

Thy will be done, Lord, Josh thought, bemused as he shook John's hand and gave the bride a kiss. *And better late than never.*

As the others strolled away, Josh caught Alex's hand and tugged her into his arms.

Except this wasn't late, he realized, basking in the glow of happiness in her eyes. God was never late. He was always there, ready to back his children up, ready to help at the call of His name. Even when the child had done something really stupid, like throw a high-priced engagement ring out in the yard in a fit of anger and lose it. God had let him stew a good two hours the following Sunday morning before that metal detector finally did its thing and Josh rushed to church, late and totally humbled.

"Our home," Alex said dreamily, tucking the deed to his grandmother's farm in his inside jacket pocket. "I'm glad I kept the décor with the original period."

Josh didn't care if she painted it purple with orange polka dots. He wanted to sweep his gorgeous designer off her feet and carry her there, right now. But the time wasn't right. And this time around, he wanted to do everything according to God's clock. For now, Josh was content to praise His holy name that there were no more *no-kissing* zones.

Dear Reader Friends,

Piper Cove is a place dear to my heart. I was born and raised in the area where I set this fictitious town. It is a mix of the small communities that have grown as a result of Ocean City, Maryland's popular barrier island resort and is populated by down-to-earth people who have, in their lifetimes, seen the area slowly change from farming and fishing lifestyles to hotels, country clubs, and retirement developments. (For a fascinating read of this hardy lot's history to present, try *City on the Sand* by Mary Corddry.)

This is not a social/political commentary on change. Life is change. Rather, it is a look at the resilient characters who sway and grow in its winds.

And what characters! I know Alex, Ellen, Jan, Sue Ann, and the townspeople. I grew up with them. They are composites of myself, friends, family, and acquaintances—flawed, funny, faithful, and sometimes, faith-challenged. For extra spice, I've added a dash of intrigue to the hometown mix of love, trial, and triumph.

Because this is an ensemble cast, all four friends are there through it all, as one of them finds or re-discovers love. All will change as a result. With regard to the spiritual journey, you will see that Jan and Sue Ann have a little farther to go than the others. Rest assured, love—both romantic and heavenly—will have its totally unexpected way with them.

In *Wedding Bell Blues,* control-freak Alex learns lessons of forgiveness, trust, and most of all, letting go and letting God. Okay, there's a lot of me in Alex. I have a phobia of crabs, and God and I have issues regarding His timing and clarifying His plans. But He's working on me . . . with a big hammer.☺

So here and now I give Him praise and glory for His patience, mercy and sense of humor. And for enabling me to do the impossible—finishing this book in the wake of my husband's death. Jim was my earthly rock and encourager. Like a wounded bird, I foundered, emotions raw, but God caught me and, with my astute and understanding editors, carried me through until the project was finished. Little did I know that, not only was the novel a work in progress, but so was the author. Unlike *Wedding Bell Blues,* I *still*

am a WIP, having grown a little stronger and wiser on this journey
called life.

May you laugh, love, and be blessed with the first story of my bosom buddies,

Linda Windsor

A merry heart doeth good like a medicine.
PROVERBS 17:22

Discussion Questions

1. There is a saying, "Make new friends, but keep the old. One is silver and the other gold." How is that played out in this book? Do you find it a stretch that four women from different social backgrounds and at different places in their faith journeys are still best friends?

2. Do you think Alex and Ellen handle their faith differences with Sue Ann and Jan well? Would you like these four women for friends? Do you have any friends like them?

3. How is Alex conflicted by Josh's return? Could you forgive and trust someone who'd abandoned you and returned years later, claiming to be different? How willing would you be to give him a second chance?

4. Can you sympathize with Josh's reasons for leaving? Do you believe that he really loved Alex? How might things have been

different, had God been part of the equation when they were first married?

5. How has Alex changed since Josh's departure years ago? How has Josh? What conflicts do they continually run into? Will that ever change?

6. How are Sue Ann, Jan, and Ellen's perspectives about love and/or finding the right man different or similar?

7. Lenora Butler changes from a depressed mother to one ready to fight for her family. What do you think prompts this change? Aside from chemical, or biological factors, what might have been at the root of Lenora's depression?

8. How would you describe B.J.'s relationship with Alex? Do you know people like B.J. Butler?

9. Alex is torn between wanting the approval and love of both her father and Josh. Is this so atypical in inter-family relationships? Do you think that honoring one's mother and father is in conflict with leaving one's parents behind to become one in marriage? What gives you hope that this conflict might not be so divisive this time for Alex and Josh?

10. At what pivotal point does Alex realize she loves and forgives Josh? What lessons does Alex learn regarding her faith throughout the book? What struggles does Josh have with his? Do you feel that these faith trials will affect the future of their marriage? How?

Turn the page for an exciting preview of

FOR PETE'S SAKE

The next book in The Piper Cove Chronicles
by Linda Windsor
Coming Soon from Avon Inspire

What a car! A 2007 atomic orange metallic Corvette swept past Ellen Brittingham's motorcycle as though in flight. It was the four-wheeled American eagle of the road, in a class all its own. Her pulse, already thrumming as she rode in the saddle of her new Harley Davidson, shot into an even higher gear. Ellen had been watching its approach in the rearview mirror as she rode past green pastures that morphed into woods, a crossroads occupied by a food and gas mini-market, or produce stand. It was just a dot of orange moving up through a herd of beach-bound cars and SUVs.

Revving up the speed of her Hog, she flipped on her blinker and swerved onto the passing lane in the sport car's wake. Talk about the perfect end to a perfect week.

The Lower Shore LOBs, Ladies on Bikes, had planned a rendezvous in St. Michaels on the Tred Avon River. A perfect opportunity to test her new bike—her first *new* bike. The gang, made up of women from all walks of life, had a blast taking day trips from St. Michael's to the farthest reaches of the Delmarva Peninsula. They'd been north to Lewis, Delaware, east to Delaware's and Maryland's beach resorts, and then south to the Chesapeake Bay Bridge-Tunnel in Cape Charles, Virginia. It never ceased to amaze Ellen how much the Eastern Shore's quaint bay and riverside towns, as well as its contrasting oceanfront resorts, had to offer—and how much locals, including her, took them for granted.

And Sheba, the name Ellen dubbed the new bike because it made her feel like a queen, had done her proud. She'd roared like a lioness or purred like a cub all the way. Not once had Ellen had to break out the tool kit she kept in the left storage bag. But then, for what she'd paid for the Harley, she hadn't expected to. It simply was wise to be prepared.

Watching the sleek Corvette swoop around an SUV like it was standing still, Ellen accelerated to close the distance between them and get a better look. She'd read in one of her mechanics magazines that the GM 'Vette had a new color and she liked it, even if some fans wrote in that resembled a mix of mustard and ketchup on a burger bun. With that metallic finish, it looked good to Ellen; from the front in her rearview mirror, the side as it passed her, and the back, as she now followed it. She'd go at least as far as Route 90 with the kid and then head for Piper Cove and home.

That is, she assumed it was a kid who'd barreled by her. Probably a college grad in his new graduation present. Or even a high school grad. Some families could swing that kind of gift. Not that she begrudged them or the fact that hers couldn't. No 'Vette in the world could give her the pleasure that she'd experienced helping her dad rebuild his classic 1967 Camaro. There were a lot of things in life that mattered more than money. Family. Faith.

Of course, money helped. And thankfully, her career as a landscape architect was lucrative enough to satisfy her meager needs and some of her wants.

With a grin as wide as her handlebar, she leaned into the wind and accelerated before her exit loomed too close. Just for one more look. Sheba came to life beneath her, growling and clawing the road as if eager to show this four-wheeled eagle what its two-wheeled counterpart could do.

A fleeting scent of the gas swooshing in Sheba's belly teased Ellen's nostrils before it was lost in the wind. Most gals got all woozy over megabuck-an-ounce perfumes, but this scent of power had tripped Ellen's trigger since she drove her first tractor at age nine. Sheba shot up beside the 'Vette. Ellen savored its sleek lines and made out a profile through the tinted windows. To her surprise, it was a mature, square-jawed one with a dimpled chin . . . that turned toward her.

Shades of 007, he was checking her out! Sheba slightly wobbled, but it betrayed Ellen's in-process shock. An embarrassed, teeth-grating smile locked on her lips, she did what she'd been taught to do since a kid. She nodded a neighborly hello and gave Sheba the gas. It wasn't flirting, she told herself, but just in case the guy thought she was, the best thing to do was to exit, blushing from bone to the leather of her vest. And if he'd been checking out Sheba . . . well, he could check out her dust.

～

"Go on, little Sheba," Adrian Sinclair chided, reading the custom tags on the back of the pearl-glow black-and-red Harley streaking ahead of him. "You might think you can run, but you can't outrun me," he murmured behind the wheel of his Z07 'Vette.

Although he had no intention of actually catching the female biker. The image of badly colored and coiffed hair, tattoos, cigarette-breath, and a voice that could grate old cheese hardly appealed to him. Passing the chrome-bedecked Harley Davidson served him just fine. It was a matter of power vs. power, nothing else. And the five hundred and five horses under his hood were as anxious to break out as his own frustrated spirit.

At least *they* could.

"In one mile, turn right onto Route 90 East to Ocean Pines," his OnStar lady told him in a pleasant, yet indifferent voice.

One mile in which to show Sheba she'd bitten off more than she could chew. He gunned the engine and shifted gears. That was definitely doable. He might even make it to the closing for his new property a few minutes early.

In a matter of seconds, Adrian caught up with the motorcycle. Once again, he couldn't help but admire the way the lady moved as one with the bike, dipping and swaying in those tight jeans as if she was glued to the seat. Sheba and her rider definitely showed a poetry in motion that a man behind a steering wheel couldn't.

Adrian wondered who the second helmet strapped on the back of the bike belonged to. A husband or boyfriend? Not likely, he decided. It matched Sheba's accessories. Would a rough-riding Harley man name his bike Sheba?

Perhaps.

"In one half mile, turn right onto Route 90 East to Ocean Pines."

Adrian grimaced, shifted, accelerated, and shot past the lady on the bike. She looked over, just as he expected. But instead of consternation on her mouth—he couldn't see her face behind her goggles—he saw a smile. Not flirtatious, but one that complemented a gracious, gloved salute of admiration.

Classy lady. A twinge of guilt pinged him for stereotyping her. He had little use for people who did that sort of thing. He subscribed that it was *who* they were, not *what* they were. But there it was.

"Turn right onto Route 90 to Ocean Pines."

"All right then," Adrian replied in annoyance.

Downshifting and slowing down, he entered the curve of the exit. A glance in the rearview mirror showed the Harley lady right behind him. Not riding his bumper, but keeping a practical distance.

Although he had no interest beyond curiosity, Adrian couldn't help but wonder both who and what Sheba was. Gracious, he knew. Adventurous. She had to be to ride a Harley. Slender, almost boyish in shape. The key word being *almost*. The wind plastering her tank top and inflating her vest revealed modest curves in the right places.

Not at all like Selena. The tall, dark, and curvaceous software marketing rep of Sinclair Group was more like the bike. An exotic tigress, built for comfort *and* speed, with an ambition that left other women in the dust. Maybe that was why she and Adrian had clicked. They were two of a kind, would settle for nothing less than winning.

Selena was the total opposite of his son's mother. Carol had complemented Adrian's ambitious personality, with her artistic nature and serene sense of who she was. And when Peter came along, she'd adapted to motherhood as if born to it, while Adrian had never quite been able to make his son the center of his priorities. Especially since Carol had sacrificed her life to give Peter his. If she'd only allowed the doctors to treat the cancer they'd diagnosed and terminated her pregnancy, things might be different today.

The decision had been cut-and-dry to Adrian. There would be other babies, but no other Carol. Yet she would not hear of doing anything that would endanger the life growing within her. And on her deathbed a year later, she'd made Adrian promise to make Peter his first and foremost priority.

The promise was easier made than kept. Of course, Adrian allocated time for the boy and saw that his nearly eleven-year-old was well provided and cared for by a nanny after Carol's death. Adrian's fingers tightened on the wheel. Had it been six years? Despite having gone on with his life, thinking about Carol still stirred a raw place in his heart that perhaps would never heal.

"Turn left in one mile at the Piper Cove Road exit."

"At your command, madame."

Adrian took the exit and stared ahead at a shoulderless county road that cut through farmland, where corn, dried yellow in the late August sun, contrasted with the green of pasture where black and white cattle grazed lazily. A farmer driving a tractor just ahead waved as Adrian cautiously eased the 'Vette around him.

Selena had chosen well. This remote setting would be a refreshing change for all of them. After a long visit to Adrian's family home in Cape Cod, it was painfully obvious that Adrian hardly knew his son, his likes and dislikes.

"Spending two evenings a week over dinner isn't exactly bonding," his mother had told Adrian. "You need to spend more leisure time with the lad, son." Thirty-eight years of marriage to Boston old money had never eradicated his Scottish mum's accent. With eighteen years of schooling at her family alma mater in Edinburgh, a bit of it still lingered with Adrian when he was animated, but no more. An offsetting twenty years of travel abroad and in the good old USA had neutralized the Edinburgh effect.

Adrian slowed again as he approached a large, rust-infested pickup loaded with debris from a construction site, toddling at its own pace around a bend in the road ahead. Glancing in the rearview mirror, he spotted Sheba in the distance still trailing him. He downshifted to make the sharp bend, the view of the road ahead now blocked by thick cornfields. As he maneuvered the curve, the 'Vette rumbled over something high enough to bang Adrian's teeth together. It scraped the bottom of the car and dragged for a few feet before the vehicle shook it off.

A post of some kind . . . or a piece of a post. Must have fallen off the truck—

Adrian broke off his train of thought, resisting watching to see how the Harley made out. Ahead, the road sharply curved in the other direction. He shifted again and hit the brake to slow down. To his horror the pedal went straight to the floor.

And he was headed toward a swaying wall of corn. No way he could make that sharp turn without flipping and—

The 'Vette shot off the road like a bullet, cornstalks passing Adrian in a blur and unmercifully whipping the deluxe atomic orange metallic finish.

"No, no, no!" he shouted, flinching from left and right, pounding the useless brake pedal with his foot as the field swallowed the car whole.

Adrian had no idea how far he'd gone before the raised rows and soft soil brought the car to a stop. Dust and field debris littered the windshield and expansive hood. Behind him, clouds of it rolled in his flattened wake.

Glancing at his gold Rolex, Adrian groaned. Two-forty-five. The settlement was at three P.M. Of all the fine fixes he'd found himself in—and some had been stellar—this one was his fault. He'd been going entirely too fast on an unfamiliar road that would have broken a snake's back.

"Continue on your current route," the feminine voice, totally unruffled, advised over the Bose sound system.

Adrian struck the wheel with both hands, then promptly shut her up before she had him running over cows as well. Exhaling heavily, he slipped a cell phone from his waist and flipped it open. Since he hadn't entered the Realtor's number, Adrian took the man's card from the visor and punched it in.

The roar of an engine behind him drew his attention to the side mirrors.

Sheba. Adrian hit the "Store" button and closed the phone, watching as the young woman hastily dismounted the Harley, kicked down the stand, and struggled for a moment to find a spot in the field firm enough to support the big bike. Once satisfied that it was stable, she started toward the 'Vette with long-booted strides and pulled off her helmet.

Dark hair, long and subdued in a braid. An oval face. All business approach, knocking aside cornstalks like gnats. Tucking the helmet under her arm, she tapped on the window. The engine stalled, and Adrian opened the car door.

"You okay in there?" she asked in an accent that took Adrian a moment to place. A surprising cross between Brooklyn and Southern.

"I've been in better spots." He climbed out of the cockpit, no easy task for his six-foot-plus frame. "A blasted time for my brakes to go out. Late for an appointment," he explained, straightening with a grunt.

Sheba lowered her sunglasses, taking him in from tip to toe and back, with a curious gaze, not quite green, but not brown either. Hazel was the color. Warm, full of depth . . . and direct. "Wow, there's almost as much of you as there is car," she observed with a snicker.

Actually it was a snort, a dainty one that embarrassed her, because she hastily covered her mouth and nose. Color crept to her tanned face, darkening it even more.

"I could say there's more bike than there is woman in your case."

Wrong thing to say. The friendly gaze sharpened. "I can handle *my* ride." *Unlike some people* went unsaid, but Adrian got the message loud and clear.

"I lost my brakes on the curve."

"Yeah, I saw you hit and drag that chunk four-by-four." She winced as though she'd felt the impact. When she looked at him again, the warmth was back, along with a hint of amusement, as though she sensed his embarrassment. "I figured right then the brake line was gone."

Made sense. Not that Adrian was mechanical. He paid someone to keep his vehicles in prime shape. "Yes, well in that case, I'd better cancel that appointment and then call OnStar to send help." He flipped open his cell phone.

"Where are you headed?"

"A real estate settlement at my new river estate in a few minutes. At the least, I'll be late."

"Where?" Sheba asked. "I live on the river nearby."

Disconcerted, Adrian glanced at the Corvette. "The address is programmed into the navigation system. The land belonged to the Addisons."

"Hey, that's right up the creek from me. Ellen Brittingham, your friendly neighborhood landscape artist and next-door neighbor," she said, extending her hand for a handshake.

Like everything else about Sheba, it was firm, self-assured. Landscape artist. That accounted for the crinkling tan lines around her expressive eyes. Brackets made by laughter in the sun.

"Adrian MacAlister Sinclair, security software analyst at your service, Ellen Brittingham." Although he had no clue why, he clicked his heels together. But then, conversing with a tall, lean, Harley-riding, girl-next-door-pretty female in a dusty cornfield was surreal in itself.

"Sheesh. You sound like a spy. Of course, you've got the car . . . American model, that is."

She gave the Corvette a look of longing that would make a man jealous. At the least, it would make his throat go dry. Suddenly those delightful eyes shifted back to him. One naturally sculpted eyebrow arched at him in challenge.

"Up to the ride of your life?"

Adrian dismissed his first thought before he made a fool of himself. There was no double entendre in her remark. She meant what she said and she meant the shiny black-and-red motorcycle awaiting her like a loyal steed.

"I'll deliver you to your appointment on time, and while you're signing your future away to a mortgage company"—she hesitated, shooting another glance at the car—"or maybe not, I'll call our local towing company for you and take care of your baby."

"My baby?" The endearment threw Adrian off for a split second. "Ah yes, my *baby*," he said, falling in behind her as she turned and headed for the Harley, as though his answer was a foregone conclusion. "I shall be forever grateful," he said nonetheless.

"You bet you will." She took off the spare helmet and handed it over to him. "And I intend to collect."

Once again Adrian mentally staggered. "Oh?" He admired the lady for her style, but she was definitely not his type. Far from it. Yet there was a deep part of him that had quickened with a mingle of intrigue and excitement from the moment the game of road tag started.

"I expect a neighborly ride in that 'Vette sometime." She climbed on the bike and looked over her shoulder. "And if you let me drive it, even if it's just for a few miles, I'll owe you forever."

Idiot. Adrian donned the helmet and got on the Harley behind Ellen's lean, lithe form. The woman wasn't hot for him. She was hot for his car.

Ellen fired up the engine and revved it. As she engineered a wide, unwieldy turn with one long, denim-clad leg extended inside as a precaution, Adrian looked for a place to hold on. A handle or something.

He was accustomed to driving some of the world's finest sports cars and was an accomplished equestrian, but motorcycles had never caught his fancy.

"You better hold on," Ellen called over her shoulder. Her white spread of a smile added, *tightly.*

Adrian complied, shoving aside disconcerting thoughts and reactions for the sake of safety. There wasn't a lot to the cycle nymph. He could nearly circle her waist twice with his arms. But seated in the low leather saddle of the giant Harley, she was as much a part of the machine as its chrome-adorned chassis, the brain to its brawn. He likened the experience to holding on to a wildcat, one that was part flesh, part steel, all spunk.

And as the Harley shot forward, bouncing across and clawing into the horizontal mounds of dirt that had eventually stopped his Corvette, Adrian held on for dear life . . . *tightly*.

Maybe he should have called OnStar and postponed the settlement.

Linda Windsor

LINDA WINDSOR, a native of Maryland's
Eastern Shore, is the author of eighteen
historical novels and nine contemporary
romances for both the secular and Christian market. A Christy Award finalist, Linda
has received numerous awards in both the
ABA and CBA, including the Romantic
Writers of America's Beacon Award. She
lives in Salisbury, Maryland.

Introducing

AVON INSPIRE

Celebrate the grace and power of Love

Discover Avon Inspire, a new imprint from Avon Books. Avon Inspire is Avon's line of uplifting women's fiction that focuses on what matters most: family, community, faith, and love. These are entertaining novels Christian readers can trust, with storylines that will be welcome to readers of any faith background. Rest assured, each book will have enough excitement and intrigue to keep readers riveted to the end and breathlessly awaiting the next installment. Each title includes reader's guide questions, a letter from the author, and a preview from their next book.

Look for more riveting historical and contemporary fiction to come from beloved authors Lori Copeland, Kristin Billerbeck, Tracey Bateman, Linda Windsor, Lyn Cote, DiAnn Mills, and more!

AVON INSPIRE

An Imprint of HarperCollinsPublishers
www.avoninspire.com

E-mail us at AvonInspire@HarperCollins.com

AVI 0507